D1435862

MASTER
of
CEREMONIES

DONALD COZZENS

in extenso

MASTER OF CEREMONIES
by Donald Cozzens

Edited by Michael Coyne
Cover design, interior design, and typesetting by Patricia A. Lynch
Photo of Donald Cozzens by Paul Tepley

Copyright © 2014 by Donald Cozzens

Published by In Extenso Press
Distributed exclusively by ACTA Publications, 4848 N. Clark Street,
Chicago, IL 60640, (800) 397-2282, actapublications.com

This story is fiction. Aside from references to well-known historic figures,
any similarity to actual people, living or dead, is purely coincidental.

Library of Congress Catalog Number: 2014953552
ISBN: 978-0-87946-993-1 (paperback)
ISBN: 978-0-87946-992-4 (hardcover)
Printed in the United States of America by Total Printing Systems
Year 25 24 23 22 21 20 19 18 17 16 15
Printing 15 14 13 12 11 10 9 8 7 6 5 4 3 2 1

♻ Text printed on 30% post-consumer recycled paper

To
Marie and Tim Glasow
and in memory of
Tom Cozzens

No grand betrayals
We lacked the impudent will
We died of small treasons.

— Kilian McDonnell

1

Kirkuk, Iraq, 2005

Like a monk in prayer, Sergeant Mark Anderlee hadn't moved in an hour. His lean body, flat against the dry dusty soil, felt weightless, suspended like a feather in effortless stillness. Trained to wait, he would wait without complaint, silently coaxing his target into the crosshairs of the Leupold scope mounted on his M24 sniper rifle. His target was a bomb specialist recruited by al-Qaeda's Abu Musab al-Zarqawi, a top lieutenant to Osama bin Laden. The target's real name, his briefing officer had said, was unknown. "He's called al-Zahidi, the one from Zahid." The name was irrelevant. It was a name adopted by at least one other al-Qaeda insurgent.

Anderlee had to admit the army had changed him, and mostly for the better. He was disciplined now and able to control the anger that had soured his soul for decades. His sniper training, moreover, had taught him patience—a virtue well beyond his grasp when he was a schoolboy in Baltimore.

He checked again the distance to target: three hundred and eighty meters—well within the 800-meter range of the M24 resting steady on its bipod. Anderlee's eyes moved from the one-floor, flat-roofed building where al-Zahidi and six other insurgents were meeting to the fuel tanks fifty meters behind the windowless structure, then on to the three trucks parked square in the middle of the baked clay road, their beds covered with canvas tarps. The sun, both friend and enemy, hung slightly behind him now. Anderlee ignored its choking heat. He judged his escape route problematic at best. Still, he told himself, his chances were good—especially since he was working without a spotter. Spotters had bungled his escapes more than once.

It might take another hour, he knew, before al-Zahidi gave him a clear and stationary target. "Come on you guys, meeting's over," he whispered. "Come on out. Come…on…out." Anderlee willed himself to stay focused, always the hardest part—now made more difficult by the creeping realization that he was waiting for more than an insurgent bomb specialist. Mark Anderlee, at his deepest core, was waiting to take revenge, waiting for the instant when his abuser, now a retired archbishop, discovered he hadn't gotten away with it after all. Just fourteen more months and he would have his twenty years of service. They would be, he was convinced, fourteen sweet months of anticipation. He would move through them with the patience of a saint, anticipating his retirement—a decent pension, clean sheets, hot showers—and the sinful pleasure of evening a score.

Anderlee wet his lips, his eyes now almost closed. Waiting, he had discovered, allowed the pleasure of anticipation; as intense a pleasure as the surging, erotic euphoria of a mission accomplished.

He peered again into his scope. In his mind's eye he saw not al-Zahidi but an aging Wilfred Gunnison—bishop's robes and all—right in his crosshairs. He couldn't miss.

Anderlee blinked himself back into the moment. Five men were now visible, two carrying semi-automatic weapons. That meant two others remained in the building. The five walked slowly toward the small caravan of trucks, his target doing the talking. The group paused, as though one of the men had asked a question or made some kind of point… It was enough; al-Zahidi was down.

2

Baltimore, Maryland 2005

Father Bryn Martin, former master of ceremonies to the retired archbishop and now chancellor of the Archdiocese of Baltimore, had heard the rumors—he was to be named a bishop. But the call that would change his life still caught him off guard. He was in the archbishop's office late in the day, summarizing a numbing auditor's report, when the phone rang. Archbishop Charles Cullen, Gunnison's recent successor and Martin's new superior, raised his eyebrows in a gesture of frustration as he lifted the handset. Martin looked down at the report in his lap while Cullen listened. He lifted his eyes to see Cullen's wide grin.

"Father Martin is in my office now, Archbishop. I'm sure he would like to hear the news directly." Cullen, his light blue eyes watering with pleasure, reached across the desk and handed the receiver to Martin. The accented voice, cultured, even lyrical, was that of Archbishop Lorenzo Tardisconi, the Holy See's ambassador to the United States—and the man in charge of the selection of all new bishops in the country.

"Father Martin? This is Archbishop Tardisconi."

"Yes, Your Excellency. This is Father Martin."

"The Holy Father has chosen you for the office of bishop, to serve as auxiliary to Archbishop Cullen." Tardisconi paused to let his message sink in. "Will you accept?"

Distracted by Cullen's obvious delight at this pivotal moment in his chancellor's life, Martin felt a rush of excitement and pleasure—the understandable but dangerous pleasure of ecclesiastical affirmation, the almost adolescent thrill of being held in favor, of being noticed.

"May I have some time to think about this, Archbishop?"

"I suspect, Father Martin, that you have been thinking about this for some time now."

Despite the vaunted secrecy veiling the process for the selection of bishops, word had made its way through the clerical network that a new auxiliary for Baltimore would be named in the near future. Bryn Martin was a presumed favorite, perhaps the favorite. In spite of the papal sanctions meant to insure confidentiality, two different sources had told him he was being vetted. Instinctively, Martin knew this was no time to appear humble.

"I am honored, Archbishop, and humbled. Yes, I will accept the appointment. And I am most grateful to his Holiness, to you, and to Archbishop Cullen for your confidence in me."

"Praised be Jesus Christ," Tardisconi replied piously. He promised to pray for the new bishop-elect and turned abruptly to matters of protocol. "Two weeks from this Tuesday the announcement will be made simultaneously by the Holy See, by my office in Washington, and by Archbishop Cullen. Until that time you should confide only in your spiritual director and with chancery staff responsible for essential preparations for your ordination as bishop. Archbishop Cullen will advise you in the matter of the customary gift of gratitude to his Holiness."

Martin repressed a smile at this last point of protocol. For centuries papal honors, especially episcopal and abbatial appointments, have been a major source of revenue for the Vatican treasury. The bishop-elect had no idea what amount would be appropriate. He would have to trust Cullen for advice.

Cullen took the phone back and ended the call with customary courtesies.

"This calls for a little single malt," he said.

It was growing dark outside and the desk and table lamps shed a soft, golden glow, much like candlelight. The two church-men sipped their whisky and talked easily—like members of a select and exclusive club—for the next half hour.

For the past six months there had been signs, subtle yet tell-ing to any astute clerical eye, that Father Bryn Martin was held in favor. He had clearly won the new archbishop's confidence, and Cullen seemed to enjoy Martin's company. But Martin never allowed himself to forget that while his working relationship with Cullen was cordial, they weren't really friends—not yet anyway. That was a mistake even the savviest of veteran priests often made. Seminarians are taught to think of their bishop as their spiritual father and, since the Second Vatican Council, as an older brother. From a *realpolitik* perspective, that is hardly the case. Their bishop is, in truth, their feudal lord who, by eccle-sial tradition and personal instinct, uses familial images and lan-guage to control his vassal priests.

It hadn't taken Martin long to grasp this reality. More than fraternal concern, more than fatherly support and encourage-ment, what really grounded the relationship of priest to bishop was loyalty—not loyalty to Christ and his gospel, but loyalty to the ecclesial system, to the culture of privilege and preference. In theory, of course, it should be the reverse. But loyalty to the gospel before loyalty to the institutional church could get a priest into real trouble. The conviction that loyalty to the institution assured a priest he was being loyal to Christ and his gospel is the great lie in the Catholic Church.

With their glasses emptied, Cullen and Martin rose from their chairs.

"Thank you, Charles," Martin said softly. "This wouldn't have happened, I know, without your endorsement."

"It's a great honor, Bryn, but you will find out soon enough the job has its burdens. And the burdens will crush you if you don't tend to your spiritual life." Cullen paused. "And the privileges? They're more dangerous than the burdens."

Cullen and Martin embraced, the brief, slightly awkward hug men often exchange, with Cullen patting Martin's back in encouragement and congratulations.

"Get something to eat, Bryn, and then make a few phone calls. Don't take Tardisconi's admonition to secrecy too seriously. You know who you can trust."

The press conference announcing his appointment was only two hours away. With his mind racing, Martin reached for the newer of his two black suits. Clerical politics, he had discovered early on, demanded of the career-minded priest an air of public piety and just the right degree of deference. There was a theatrical dimension to the hierarchy that bordered on camp. There were roles to be played. It would never do for a priest to go around saying he wanted to be a bishop or a chancellor or even a monsignor. No, a climber had to channel his ambition carefully, had to be noticed, had to project an air of gravity, and above all had to project an air of absolute, unquestioning loyalty to the minutest of the church's teachings and policies. Maybe this was what was bothering Martin. Maybe this was what made his mind race and his stomach tighten. Had he become the kind of climber he despised?

He couldn't finish his usual breakfast bagel and coffee. He returned to his room and sat down. He couldn't pray, couldn't think. His inner turmoil displaced any possibility of a peaceful interlude before the press conference that would forever change his life.

He should have insisted on more time to think about it. To pray about it. That's what he should have said. And that's what he should have said when Archbishop Gunnison had first asked him to be his master of ceremonies. Instead, Martin had acquiesced on the spot both times. It was the beginning of his rise to the office of bishop—and the end of his innocence.

As he sat alone, Martin remembered it all—the appointment as Gunnison's master of ceremonies, the call from Tardisconi, and his own obsequious response. Yet another scene, this one rife with the musk of guilt, came into focus. Martin squeezed his eyes shut, trying to block out what happened so long ago in that dark car parked in shadow outside the archbishop's residence. Was the archbishop's bizarre behavior that night behind Martin's rise from master of ceremonies to chancellor and now to bishop in just two and a half years—an astronomical assent as church careers go?

Bishop-elect Bryn Martin got up, left the rectory through the side entrance, and with his hands buried deep in his overcoat pockets walked the short distance to the Catholic Center. On this day, of all days, the incident he was trying to forget should be left to the mercy of God. Waiting for the light at the corner of Cathedral and Mulberry, Martin told himself he wasn't sad at all.

3

Baltimore, 2007

Dan Barrett and Paul Kline half raised their long-necked bottles of beer in a subtle man-toast to Mark Anderlee.

"It's great to have you back home," Dan said.

"Yeah," Paul added, "it really is. Twenty years of army life. I don't know how you did it."

The three men meeting for drinks in the Belvedere Hotel's Owl Bar had known each other since Blessed Sacrament elementary school. But it wasn't until their high school years at Loyola Blakefield that their friendship took hold. After graduating, Barrett and Kline went on to college and eventually to teaching careers in two of Baltimore's Catholic high schools. Anderlee had enlisted. Now, more than two decades since their years at Blakefield, they were gathering for beer and wings to celebrate Anderlee's retirement from the army and his return to Baltimore.

"I feel bad I never wrote," Paul said sheepishly.

"Forget it. If you had written I would've felt I had to write you back. You did me a favor."

The three smiled weakly.

Barrett and Kline had looked forward to the evening and hearing about Anderlee's two tours in Iraq.

"We heard you were the leader of a goddamn sniper unit, for Christ's sake," Dan said, coaxing him on. After the first round of drinks, Mark opened up a little but spoke only in generalities, never once hinting at any heroics on his part. It was clear to the two civilians that their old friend wasn't into recounting his experiences as a soldier—at least not tonight.

"What're you going to do now?" Dan asked.

"My army pension is pretty good so I don't have to look for a job right away. I'll be staying with my Aunt Margaret until I find a place I like. Maybe in a few years I'll go someplace where I won't freeze my ass off during the winter months. My mom is living in South Carolina. I'll check it out. But right now I have some business here in Baltimore."

Barrett and Kline exchanged a glance.

"What kind of business?" Dan said.

"Church business."

"What the hell are you talking about, Mark?" Paul asked.

Anderlee looked over his shoulder to make sure their waitress wasn't heading for their table.

"One night I was on patrol in Tikkrit, Saddam Hussein's hometown. It was routine, nothing out of the ordinary. But on that patrol, on that quiet night, I realized that as much as I hated Hussein, there was someone I hated more. And I swore to myself I would square things when I got back home."

The three men leaned in across the table as Anderlee, his voice just above a whisper, said, "The summer before we started at Blakefield, I spent two weeks at Camp Carroll, the summer camp run by the archdiocese. There was a priest, Father Wilfred Gunnison, an older guy in his fifties or so who was like the chaplain or something. The prick messed with me."

"Mark," Barrett interrupted, "Archbishop Gunnison?"

"Yeah, I'm talking about the Most Reverend Wilfred Freakin' Gunnison, the retired archbishop of Baltimore. One and the same."

"Damn," Dan said.

Kline was speechless.

The two men, their stomachs suddenly cramped, sat staring at their beer bottles. Anderlee, without raising his eyes, broke the silence.

"It was the summer I turned fifteen, Father Wil, as we called him, tells me he has to do weekend Masses at some parish in a small town in Pennsylvania, about two hundred miles north of here. Do I want to go with him, give him some company? I said okay 'cause I couldn't think of any reason to say no. He goes to tell one of the counselors I'd be away for two nights and I go put some stuff in my backpack."

He took a swig of beer. Neither of the others touched theirs.

"Gunnison says to be ready to leave in an hour—around four o'clock. He had it all figured out. We'd drive for about a hundred miles or so and stop for dinner, spend the night in a motel, and drive the rest of the way to the parish on Saturday.

"'I need to be at the parish in time for confessions and the Saturday vigil Mass,' Gunnison says, all piss pious and friendly like. The plan was to spend Saturday night at the rectory and then, after the two Sunday morning Masses, we'd drive back to Camp Carroll.

"It started out okay. He isn't that hard to talk to, and he can be funny. And I was kinda pleased he asked me to go along with him. Well, we got this motel room, two double beds, TV, nothing special. I thought we might go to a nice restaurant but there weren't any nice restaurants around. We found a family-owned place that was okay and then went back to the motel. There was really nothing else to do.

"Gunnison kept saying I should consider it a mini-vacation, but it was a mini-trip to hell," Anderlee said coldly. "Then he said since we were on vacation, a drink or two was in order.

"I was almost fifteen. Yeah, I thought, I can handle a few drinks. He had this plastic shopping bag with two bottles of Jack Daniels and a six-pack of ginger ale. Then he sends me out to the ice machine while he gets the plastic glasses from the bathroom."

"Another round?" the waitress asked, appearing from nowhere.

"Sure," Paul said without looking at her. They waited while she left.

"So we sipped whiskey and ginger ale and watched a little television," Mark continued. "Gunnison had a second drink and so did I. This one was stronger. But booze wasn't the only thing in the shopping bag. He had a bottle of skin lotion in there too. He goes, 'What's really relaxing, Mark, is a massage. Have you ever had one? I'll give you one and then you can give me one.'

"I'm getting a funny feeling now but I don't say a damn word. It's dark outside by this time, and Gunnison gets up and closes the drapes and puts the safety chain on the door.

"'Let's get undressed,' he says, but then he says, 'but it's a good idea to wear jockstraps.'"

The waitress came with their beers. Anderlee waited until she left, neither Barrett nor Kline said a word.

"Gunnison produced two jockstraps from his suitcase. I'm not thinking so clear and my stomach was tightening up. But then I got undressed and there we were, wearing nothing but these jockstraps. He takes the bed spread down and the blanket and has me lie face down on the sheets. Neither one of us was saying anything. He put lotion on my back and shoulders and started rubbing. He rubbed my neck and arms and then moved down to my lower back. I'm starting to freak out. He put lotion on the back of my legs and massaged them down to my ankles... and then my butt.

The other two looked at each other, and then down at the table.

"'Roll over,' he told me, but I didn't want to roll over. By this time I had a hard on. He rolled me over and I'm glad I have the jockstrap on but he could tell I'm excited. He massaged my chest

17

and I'm lying there with my eyes closed. His hands moved down to my stomach and he's breathing heavy now. He says something about giving a massage is hard work. My eyes were still closed but now his hands were just above the waist band of the supporter. Gunnison was no longer straddling me. He seemed to be kneeling at my side and leaning over me. Then he rubbed my stomach, but his left elbow is right on my prick. His hands stayed on my stomach but his elbow kept pressing down on me." Mark paused. "And then I came."

Kline and Barrett hadn't moved. They lifted their eyes from the table, knowing they just had to look at Anderlee. They wanted to say how sorry they were. But they didn't know how.

"Gunnison reached for the towel he'd placed on the bed and says he's going to get the lotion off me. He wiped the lotion and mess I'd made without saying another word—like what he's doing is the most natural thing in the world."

What Anderlee didn't tell his two friends was that he was so upset and confused he had almost cried.

"Okay, Mark," he says to me, "it's your turn to do me."

"Gunnison went over to his bed, pulled the spread down and stretches out on his stomach. I said I wasn't very good at it and was going to go to bed.

"Gunnison didn't say anything at first. Then, like after a moment from hell, he said it was okay and he was a little tired too.

"He got up, took his jockstrap off and headed to the bathroom, making sure I saw his boner. He was in the shower a long time and I cleaned up a little and got into my T-shirt and shorts. I hadn't brought any pajamas. My back was to the bathroom and I pretended I was sleeping when he came back in the room. He got in bed and turned out the light and said good night. That's what I said too.

"'Good night, Father.' I should've said, 'Hey, you forgot to say your night prayers.'"

Kline and Barrett gurgled little nervous chuckles and sipped their beers wondering what the hell you say to a friend who has been messed with by a priest.

"I was sick and scared and felt like shit. I didn't sleep at all that night. I don't know what time it was but I heard him get up and go into the bathroom. I could hear him pissing. He turned the bathroom light out then came back and tried to get into my bed.

"I just said, 'You've got the wrong bed, Father,' but like I meant it, and he backed off. After that I was terrified he'd try to get into my bed again. That was the worst night of my life."

Dan slowly shook his head. "The bastard," he said.

Paul nodded agreement. The eyes of both men seemed to shrink and grow dark, their lips pressed so thin and inward they were invisible. They sat, frozen, for a while. Mark signaled the waitress for another round.

"Gunnison didn't try anything the next night at the rectory. He stayed in the pastor's bedroom and I had the guestroom, but we had to use the same bathroom. I found it hard to look at the guy. And listen to this. Before the Saturday evening Mass he asked me if I wanted to be one of the altar servers. I couldn't believe it. I said no, I'd skip it that time, and next day we drove back without saying hardly anything. When we finally got back to Carroll, it was too late for supper and he asked me if I wanted to go out for pizza. I told him, no, I wasn't hungry and grabbed my backpack and headed for my cabin. I was sick and tired and starving."

"So what did he say when you left?" Dan asked.

"He said, 'Hey, remember you owe me a back rub.'

"Then when I saw him Monday morning he acted like nothin' had ever happened. I didn't know what to think. Did he just give me a massage and I got so excited I came? I felt confused, I felt guilty... I felt like shit. So I pretended it didn't happen and tried to act like everything was okay. After a while I didn't think about it so much. But I had a secret and it wasn't a good secret. I never thought of telling anyone—not even you guys."

Outside the three men let the night air wash over them. Before moving to their cars, Paul asked, "Are you going to talk to Gunnison?"

Mark looked at each of his friends, and as he did his expression changed.

"Oh, yeah. I'm gonna to talk to Gunnison. You bet your ass I am. He lives in that stone house next to the Basilica. I've spent a few days watching the place. I know when he comes and goes. I'm going to pay the pervert a surprise visit and, believe me, I'm gonna do more than talk to him."

Kline and Barrett exchanged an anxious glance.

"First I'm gonna get some money from him. Then I'm gonna make him shit in his pants. And then, when I'm ready, I'm gonna take him down."

4

The Johns Hopkins University faculty convocation was as tedious and interminable as professor Ian Landers had anticipated. He had distracted himself from the ordeal by stealthily admiring a faculty member he hadn't noticed before. She sat three rows ahead of him in the tiered auditorium, off to his right. He had spotted her before she had taken her seat. There were quite a few attractive women on the faculty, and some were clearly available, including a few with husbands. But this woman caught his attention as others hadn't. While his line of sight was restricted to her left profile, it was enough to draw his glance again and again.

Landers had planned to skip the wine and hors d'oeuvres reception that followed the convocation, but changed his mind so he could meet her.

"Hello," he said simply, approaching her with an outstretched hand, making the most of his British accent, "I'm Ian...Ian Landers. I don't believe we've met."

"No, I don't think so." Her grip was firm and brief. "I'm Nora Martin. I'm in the psychology department, one of two new hires."

"I'm in history, medieval history."

They chatted for the next quarter hour while sipping white wine and nibbling at vegetable egg rolls. When Landers suggested meeting sometime for coffee, Martin didn't hesitate.

"I'd like that."

Over coffee four days later Ian said rather directly, "Tell me about yourself...no, let me guess. From your figure—I don't mean to be too personal here—you're an athlete."

"I was an athlete," Nora responded with a blush. "I went to Penn State on a track scholarship. The 400 meter. I try to keep in shape, but I won't let anybody time me anymore."

"And what drew you to psychology?"

"This might surprise you. It was spirituality. In fact, my major research interest is the nexus between psychology and spirituality. I'm coming to see that the healthiest people, from a psychology perspective, are people who are spiritually alive. Right now I'm trying to find the language to write about this without sounding overtly religious. I'm struggling for words that will capture what the mystics speak of as spiritual transcendence that will be acceptable, or at least make some sense, to my secular colleagues and students. Wish me luck!"

"I find that fascinating, Nora, really I do. Here's why. I'm looking into ambition and power in the prelates of the medieval church. So many of these men were outwardly devout and pious, but spiritually, from the evidence I've uncovered, they appear frighteningly shallow. I find little evidence of any authentic spiritual experience. And, as I'm sure you know, most were very suspicious of the mystics of their time...and not a few were sexual libertines."

Nora sipped her coffee, feeling torn between wanting to know more about Lander's research and wanting to know more about the man across the table. Trying to sound light and playful she said, "Well, Ian. Your turn. Tell me about yourself."

"All right," Landers said with a shy smile that Nora took to mean he might go beyond the British penchant for privacy. "I was born in Leeds thirty-eight years ago. If you've ever been to

Leeds you know it's never confused with Oxford or Cambridge. It is…" he took a breath "…a bit dreary. When I was a teenager," he hesitated, revealing some discomfort, "I discovered that my mother had miscarried twice. I've always regretted not having siblings. It was difficult for my parents and difficult for me. My father, Owen, a non-church-going Anglican, was a senior editor at the University of Leeds Press. He loved his job, and he certainly loved books.

"Our apartment was literally filled with books and, for some reason I don't fully understand, I was drawn to the ones on medieval history. Instead of playing cricket, I spent a lot of time reading. I remember my father boasting, to my embarrassment I must add, that I was the only twelve-year-old in all of England who had read Bisticci's *Lives of Illustrious Men of the 15th Century* or Burchard's *At the Court of the Borgia*. I'm not sure my father knew how much my sexual education was furthered from reading about the Borgias."

Nora tried to hide a smile. This Englishman, while a little on the formal side, was indeed interesting.

"My mother, Ella Crawford Landers, an American Catholic," he continued, "was born and raised in Baltimore and met my father when she was a Foreign Service officer posted to England. She was far more socially visible than my father—she served on several of Leeds' civic and artistic boards. And," Ian said, almost in a whisper, "in spite of their differences in temperament, they never lost the romantic, even sexy edge to their relationship." And with hint of a smile that drew Nora in, added, "It was very un-English of them, you know."

Nora looked at her companion, "Hmm…a rather lonely childhood but a happy and stimulating home life."

"Yes, yes it was."

They held each other's eyes for second or two before glancing down at their plates. Feeling the heat in his face, Ian continued.

"During the Cold War years mother was the Information Officer at the U.S. Consulate in Leeds. And while she certainly wasn't anything close to a James Bond type, it was rumored that my mother was also CIA. This gave her a certain panache within her circle of friends."

"Was she?"

"If she was, she really couldn't talk about it, of course. But there were enough late-night, whispered conversations between my parents to lead me to believe the rumors to be true. When I brought the possibility up with my father, he just wouldn't go there. He didn't outright deny that my mother was CIA, but rather brushed it off as a 'rather silly notion.'

"Not long after my father died, my mother moved back to the States. She has some distant cousins, but there's really no family left. Just me and her best friend, Margaret Comiskey, a high school classmate. The two are like sisters. After their first year of college together, Margaret's mother died, and she dropped out of college to take care of her father. She's worked forever at the archdiocese as a secretary. Mother says she's now the secretary to the chancellor. The two stayed in touch during the years Mother was across the sea, and now they're only an hour's drive apart. Margaret lives here in Baltimore, and my mother has a condominium in Silver Spring. Mother wanted to live near D.C. because she still has friends there from her Foreign Service days... but what she really did years ago is still a mystery to me.

"How about your family?" Ian asked, realizing that he had been monopolizing the conversation.

"Well," Nora said, her voice softening, "Both of my parents are gone. They had a good marriage, too. I have three brothers— all older, all close. One of them is an auxiliary bishop here in Baltimore. I hope you can meet Bryn someday. He would love to hear about your work."

"I'd like that," Ian responded.

"How did you find growing up an only child?" Nora asked turning the conversation back to Ian. She was nowhere near ready to tell him the rest of her story, especially the years following Penn State.

"Well," Ian said, "since my coffee's cold and I need to get back to campus, let's save that for another time, shall we?"

5

Archbishop Wilfred Gunnison reached to put his key into the lock of the front door to his sandstone house next to the Basilica of the Assumption.

"Open the damn door, Gunnison," a firm voice from over his shoulder demanded. Gunnison felt the man's weight against his back, pushing him flat against the door. The lock turned and he was shoved inside. The intruder closed and locked the door.

"Sit down, Wilfred," the man said with a sneer. "My name, in case you can't remember me, is Mark Anderlee." He stood directly over the shaken old man. "When I was a kid at Camp Carroll, you messed with me. You sexually abused me, you sick old bastard. And I'm here to tell you you're going to pay. You're going to pay big time."

Gunnison's hands were shaking as he called the office of Monsignor Aidan Kempe, financial vicar and recently appointed chancellor of the Archdiocese of Baltimore.

"Aidan, I need to see you now, right now! Something terrible has happened." Gunnison's voice was thin and jerky. "Oh, thank God...yes, I'll be there as soon as I can."

Putting the phone down, Gunnison carefully approached the window facing Cathedral Street. There was no sign of Anderlee. The retired archbishop was still shaking from the awful accusation made by the man he was sure he had never met. The man is mistaken. He has to be mistaken. Yet Gunnison knew he really wasn't sure. It was so many years ago...

What he didn't know, couldn't know, was that this was just the beginning of Mark Anderlee's strategy of revenge, a strategy planned with military precision.

Twenty minutes later, a cowering Wilfred Gunnison slumped into one of the four leather chairs in Monsignor Aidan Kempe's office.

"Hold my calls, Margaret," Kempe said crisply to his secretary, and closed the big oak door to his office.

The former archbishop knew if anybody could save him, if anybody could make this go away, it was Aidan Kempe, the leader of a very private, in fact secret, band of priests who called themselves the Brotherhood of the Sacred Purple. Their mission, their sacred duty, was to work quietly behind the scenes in order to save the Catholic Church from its misguided leaders, leftist bishops, and lax priests who were dragging their beloved Roman Catholic Church into the bosom of Protestantism and worse—into the clutches of relativism, secularism, and the paganism of Western society.

The Baltimore Brotherhood consisted of six priests, including Kempe and Gunnison. As an archbishop, albeit retired, Gunnison far outranked Kempe, but he had long ago come to understand it best to concede the leadership of the Brotherhood to Kempe. Kempe's Italian, far from fluent, was still better than his own, and Kempe had better Roman connections. Both Gunnison and Kempe took considerable, even illicit, delight in the Brotherhood's power to influence the appointments of American bishops, a power Kempe cultivated through his network of like-minded American bishops.

Moreover, Gunnison understood that it was Kempe alone who enjoyed access to the Brotherhood's supreme leader and protector, the mysterious Vatican bishop known to the Brotherhood only as Murex, or simply M. And it was Kempe who had sole control of the Brotherhood's treasury, the purple purse. The bulk of the purse came from wealthy, mostly conservative Catholics in the Baltimore-Washington area Kempe shrewdly, patiently cultivated. In the minds of his benefactors, if you could claim Monsignor Aidan Kempe as a personal friend, you had arrived among the elite of Catholic society.

"A half hour ago," Gunnison began, trying to steady his voice, "a man appeared at my door as I was coming back from breakfast and pushed his way in. He ordered me to sit down. He stood so close I could see the veins bulging in his neck." He waved a shaking hand at his own throat. "He told me I had molested him when he was a teenager. I need some water," Gunnison pleaded.

Kempe rose, crossed the room, and returned with water in a crystal tumbler.

"He was alone?"

"Yes."

"Did he say anything about going to the police or hiring a lawyer?

"No."

"I need to know his name, Wilfred."

"Mark Anderlee. His family belonged to Blessed Sacrament parish. He graduated from Loyola Blakefield. I vaguely remember him from my summers at Camp Carroll. He said he's just out of the army, retired after twenty years. He was very intent, Aidan, very intent." Gunnison put the tumbler down. "He wants money. He wants a hundred thousand dollars!"

Kempe's eyes, cold and clear, bore into Gunnison.

"Tell me what happened, Wilfred."

"He's blowing this way out of proportion. I may have given him a back rub. A back rub. That's all there was to it."

Kempe shook his head. Gunnison knew what he was thinking. Yes, he was thinking of the other young men who had back rubs from the archbishop. Their parents had made no formal allegations nor had they filed police reports. Thank God. After Kempe had provided counseling for the boys and assured their parents their abuser would never be in a position to abuse again, the cases seemed to go away.

Kempe, to the Brotherhood's great advantage, was part of the archdiocese's response team created in the wake of the first clergy abuse scandals. Gunnison, of course, while he was still archbishop, had appointed him to the post. And Gunnison knew that on a few occasions, including the earlier allegations against him, Kempe acted quietly, alone, not even informing Cullen, the new archbishop. It was risky, but Kempe found that a little money, a few months of counseling, and a promise to make sure the priest wouldn't offend again always did the trick.

What Gunnison didn't know, however, was something that Kempe was beginning to understand all too clearly. Wilfred Gunnison was no longer an asset to the Brotherhood. His prominence and his weakness were a danger to their mission, a mission under attack on every front. Aidan Kempe knew his next step. He would, and very soon, have to seek advice from M.

Gunnison rose slowly from his chair.

"Can we talk tomorrow, Aidan?" he said, "But not here. Not in your office. Somewhere less...official."

Gunnison waited for a hint of sympathy that never came.

In the outer office, Gunnison nodded peremptorily to Margaret Comiskey and headed to the elevator. He had seen Comiskey almost daily for the eleven years he was archbishop. Even had he not been preoccupied with Anderlee's allegation, it never would have occurred to him to ask her how she was.

Walking back to his residence, Gunnison found himself coping with a swirl of emotions. In addition to the fear that clung like a heavy, black vestment, he was now swallowing resentment, a resentment that wouldn't stay down, a bile rising in his throat.

It was he, after all, who had furthered Aidan Kempe's career. He sent him to study in Rome. He named him financial vicar. He recommended him to Cullen for the chancellor's position. Now the chancellor was treating him like some clueless priest. The hubris of the man!

Kempe, Gunnison knew, had taken as many risks as any of them. He thought of his weekend trips to the Boys Town area of Chicago, where Kempe and some of his priest friends frequented the gay bars on Division Street. Their intention, of course, was simply to have interesting conversation with like-minded men.

Gunnison paused in front of the Basilica. There was no sign of Anderlee. Perhaps it had been a little more than a backrub. One thing was certain, however. He never, never, never sodomized the boy.

Kempe and Gunnison met the next day at a restaurant a block from the Catholic Center, well after the lunch crowd had thinned.

"I'm doing all I can to make this go away, Wilfred."

Gunnison still looked anxious and drawn. "This couldn't come at a worse time," he whispered.

Kempe tried not to look cynical. *Yes, in a few weeks you'll be celebrating your fiftieth ordination anniversary with a Mass at the Basilica and a Catholic Charities fundraising dinner. Let's hope nobody finds out that half the proceeds go to you, Wilfred, you goddamn phony.*

"I understand the timing couldn't be worse," Kempe said, trying to sound sympathetic. "But we can't do anything about it—unless you postpone your celebration."

"I'm not going to postpone the celebration," Gunnison said emphatically.

"You could claim a medical emergency."

"Aidan, the anniversary Mass and dinner will go on as scheduled. We'll just have to deal with this Anderlee. Can you come up with the hundred thousand?"

Both men knew the money was a major hurdle.

"I think so," Kempe answered lowering his voice. "I could take half of it from the purple purse." His tone changed as he said sternly, "You understand, of course, this puts a very big dent in our resources."

Gunnison didn't appreciate this little lecture and fought to keep his buried resentment toward Kempe from showing. He had given his life to the church and in his eyes had served it well. He was an archbishop, for God's sake, and entitled to Kempe's respect and best efforts to get him out of this mess. And not just for his own sake, but for the good of the church and for the good of the Brotherhood.

"And the rest?" he asked petulantly.

Kempe ignored the tone. "I'll call on some of our faithful benefactors and tell them the archdiocese is faced with an unexpected financial emergency. Let's hope their trust is still such that they won't ask questions. And let's hope our lay friends can get their checks to me in a matter of days."

Gunnison took a deep breath. Maybe this will, please God, go away.

"When Anderlee contacts you, and you can be sure he will be contacting you soon, tell him you need to meet with him in the Basilica, in one of the pews where you can talk privately—and still be seen by anyone making a visit."

"That's a good idea," Gunnison said quickly. "I don't want to be alone with him."

"Give him the impression," Kempe went on, "that the money has come from your personal savings and that you want to help him out until he gets settled and established. How you play this, Wilfred, is critical."

Again, Gunnison scarcely concealed his rising irritation at the lecturing tone. "Yes, of course."

"If Anderlee brings up the incident, you should say you're sorry if the backrub disturbed or upset him…that you never meant to harm him. Above all, do not ask for his forgiveness."

Gunnison nodded his agreement.

Kempe wasn't finished, "We're banking that Anderlee is working on his own, that he hasn't hired a lawyer. So we can't ask for a letter promising silence. He'd almost certainly seek legal advice."

"Yes, you're probably right." Gunnison conceded. There was sadness in his voice and his eyes were watery and tired.

"Wilfred, this is more money than I've ever given to anyone making an allegation. We can only pray he takes it, keeps his mouth shut, and moves on with his life."

Gunnison could barely tolerate this last preachy piety. He sat still, with his eyes lowered, too tired to eat, too exasperated even to pray.

6

Ian Landers rose to greet Nora Martin as she approached his table. He thought of greeting her with a light embrace the way Americans do even with casual friends. Instead he offered her his hand. It was too formal, too British a gesture—and he knew it. Martin wore a light, powdery fragrance that led Landers to imagine she had just showered after a five mile run. He liked the cut of her hair, on the short side, and her simple earrings. Her sky blue eyes, not really large, but clear and intelligent, were her best feature. She wore no other jewelry except a small emerald ring on her right hand. Her white open-necked blouse revealed the exquisite, dimpled juncture of her smooth neck and upper chest. Martin's brushed-pink Irish skin, Landers noted with a swallow, suggested a youthful wholesomeness, even innocence.

"Good choice of a restaurant," Ian said smiling. Nora had suggested a small, not yet trendy place on Charles Street.

"I've never found it noisy," she responded, glancing around at the tables closest to theirs. "We should be able to talk without shouting at each other."

They sipped a 2004 Argentine Malbec and shared some fairly harmless university gossip and compared positions on the current policy issues raising the ire of their colleagues.

"You promised to tell me more about your life in England," Nora said after the first pause in their conversation.

"All right, I'll go next." Ian glanced at his wine glass but instead took a sip of water. "After Leeds, I found myself at Oxford.

When I finished my undergraduate studies at Balliol College, I continued on for the doctorate in medieval history.

"To be honest, it wasn't quite that seamless. My last year at Balliol I shared my flat with another doctoral student, a very lovely woman. It was my first serious relationship, and it was liberating and intense and wonderful. I should have been a very happy chap. But I felt something wasn't quite right. There were days when I felt confused and even sad." Landers furrowed his brow and reached for his wine. "Now I think I understand. The whole time we were together I was having a rather intense spiritual awakening. Don't ask me to explain it. I just had this need to sit still in prayer. I really don't know if it was even proper prayer. I just needed to sit still and be still."

Nora nodded and flushed at the budding intimacy between them, trying hard to hide her own confusion in hearing this personal and private episode in Ian's life. She understood his desire for contemplative stillness well enough—but the affair, and his telling her about it now, caught her off guard.

"After she moved out," Ian continued, "I even spoke to a Dominican on the history faculty about the possibility of entering the Dominicans and studying for the priesthood."

He shook his head and smiled, saying without saying: *That never happened, of course.*

"Perhaps we should look at our menus before the server thinks we're here just for drinks," Nora said, to fill the sudden void.

Their orders placed, they nibbled at the bread while Ian struggled not to stare at that delicious point at the base of Nora's throat.

"So you thought of becoming a priest."

"It was a long time ago," Ian said crisply, an apparent signal he didn't want to say anything more about the subject. Nora nodded her silent understanding, a slight smile softening her gaze that seemed to say: *Of course.*

"Well, Professor Martin, I'm waiting."

"Well, Professor Landers, I could tell you that after graduating from Penn State I did graduate work in psychology at The Catholic University. I got my Ph.D. there four years ago. And that would be true. But I would be leaving out an important part of my story."

Nora was thankful to be interrupted by the server filling their wine glasses.

"Don't leave me hanging."

"After college, my parents, brothers, friends…they all expected me to do graduate studies in psychology. They had good reason—I talked about it a lot. But instead, I entered the convent."

"*You* entered a *convent?*" Ian repeated lamely.

"Yes, a contemplative monastery to be precise. The Carmelite Monastery just north of the Beltway, not far from Goucher College."

"I've heard of it," Ian said. "One of my graduate students recommended the 9:00 Mass on Sundays."

"If you go, you won't be sorry," Nora said. "When you mentioned your need for stillness, as you put it, I smiled to myself. I thought of Pascal's maxim, 'All the evil in the world can be traced to our inability to sit still in a room.' During my last two years at Penn State, I felt something very similar—a need for contemplation. I wanted to try a simpler way of living, a less driven way, a less competitive way. On the positive side, I wanted a more radical way of being a Christian. I believe I got a taste of that when I went to Mass at the Carmel. So, one Sunday after Mass I decided to speak to the prioress."

The arrival of their entrees broke the flow of Martin's story.

"I'm very glad I did. Six months later I entered the novitiate. The Baltimore Carmel is one of only about a dozen Carmelite monasteries in the world that renewed or updated after the Second Vatican Council. The sisters still wear cowled white robes for Mass and the chanting of the office, but they dress in ordinary, functional clothes when not in chapel for liturgy. The order of the day is pretty much what it's been for centuries—common prayer, two hours of contemplative prayer, common meals, common recreation, house responsibilities of various kinds. Some of the sisters offer spiritual direction to people outside the cloister."

"Didn't the deadly silence get to you after a while?" Ian asked.

"I thrived on it. It was *anything* but deadly. The renewed monasteries have a different understanding of cloistered life. It's less a matter of geography—sacred space within closed walls—than it is of a commitment to living in the presence of God in a monastic setting, in a monastic community. So we talked when necessary and when it seemed the healthy and human thing to do. We went to the dentist and doctor, we shopped for groceries and other necessities, we might visit our families for anniversaries and funerals if they lived nearby.

"No, it wasn't the silence that got to me. I came to see that my truth—that's how I think of vocation or calling—was to lead a contemplative life beyond the monastery."

"So you left."

"Yes, I left after my temporary vows expired. A few of the sisters remain dear friends. I visit as often as I can."

Landers sat back in his chair. He was moved. So this is where her spiritual depth came from. A line from Cicero's *De Amicitia* came back to him, a line he had memorized in his first year of Latin studies: *Nihil enim virtute amabilius.* Nothing is more lovable than goodness. Yes, Nora Martin was attractive, but what really quickened his pulse was her unvarnished goodness.

They walked together south down Charles Street, looking for some quiet place to stop for coffee or an after dinner drink, their shoulders and elbows lightly touching.

"What are you teaching this semester?" Nora asked, breaking the comfortable silence.

"It's a graduate seminar, Politics and Power in the Medieval Church. It fits nicely with the book I'm working on."

"Tell me about it."

"I'm not sure I should. It has a ring of the cloak and dagger about it."

Nora gave him an encouraging smile.

"We've known for a long time about secret clerical societies in Europe during the late Middle Ages and well into the early modern era. They claimed to be committed to identifying and rooting out heretics and to fighting the external enemies of the church. What I'm trying to do is not only understand the social dynamic at work there but to measure, in so far as any historian can, their influence on the church. The more I dig, the clearer it is that most were ambitious men eager for ever more lucrative, high-ranking appointments in the church. Many of the lower clergy desperately wanted to be bishops or abbots and get their hands on the riches such appointments would afford them. They all were rigidly orthodox theologically, but some of the prelates and priests I've come across had quite unorthodox views on sexuality, especially physical affection between members of their own clandestine society."

"Ian," Nora asked with rising energy in her voice, "have you heard of a secret society known as *Fideli d' Amore*—the Brotherhood of the Faithful in Love?

"How in the world did you ever hear of *Fideli d' Amore*? There are church historians who don't know a thing about the *Fideli*."

"I just know a secret Brotherhood existed," Nora said quickly. "I wouldn't say I know much about it."

"I really don't know that much about it, either. But then, who does? Kind of the point of a secret society. There's considerable evidence that the *Fideli* were an offshoot of the Knights Templar, the secret society of poets and financiers who considered themselves 'guardians of the supreme center'—the very heart and soul of the papacy and the Holy Roman Empire. This is quite a coincidence...the *Fideli* are on the syllabus for my graduate seminar."

Pleased too at the coincidence, and with herself, Nora had to tell Ian how she had come to know of the ancient secret society.

"The Baltimore Carmel is the oldest order of religious women in the colonial U.S. Our nuns arrived in Baltimore, actually Port Tobacco, in 1790, and moved to Baltimore proper twenty or thirty years later. The monastery's archives are in very good order. I came across the *Fideli* while trying to acquaint myself with the monastery's history. You really should take some time to see what's there."

Suddenly Nora wasn't pleased with herself at all. This discussion of *Fideli d' Amore* had smothered any romantic embers their dinner had fanned.

"I'd like very much to visit the archives. Can you really help me there, Nora?"

"I believe I can," Nora said. "Yes, I certainly can."

7

It took a half-dozen calls to raise the money, and the tedious process anchored Aidan Kempe to his desk until late in the afternoon. Now alone in his office, he stood at the corner window surveying the intersection of Cathedral and Mulberry Streets. It was almost five and the late January clouds layered the low sky in feathery bands of blue and gray. Streetlights were on, and Kempe drew a strange comfort from the stalled rush hour traffic and the anonymous figures filing heavily along the sidewalks. Few if any of the people below his window had the sense of mission and purpose that made his life so fascinating, so heroic. They were making a living. Monsignor Aidan Kempe was saving the Roman Catholic Church.

He loved these short days of winter, especially when the streets were wet with snow or rain. He did his best thinking and praying in this silent after-glow of twilight.

The Catholic Center staff was closing down for the day. Another fifteen minutes and he would be alone in the building. Only he and Bryn Martin regularly worked well into the evening. He clenched his teeth at the thought of Martin, the new auxiliary bishop of the archdiocese. Kempe had been informed by M and a local priest with Roman connections that his own name had made the short list. He had believed his chances were very good. Both he and Martin were protégés of Gunnison, but Kempe was Martin's senior in terms of ordination and Gunnison surely would have spoken up for him. It would have strengthened the Brotherhood to have a second bishop in its inner circle.

Kempe couldn't help it. He was still bitter at being passed over. It was no doubt Charles Cullen who had tipped the scale in Martin's favor. Cullen and Martin, he feared, were not good for the archdiocese and not good for the Church of Rome. They were among the diminishing breed of democracy-tainted American bishops and priests—too naïve to see the dangerous liberal underside to the Second Vatican Council, too trusting in the laity and the secular order. Their numbers were shrinking, Kempe thought, but not fast enough. He turned from the window and went back to his desk to call Gunnison.

"I've raised the money."

"Thank God," Gunnison whispered into the phone.

"I'll have a registered bank check drawn up and have my secretary bring it directly to your residence. You remember Margaret Comiskey, don't you?"

"Yes, she was one of the chancery secretaries when I was named archbishop."

"She will hand deliver a large envelope with your name and the word 'Confidential' printed on it. Inside will be a business size envelope with the check. Let me know the moment you hear from Anderlee."

Kempe hung up and took a black leather key case from his suit coat pocket and selected the key to a file drawer on the right side of his desk. There were no duplicates, and the key was always on his person. The drawer rolled open smoothly. Kempe kept at least ten thousand in cash in the drawer and the checkbook to the purple purse. The account bore the name Archdiocese of Baltimore, Emergency Fund. A small suburban bank held the account, and he was the only signatory. It had a balance of over seven hundred thousand dollars. Kempe's goal was to bring the purse up to a million in the next few years. But the file guarded something arguably as useful to Kempe as the influence and power the money could wield. It held his hand-written notes of allegations brought directly to him as vicar and chancellor against a dozen or so priests, a veritable spectrum of sins of the flesh—sexual misconduct with married women and adult men, with teenage boys, with pre-pubescent children; arrests for solicitation and possession of child pornography; allegations against pastors for skimming money from the Sunday collections and abusing their parish credit cards. At considerable risk to his own career, Kempe had deftly handled these allegations and arrests without informing other archdiocesan authorities, not even the archbishop. Kempe reported none of the allegations, including those of abuse involving minors, to the police. He took these risks to protect the church from scandal. The anti-Catholic media feasted on the sins of a small minority of Catholic clergy, and he wanted to save his weak brothers from public humiliation, from losing their pastorates, and, in some cases, from prison time.

Included in the file were three allegations of inappropriate sexual contact against Wilfred Gunnison, the retired, jubilee-celebrating archbishop of Baltimore.

Kempe removed his confidential journal and wrote: *Situation involving senior member of the Brotherhood may be resolved. Fifty K withdrawn from purple purse. Situation still a threat to the Brotherhood.* Kempe added the date and placed the journal into the file. He rolled the drawer shut and locked it, returning the key case to his pocket. With elbows on his desk, Aidan Kempe rested his head in his hands and rubbed his eyes. It had been a long day.

In spite of his fatigue, he was pleased with himself. Years before, when he had started working at the Catholic Center after his studies in Rome, a senior chancery priest had taken him aside. "The way to survive down here, Aidan, is to get something on your colleagues." Kempe remembered raising his eyebrows at the Machiavellian advice, but had said nothing, giving his seasoned advisor the barest hint of a smile. He was, he knew without the least bit of exaggeration, way ahead of his older colleague on that score.

Kempe rose from his chair and glanced around his office. It was without question the most elegantly appointed office in the Catholic Center, more tasteful, he believed, than even the archbishop's. His eyes moved from the deep purple drapes to the carefully chosen purple tones in the oriental rugs. The desk lamps had been chosen to give his book-lined office the feel of a study. He was seldom in a hurry to return to his suite in the Cathedral rectory. He moved back to the corner window, pleased with his day's work. The rush hour traffic had given way to the normal late evening volume. There was so much chaos out there, he thought, so much infidelity and cruelty. He shivered, though his office was comfortably warm. He was safe here, protected from the late winter wind.

He stood still at the window. Someone looking out from an office across Mulberry Street might see a dignified churchman standing as if in a portrait, the window casing serving as its frame. The image Kempe projected, however, was not that of a pastor. It was more of a corporate CEO or a U.S. senator. He was tired, but looked forward with pleasure to the unscheduled evening—a good meal, a glass or two of Pinot Noir, and the haunting spiritual power of Rachmaninov's *Vespers* awaited him.

The shimmering of red and white car lights in the slow-moving traffic kept Kempe at the window. It had rained a few hours earlier. Perfect. The red taillights, if he squinted a bit, seemed like vigil candles burning in all the churches of the archdiocese, and the white headlights seemed like so many candles standing guard at a church's altar. Many, maybe half, of the people in the cars and on the sidewalks below were Catholic. And he, financial vicar and chancellor of the Archdiocese of Baltimore and leader of the Brotherhood of the Sacred Purple, had to make sure their faith in the church was not disturbed. Most of the laity didn't know who Monsignor Aidan Kempe was. But he knew. He was, by the grace of God, their true spiritual father. At least in this archdiocese, he and the Brotherhood would save their church from the dissenters who wanted to replace the fear of God with the so-called "freedom" of God's people. They had no idea, he felt certain, just how dangerous freedom could be.

A dark figure moving toward the rectory's garage down the street caught his eye. Bryn Martin. Yes, he was certain it was Martin, dressed in jeans and a dark bomber jacket with the collar turned up. Kempe glanced at this watch. 6:30. Where was young Bishop Martin going? What was he up to? Jeans and a dark jacket, after all, were the cruising attire of the more worldly clergy. If he could have reached his car in time, Kempe would have followed him. Did Martin have a double life? The idea intrigued him. Kempe's heart was beating now with a rush of curiosity. And yes, if he were honest, with hope.

Before leaving his office, Kempe unlocked the file to make another entry.

Bryn Martin pulled up to the side entrance of the archbishop's residence, the same entrance Gunnison had used on the night that, in spite of all his efforts, Martin couldn't forget. The flashback lasted but a few seconds. Charles Cullen got in the car, dressed in dark slacks and an L.L. Bean cargo coat.

"Good evening, Charles."

Cullen nodded a greeting but looked uncomfortable. "I hope this goes all right."

In a matter of minutes the two bishops were driving north on Cathedral Street heading for the Loyola University campus.

"Tell me again how you got me into this," Cullen said.

"The director of campus ministry at Loyola asked me to give a talk on the church's social mission. Afterwards I met with the student justice commission and heard about their ministry to the city's street people. They invited me to come along and I found it was good for me. There was something…I don't know… *real* about it. And the students are terrific. They're my hope. So when my schedule permits, and it's seldom more than one night a month, I join them. They were excited to hear that you agreed to go out with them. I told them what the ground rules were, but you might go over them again yourself."

Cullen nodded in agreement.

"By the time we get there, the sandwiches and coffee will have been made and loaded into the campus ministry vans. I'll introduce you, you can say a few words, one of the students will lead us in prayer, and we'll head into the city."

Martin pulled up to the back entrance of the Student Union building. The bishops got out of the car and set matching green Loyola College caps low over their brows.

"Thank you for the invitation to join you this evening," Cullen began. "I've heard wonderful things about you and your ministry from Bishop Martin. He's said that you not only offer food and coffee to the homeless, you spend some time visiting with them. This effort to get to know these men and women as individuals impressed me. Help me to do that too. If they ask who I am, say I'm your godfather."

"Archbishop Cullen and I don't want our evening with you to become a distraction," Martin said. "I think you can imagine the lead on the local TV news: Two bishops feed Baltimore's homeless. That's the last thing we want. So, it's important, whenever Archbishop Cullen or I join you, that you keep it to yourselves."

44

The students nodded their understanding.

Martin turned to Cullen, "Archbishop, when I'm in the city with these young men and women, I've asked them to call me Bryn."

Cullen picked up the cue and said with a wink, "Well then, when I'm able to be with you, I'd suggest you simply call me 'Archie.'"

A few of the students said half aloud, "Cool."

"That means, of course, that this old man wants to get to know your names. Help me with that, will you please?"

Most of the students had never talked with an archbishop before. And with those few words, Charles Cullen became, in reality as well as title, archbishop and shepherd and friend to the Loyola students. They were slowly growing comfortable with him, and they sensed that he took them seriously. The archbishop was feeling the same way about them.

In the van during the drive into the city, Cullen asked, "What's it like being a young Catholic in today's world—and in today's church?"

The students went silent. They were already pretty comfortable with Martin when it came to talking about their lives and what mattered to them and disturbed them, but with the archbishop, it was a different matter.

A voice broke the uncomfortable silence.

"Archbishop, I'm Mary Ellen." Cullen was thankful that she was thoughtful enough to repeat her name. "I think most of us, at least the students I hang with, are trying to escape the success trap—making a lot of money and living in a big house in the suburbs. That's okay, of course, but we want to do something a little radical, like living simply and helping folks who don't have as much as we do."

"Yeah," another voice said from the back of the van. "I'm Matt, Archbishop. We're really turned on by the church's teaching on social justice, on peace in particular. That really gets to us. We admire Dorothy Day, Thomas Merton, Pope John Paul, and Archbishop Tutu. Maybe Bishop Martin told you that most of us have spent our spring breaks on service trips to El Salvador and Honduras. And Mary Ellen has gotten some of us to spend Wednesday evenings at the Catholic Worker house."

Matt stopped suddenly, thinking he was making himself and the others sound weird. "Don't get me wrong," he continued. "We do our share of partying and we know most of the bars in the Harbor area. But these food trips to do something small for the homeless, and the evenings at the Catholic Worker house...I don't know how to put it, but there is something real about it."

Cullen had the front passenger seat and he turned his back against the van's door so he could see the students in the rows of seats behind him.

"I don't think we're cynical," Mary Ellen said, "but we don't really trust institutions—like big business, big government, even big church. No offense, Archbishop."

"None taken," Cullen said, catching Martin's eye.

On the way back to Loyola, one of the seniors who had pretty much stayed at the archbishop's side throughout the evening suddenly said, "What we don't understand is much of the church's teaching on sex. You tell us that every sexual fantasy, desire, or act—if we're not married—is a mortal sin, like a spiritual felony. Man, aren't there any misdemeanors when it comes to sex?"

The others laughed nervously at the unintended informality, but they were glad for the senior's nerve in bringing up sex. Cullen and Martin were smart enough to just listen, and to say that they understood the student's concerns. A conversation had been joined.

Both Cullen and Martin knew how easy it would be for

the students to let it slip that sometimes when they went into the city to meet and feed the homeless they were joined by the archbishop of Baltimore himself. The students, it turned out, were mature enough to keep the bishops' involvement in their ministry to themselves. From the students' point of view, Martin learned later, it was a special night when he and "Archie" were able to join them.

8

Nora Martin made a left turn off Dulaney Valley Road onto a private, gently rolling drive that led to the Carmelite Monastery of the Sacred Heart, originally a mansion of colonial-style elegance constructed of craggy tan and brown Maryland stone. The additions the sisters made to accommodate the needs of the monastery blended the old and the new without distraction. The low-slung tile roof of the chapel caught Ian Landers' eye as he stepped out of the passenger door of Nora's car.

"The prioress is expecting us," she said to Ian as they approached the modest entrance. "She's Sister Miriam and a good friend. Before the renewal we would have addressed her as Mother Miriam. But now it's 'Sister.'"

They waited in a parlor warmed comfortably by the afternoon sun while the sister at the reception desk rang the prioress' bell code. Landers stood at a French window offering a broad view of the enclosure lawn and let the spirit of the place come over him. The monastery's footprint was a giant U, with the open end facing a grassy knoll on which a large crucifix stood facing the enclosure. Beyond the crucifix, Landers could see the monastery's wall, which eventually gave way to a wire fence. He would have loved a glimpse of the rolling meadow behind the monastery that Nora had described during their drive to the Carmel.

"First impression?" Nora asked now standing at his side, slipping her arm easily into his.

"It's a monastic gem," Ian said thoughtfully, putting his hand over hers on his arm. "From the towering trees to the striking architecture to the location in this wooded area."

"I thought you would like it. Really, most visitors are rather taken with the beauty."

"Welcome," said a soft but confident voice from the doorway behind them. Sister Miriam approached Nora and the women embraced.

Nora turned to Landers. "Miriam, I'd like you to meet my colleague at the University, Ian Landers. He's a professor of history, medieval history."

"I'm happy to meet you," Miriam said, catching Nora's eye with a smile.

"Thank you for making time for us, Sister," Ian responded, looking into the alert dark eyes of an attractive woman in her mid-fifties. As Nora had predicted, the nun was dressed simply—almost Amish-like—in an ankle-length dark brown skirt and an oxford blue, long-sleeved cotton blouse. "Your monastery is quite impressive."

Miriam smiled at the compliment and gestured to the linen-upholstered chairs.

"Nora mentioned you would like to view our archives."

"I would, very much."

"We've had a number of scholars interested in them. We like to think there's a good bit of history tucked away in them, and you're most welcome to spend as much time here as you need. Nora is familiar with their contents and will help you get acquainted with our cataloging system." Miriam glanced at Nora and added, "Let's have some coffee—or tea."

They moved to the guest kitchen used primarily for retreatants, where the prioress boiled water while Nora opened a box of cookies.

"Tell Ian about Father Combier," Nora said, placing a plate

of cookies on the table. "He was one of our first resident chaplains."

"Well," Sister Miriam began while pouring the tea, "Father Gilbert Combier, a Jesuit, arrived at our monastery in 1897. Apparently he came to America after working in the Vatican Archives and library for many years. He arrived, according to our oral history, with only two suitcases. The smaller of the two contained his breviary, bible, and a half dozen or so books. It also held a sheaf of papers, church documents of various sorts, carefully wrapped in sturdy paper and bound with heavy string. We know of these details from Mother Bernard, the former prioress, who was a novice when Father Combier arrived. Two of our older nuns, Benedicta of the Holy Cross and Ann of the Child Jesus, were novices under Mother Bernard. They are our last living link with our scholarly chaplain.

"They rather enjoy keeping his memory and legacy alive. I know they would enjoy meeting you. They're both up in years, but quite alert."

"I'd love to meet them if possible," Ian replied.

Sister Miriam went to the intercom and asked the receptionist to invite Mother Benedicta and Mother Ann to come to the guest parlor. "Both sisters," she said, returning to the table, "served as prioress many years ago, when the prioress was addressed as 'Mother.'" Ian smiled at Nora, aware of this fine point in Carmelite nomenclature. "They carry the honorific titles with graceful dignity," Sister Miriam said, almost winking.

"What seemed mysterious to the sisters when Father Combier arrived was his apparent haste in leaving Rome," Nora said, injecting a little mystery into the story.

Ian didn't pursue this bit of information. But he wouldn't forget it.

"Perhaps Nora mentioned that I'm working on a book on the dynamics of clerical ambition, politics, and power in the late

Middle Ages, Your archives, and especially the papers of your chaplain, might turn out to be very helpful to me."

The intercom rang and Sister Miriam rose to answer it.

"Mother Benedicta is able to join us, but Mother Ann is resting."

"Well, I'll let you two visit with Mother Benedicta, and then Nora can take you to the archives. She's quite familiar with them."

"Thank you very much, Sister Miriam," Ian said.

"I'll let the sisters know you're here," and then added with smile, "and that you might return." Then turning to Nora. "Show Professor Landers where the copy machine is. I suspect he'll want to use it."

She said to Landers, "You're welcome to copy any of the Combier papers that might relate to your research." Then, pleasantly but abruptly, the prioress said, "Now, please excuse me."

When Mother Benedicta arrived they moved back to the parlor and more comfortable chairs.

"Thank you for meeting with us," Ian said, "I hope this isn't inconvenient for you."

"You caught me at a good time. I was reading in my cell. Nora will probably tell you later that 'reading in my cell' is sometimes code for 'napping in my cell.'"

Landers liked her immediately. She struck him as an archetypal grandmother—at home with herself, beyond judgment, exuding a quiet but unmistakable delight. It was, he thought, delight at seeing Nora and meeting a friend of hers, but even more a fundamental delight with life itself.

Mother Benedicta understood immediately why Landers was interested in Father Combier and his papers. All Nora had to say was that Ian was writing about the ambition and power dynamics of medieval clergymen.

"Well, I never knew Gilbert Combier, of course, but I feel like I did. When I came to the monastery in 1942, Mother Bernard was still with us. She was a novice when Father Combier arrived, and the two became dear friends. It's clear they loved each other." Then she added, "Their relationship was a striking example of honest celibate love and loyalty. She was his confidant, and over time she came to know a great deal of his life at the Vatican and his work in the archives there."

"Do you have any idea," Landers asked, "why Father Combier left the Vatican?"

"Mother Bernard believed he had been disturbed by the intrigue there. I remember she used the word 'treachery,' which I've never forgotten. It seems Father Combier's faith had been shaken, not only by the mostly hidden scandals of the medieval church that he came across in the archives, but by the vices he came to see in the Roman clergy in his own time. Just why he left Rome, I can't say. Some of the sisters thought his health was the main reason for his leaving."

Nora could see Benedicta was tiring. "Thank you, Mother," she said. "It was very kind of you to meet with us."

"Mother, I am delighted to have met you," Landers added, eager to get to the Combier papers. He helped the elderly woman out of her chair. The light in her eyes had dimmed, but she replied crisply, "Oh, I enjoyed our little visit very much."

Nora placed the Combier papers in front of Ian and sat down next to him at the work table in the center of the second floor room that housed the monastery's archives. At first glance, Landers could see there were perhaps a hundred pages of letters, reports, journal entries, financial ledgers, including a few papal declarations and condemnations. Scanning the papers at the top of the pile, Ian concluded that Combier had hand-copied most of them from original archival material. But not all. The priest had taken quite a few original documents with him when he left for America. That took nerve and cunning. Landers' curiosity soared when he discovered, interspersed among the papers, Combier's own notes, some lengthy, written in French.

"Mother Bernard was one of the few sisters fluent in Italian and French. And she could read Latin. So we think she was somewhat of an assistant to Combier as he worked on his papers. We believe he was writing something, whether for publication or not, we don't know. Whatever it was, it's been lost."

Nora reached over, her elbow brushing against Ian's chest, and thumbed through the documents.

"I know you're searching for anything about the *Fideli d' Amore*, but there's a letter in here I want you to see." She pulled a page from a manila folder and handed it to Landers. Getting up from the chair next to Ian's, she walked around the table and sat across from him. Nora saw him look up, puzzled by her abrupt move. She tried to hold his gaze, but he quickly returned to the page in front of him. She wanted to see Ian's reaction as he read the letter written in 1477 from the bishop of Orvieto to the cardinal archbishop of Genoa. Ian furrowed his brow as he put the letter down. He was feeling the familiar rush of energy that accompanied the discovery of fresh evidence. "Nora, would you turn on the copy machine, please?"

9

Dan Barrett and Paul Kline spoke quietly into their cell phones, not wanting to be overheard by their wives or children.

"Mark called you, too?" Barrett asked.

"For Christ's sake, he's bought a condominium at the Harbor. Do you have any idea how much those condos cost?"

"He has his army pension and he probably saved a lot over the last twenty years."

"Still, those things are out of sight," Kline said. "I think you're thinking what I'm thinking...that he got a load of cash from Gunnison."

"I don't like this, Paul. I suggested the three of us get together and he said 'not for a while,' that he had some things to take care of. I should've asked him 'what things?' but I didn't. I can't forget what he said when we were leaving the bar, that he was gonna really scare Gunnison, make him shit in his pants. And maybe bring him down. Whatever that means."

"I know. I know. I don't know about Gunnison, but I think Mark is scaring the hell out of both of us," Kline said. "What do you think we should do?"

"I don't know," Barrett answered. "What can we do? Call Gunnison and say 'watch out, somebody plans to really scare you?' Or say, 'be careful, someone has threatened you?' I keep telling myself Mark hasn't hurt anyone."

"Yet," Kline added. "Maybe we should call him and say we

have to get together whether he wants to or not...that it's really important."

Barrett thought about this. All he could muster was, "I wish he was still living with his Aunt Margaret."

"Father, in your loving plan," Aidan Kempe prayed in a soft monotone, "Christ your Son became the price of our salvation. May we be united with him in his suffering so that we may experience the power of his resurrection in the kingdom where he lives and reigns with you and the Holy Spirit, one God, for ever and ever."

"Amen," answered the priests of the Brotherhood to the closing prayer of vespers.

"The Lord be with you," Kempe continued without raising his eyes from his breviary.

"And also with you," each responded.

"May Almighty God bless you, the Father, and the Son, and the Holy Spirit," Kempe intoned, making the sign of the cross over the Brothers of the Sacred Purple.

The five priests sat in the rectory study of Father Thomas Fenton. Kempe and Fenton sat in two leather wing chairs on either side of the gas fire that was the centerpiece of the book-lined room. The others, veteran priest Herman Volker, a personal friend of Wilfred Gunnison, and two of the archdiocese's younger pastors, Eric St. John and Paul Carafa, sat in Chippendale chairs arranged in front of the fireplace. The younger men were recruited because in Kempe's mind they had the potential to be players in the internal battle to keep the church orthodox. St. John held a master's degree in Liturgy from the University of Notre Dame and was perhaps a future master of ceremonies to the archbishop. Carafa, who did his seminary studies at the North American College in Rome, maintained good contacts at the Vatican.

The Brotherhood met monthly on a Sunday evening. Without fail, they began their meeting with vespers, the evening prayer of the breviary. Kempe then presided at a sort of business meeting which mostly came down to discussing tactics for promoting the appointment of orthodox priests to the episcopacy or, on the local scene, to positions of influence in the archdiocese. But the Brotherhood had an even loftier purpose—to save their archdiocese and the Catholic Church itself from the moral chaos and doctrinal unraveling fostered by the Second Vatican Council. By any means necessary.

On more than one Sunday evening, St. John and Carafa were made to listen to some of the Brotherhood's more memorable triumphs. "During the eighties and nineties," Kempe would begin with the precision of an academic, "perhaps even earlier, but we don't have the evidence to be sure, a group of maybe forty liberal bishops tried to take over the U.S. Conference of Bishops. I like to refer to them as the Brotherhood of Luther. They were really more Protestant than Catholic. They met two or three days before the U.S. bishops meetings in the spring and fall of every year, plotting various strategies and tactics to further the misguided policies and vision of Vatican II."

Kempe would pause here to see if Fenton or Volker wanted to add something about the demonic plot.

"Here's an example of how they operated. As you know, a little more than ten years ago the pope released an Apostolic Letter, *Ordinatio Sacerdotalis*, stating definitively that women could not be ordained to the priesthood. The Congregation for the Doctrine of the Faith said emphatically that the Apostolic Letter was to be considered to belong to the Deposit of Faith—to the supreme center of Catholic dogma. That wasn't good enough for the Brotherhood of Luther. These liberal bishops drew up a confidential paper for the bishops of the Conference titled "An Expression of Pastoral Concern" criticizing the theological and biblical foundations of the Congregation of the Faith's teaching that the Apostolic Letter was to be considered a matter of faith. Thank God the rogue bishops' statement didn't have any impact on the majority of the bishops, but it is a good example of how the Brotherhood of Luther tried to undermine the teaching office of Rome."

Fenton added, "It's fair to say that if it weren't for the Brotherhood of the Sacred Purple, the Brotherhood of Luther's statement of dissent may have gotten to the media. That would have caused all kinds of confusion and scandal."

"We can take some credit for the demise of the Brotherhood of Luther," Volker said confidently. "Maybe a *lot* of credit."

"Herm's right," Kempe said, "we have helped to ensure that the American bishops are unquestionably loyal and faithful to Rome, to the supreme center. Thanks to our work, the number of liberal bishops has dropped significantly. But we can't let down our guard. There are countless priests, religious, laity, and God knows still how many bishops we haven't yet identified who continue to believe the church can change, and should change, her timeless teachings."

The reminiscing was over.

"Perhaps you're wondering where Archbishop Gunnison is this evening," Kempe said, looking at St. John and Carafa.

"I'm afraid the Brotherhood may be faced with some danger," Kempe continued. "A man has approached the archbishop claiming he was sexually abused by him decades ago.

"The accusation is false," Kempe assured them. "The accuser is misinterpreting an innocent back-rub—most likely to achieve a financial windfall. For a number of reasons, not the least of which is the archbishop's approaching fiftieth ordination anniversary, we have made a sizable payment to him from the Brotherhood's purse. It appears he hasn't gone to the police and we believe he hasn't hired an attorney. The archbishop hopes, of course, that the money will mollify him and dissuade him from taking his accusation to the authorities or to the media. But we just don't know.

"It's best, I...we...thought, that the archbishop not attend our meeting this evening. Nor will he be coming to our meetings for the foreseeable future. He's thinking of what is best for the Brotherhood, even though, at least for now, the danger seems minimal. Obviously, we need to keep this situation in our prayers."

St. John and Carafa exchanged a nervous glance.

"There are a few priests who know we meet regularly and that the archbishop is part of our group," St. John said.

"Yes," Fenton responded. "But they think we're just another priest support group...a very orthodox and faithful group, to be sure, but nothing out of the ordinary. Our brother priests must never discover—they wouldn't understand—that we are committed to protecting the supreme center and working discreetly to assure that only faithful priests are named bishops."

"Don't be troubled, Fathers," Kempe said to the two junior priests, "the Holy Spirit is with us."

But Kempe himself was troubled, very troubled. There were signs that Gunnison was weakening under the pressure of Anderlee's threats. A public accusation against a member of the Brotherhood and Gunnison's fragile psyche could seriously threaten the mission, and secrecy, of the Brotherhood of the Sacred Purple.

"Please tell the archbishop we are praying for him," Carafa said sincerely to Kempe.

The Brotherhood sat quietly for a few minutes gazing at the fire.

"Well," Kempe said breaking the mood, "it's time for drinks." After half an hour of drinks, shrimp, goat cheese and crackers, and a generous serving of clerical gossip, each of the priests approached Kempe and placed an envelope in his hand containing a bank check for one thousand dollars.

"Your support of the purse is more important than ever," Kempe said seriously. "The archbishop's accuser has, quite regrettably, weakened it."

Fenton and Volker had coached the new pastors on ways to circumvent the parish finance council's oversight function. Your parish is your benefice, they instructed St. John and Carafa. As such, you have discretionary control over your parish finances. "Don't hesitate to exercise that power for the good of the Brotherhood," they had been told repeatedly.

Both young pastors respected Gunnison, Fenton and Volker, but they were in awe of Monsignor Aidan Kempe. He was a true defender of the church, and in their eyes he towered over Archbishop Gunnison. He spoke Italian and, more importantly, knew better than most how the Vatican bureaucracies worked. And it was Monsignor Kempe, not the archbishop, who was the Brotherhood's link to their Vatican protector, a bishop known only as M, whose identity was secret save to Kempe.

It was just a matter of time, both felt sure, until Kempe would be named a bishop. They had been deeply disappointed, even angered, when he had been passed over in favor of Bryn Martin.

And once Kempe was a bishop, who knew what the future might hold for their own careers?

10

In the early summer of 1477," Ian Landers said to his seminar students, "during the reign of Pope Nicholas V, a young nobleman in service to the bishop of Orvieto delivered a letter to the cardinal archbishop of Genoa. Along with the letter, the tonsured messenger carried a monetary gift for the cardinal, and a personal gift—himself.

"I have a translation of the letter here for each of you. Take a minute to read it."

Alfonso Cardinal Colonna
Archbishop of Genoa

Your most esteemed Eminence,

> *Grace and peace to you as you celebrate the fifth anniversary of your elevation as Prince of the Church. May God sustain you in health and prosperity in your faithful service to Jesus Christ and in your governance of His Holy Church.*

> *The bearer of this letter, Ascanio Sforsa, my personal secretary for the past year, brings into your exalted presence my humble gift of one thousand ducats. May it please your Eminence to use this expression of my respect for the works of mercy and charity for which you are rightly renowned or for any other purpose that may please you.*

> *Ascanio desires a life of service to the Church and has the blessing of his family, the ruling family of the Duchy*

of Milan. He is a pious, pleasing, and comely young man. His Latin and Greek are superior and he is fluent in both French and Spanish. In spite of his youth and inexperience, Ascanio has assisted me with prudence and discretion in the governance of my humble diocese. Moreover, he oversees the ordering of my household, and his daily presence has proven to be a source of comfort and solace to me.

May I humbly propose that your Eminence admit Ascanio to service in your household if this be pleasing to you. You will find that he is indefatigable in his desire to please. And I assure you of his total discretion in ecclesiastical and personal affairs.

Should you find Ascanio worthy of a place in your household, the Sforsa family would be eager to express their gratitude to you and I would be deeply honored.

I remain ever ready to be of service to you, your Eminence, and to your family. May Almighty God fortify you and the house of Colonna with His strength and protection.

Kissing the sacred purple, I remain

Your humble servant,

+Francesco Barbiano
Bishop of Orvieto
June 30, 1477

The graduate students in Landers' seminar looked up as they finished reading. There were a few cynical smiles but most were waiting to see how their professor would respond.

Landers hesitated. The two students from St. Mary's Seminary seemed on edge.

"Well, what do you think?"

"Bishop Barbiano was a shrewd, calculating climber," began

John Pointer, one of two doctoral students who regularly intimidated his masters-level classmates. "I give him credit for knowing how to play the game."

Ellen Stark, the other doctoral student, was less generous. "This is pandering at its worst. Do you think Machiavelli could have been a nephew or relative of Barbiano?" she asked. Landers raised his eyebrows—a sure sign he was pleased with the allusion to the cunning master of political strategy and tactics. Stark continued, "It's too bad we don't have any idea how Ascanio Sforsa felt about this arrangement. Was he, too, making his way in the church circles of his day? Or was he being exploited by Barbiano?"

"Maybe he just wanted to be a good priest one day and was being obedient to his bishop," Nolan Connors, one of the seminarians, interrupted.

"Okay, sure," Stark shot back. "I'm not trying to judge the guy's motives. I'm just wondering if this is another incident of a patriarchy's abuse of power."

She paused and looked at Landers, then continued, "Is this kind of thing typical of the period? It seems like a carry-over of the greed and lust for power we saw in the ninth-and-tenth-century papacies."

"You're right," Landers said. "It is. The corruption in the church during the fourteenth, fifteenth, and sixteenth centuries has many similarities to the period you mentioned. In fact, Sforsa's case is telling. I don't think we need to feel too sorry for Ascanio. He eventually became a cardinal, a very wealthy cardinal, and was the only real rival to Cardinal Rodrigo Borgia of Valencia in the papal election in 1492. There's evidence, by the way, that Borgia bought the votes of at least thirteen cardinals before or during the conclave. And I don't have to tell graduate students that Alexander VI was not the first cardinal to buy the papacy."

The seminarians looked uneasy.

"I think we're missing something here," Connors said. "Men like Bishop Barbiano may well be reprehensible, but I don't think he and others like him were typical of the majority of bishops. They may not have been as outstanding as Saint Charles Borromeo, but shouldn't we assume most bishops were good men?"

"That's a fair point, Nolan, in fact, an important point," Landers said, affirming him. "As we look at this period from the perspective of clerical ambition, the sources we have tell only a partial story. They miss a lot of greed and ruthlessness as well as a lot of virtue and holiness. And we shouldn't be surprised that goodness and virtue are more difficult to recognize—and less interesting—than greed and ruthlessness. But let's stay focused on the churchmen who wanted to rise in the ranks of the hierarchy. It's time for our break, however. When we return, Mr. Pointer will give us a progress report on his research paper."

The students pushed their swivel chairs back from the table and headed for the coffee machines or the rest rooms.

"If you are ready, John…?" Landers said politely.

"What's fundamental to our understanding of clerical ambition, wealth, and power in the late Middle Ages," Pointer began, "is something Professor Landers has emphasized from the first week of the seminar. The structure of the church mirrored the economic, social, and political structure of Western Europe at the time. And that structure, as you know, was monarchical and feudal. In my paper, I'm focusing primarily on the feudal nature of the church and only indirectly will I address the church as monarchy, or perhaps more precisely, the church as a spiritual empire." Pointer paused, made eye contact with Ellen Stark with a look that asked, *You're impressed, aren't you?* Stark returned his glance with exquisite indifference. Pointer recovered quickly, "It might help to think of a country priest as a vassal to his bishop.

And a bishop, say Bishop Barbiano, as a vassal to the pope, or in his case, as a vassal to the archbishop, Cardinal Colonna."

"And what is the fundamental, operative virtue in feudal societies?" Landers asked.

"Loyalty," Ellen Stark said confidently.

"Yes," Pointer said, annoyed at Stark's competitiveness. "And while loyalty was essential for holding feudal societies together and keeping them safe from invaders, there was a shadow side to it. Loyalty on the part of an inferior to a superior can repress honest communication. Vassals know it can be dangerous to speak too candidly to their lord. And it can further an unhealthy docility. If you're a vassal, you don't want to cross the lord of the manor or the duke or the king who has granted you your benefice or your little fiefdom. It's obviously a hierarchical system." Pointer looked at Stark and added, "And with few exceptions, patriarchal to its core."

Landers noticed that Nolan Connors was listening carefully to Pointer's presentation. Perhaps some lights were going on in the seminarian's mind.

"So," Pointer went on, "how does an ambitious priest or bishop get ahead in a clerical system that is essentially feudal? First of all he has to get noticed. Some of the methods I've discovered include flattery, especially the kind we saw in Barbiano's letter, and, if he can afford it, discreet and tasteful gifts. It's a system that operates indirectly—by currying favor, by gossip, by exaggerated deference. Of course, the clerical climber has to have a certain level of intelligence. After that, language skills and family connections help immensely."

"Thank you, John," Landers said with a nod. "That's what I'm looking for in these reports. What John didn't have time to discuss is the last section of his paper in which he examines the role sex played in climbing the hierarchical ladder. You noted, I'm sure, the sexual overtones in the letter to Cardinal Colonna.

"We have a few minutes left. Any questions?"

"Professor Landers," one of the masters-level students asked, "What's the meaning of the closing to Bishop Barbiano's letter? What's 'kissing the sacred purple?'"

A few students smirked. If they didn't know the answer, they had the imagination to come up with one.

"I thought you might be wondering about that," Landers responded, without any acknowledgment of double entendre. "It's an ecclesiastical expression that is common even today in some church circles. The cleric of a lower rank or a lay person is saying in effect, 'I kneel and kiss the purple hem of your sacred robe.' A little over the top to us moderns. But in Barbiano's era, it was simply part of church etiquette."

Landers paused. Some of the students looked as if they found the expression ludicrous.

"By the way," Landers went on, "You should know the significance of the color purple."

Nolan Connors shifted in his seat. I know where he's going with this, the seminarian said to himself, as he thought of Jesus' parable about poor Lazarus and the "rich man who dressed in purple garments and fine linen." He almost interrupted with this bit of biblical corroboration but thought better of it and let Landers continue.

"Before the modern era, there was a substance that was as valuable as gold, a substance that provoked wars and toppled kingdoms, a substance that made fortunes and opened doors to the inner circles of power." He paused for a few seconds. "I'm referring to murex purple, or Tyrian purple—made from the dye obtained from murex shellfish. Some of the best murex species were found on the coast of Tyre. When crushed alive, they produce a purple liquid that is the base substance of the dye. Thousands of snails had to be killed to make enough dye for a single purple robe or garment. It was, of course, extremely expensive.

Purple, we shouldn't be surprised, became the color of royalty and the very rich, and later the designated color of the church's princes. It didn't take long before the color purple, especially in higher ecclesiastical circles, became 'sacred purple,' *sacra purpura*.

"When we meet next Thursday, Ms. Stark will make a progress report on her paper. Her working title, you might be interested in knowing, is "Homosexual Courtly Love and Clerical Ambition in Sixteenth Century Europe."

11

Wilfred Gunnison didn't think of himself as vain—just appropriately concerned about his episcopal appearance. He wasn't pleased with his weight, but the dinners that filled his calendar, especially since his retirement, had taken their toll. Still, at six-feet-one he was, he thought, only slightly heavy. His clear, Nordic blue eyes looked out through rimless glasses and were guarded by full, grey-white eyebrows. Wavy white hair, trimmed twice monthly by a stylist, provided a striking contrast to the fuchsia zucchetto he wore when vested. With a miter on his head and a crozier in hand, he knew he cut an especially handsome figure. In fact, not a few of Baltimore's leading Catholic women had told him he epitomized the archetypal bishop—a dignified, even stately demeanor, a congenial yet reserved personality. He never took these remarks to be flattery.

Gunnison pulled on a black cashmere overcoat and caught a glimpse of himself in the full-length mirror on the closet door just inside his small but elegant residence nestled next to the Basilica. Not bad, he thought, for a man in his late seventies. Tonight he was scheduled for the sacrament of confirmation at St. Bernardine's Parish, a task he still enjoyed for the most part. The pattern seldom varied—a passable meal in the rectory with the pastor and his staff, the photo-op at the reception in the parish hall, the mostly pleased but out-of-their-element parents, and of course the nervous, somewhat dazed *confirmandi*—although one had to be on guard about any touching of children since the sexual abuse scandals. Strangely, Gunnison's own "randy behavior," as he chose to think of it in recent years, didn't factor into his concern about interacting with parents. There would be just two more confirmations before his Jubilee Mass and dinner, now just three weeks away.

Mark Anderlee arrived at St. Bernardine's forty minutes before the beginning of the Confirmation Mass and secured a place in the choir loft, directly in front of the loft rail and up against the right side wall of the church. His position gave him a clear line of fire to the altar and the center aisle of the church. The stairs to the loft—his planned escape route—were no more than fifteen feet away. Anderlee wore a knee-length, bulky parka and had a soft Irish cloth cap in his pocket that he would don right after the hit. The choir members who noticed him more than likely thought he was as a divorced parent who felt compelled to attend his son or daughter's confirmation but didn't want to intrude on the family celebration. Anderlee was certain this could work— that he could make his way down the choir loft stairs and out of the church without being noticed or at least described in any detail to the police.

Before the final blessing, Archbishop Gunnison congratulated the *confirmandi* and started the applause that was sustained by proud parents and relatives. He thanked the parents for their example of Christian living, which, he said, had undoubtedly influenced the young men and women in their decision to be confirmed. The litany of gratitude that followed was one Gunnison knew by heart. He directed thanks to the parish staff and the religious educators who had prepared the young adults for confirmation, their sponsors, the servers, the choir, and finally offered a warm affirmation of St. Bernardine's pastor, Father John Krajik. Another round of applause. At this point, it was common for the pastor to move to the ambo and thank the confirming bishop.

Krajik gently nudged Gunnison aside with a smile.

"On behalf of the parish of St. Bernardine and our newly confirmed members, I want to thank Archbishop Gunnison for his presence this evening and for conferring this sacrament on our *confirmandi*." Krajik paused but a few seconds. "As many of you know, in just a few weeks Archbishop Gunnison will celebrate the fiftieth anniversary of his ordination to the priesthood." Turning to Gunnison, he said sincerely, "Congratulations, Archbishop. You have our prayers and best wishes."

The applause that followed was genuine and sustained. Gunnison was moved.

After the final blessing and dismissal, Gunnison kissed the altar, genuflected to the tabernacle, and turned to take his place at the end of the recessional. As he left the sanctuary, he began turning alternatively from the right bank of pews to the left, imparting a silent episcopal blessing as he processed down the center aisle. His smile was kindly yet reserved.

Anderlee opened his parka and readied himself. The choir's attention was focused on their director. He rested his elbows on the choir loft railing, steadying his aim. His target was dead center in the crosshairs of his Leupold scope.

As Gunnison passed the fifth row of pews, a laser beam suddenly appeared on his chest. Gunnison's first awareness that something was amiss came from the startled expressions on the faces he was blessing. People turned but didn't know where to look. Most in the church had missed it, but enough of the assembly had seen the red dot resting squarely over the heart of the archbishop to cause gasps of alarm and whispers of confusion and concern.

In self-conscious slow motion, Archbishop Gunnison unvested in the sacristy. What could the laser beam have meant? Was he a target of some deranged anti-cleric? What made him visibly shake was the rising fear that the beam that rested on his chest was a warning, or some kind of message of an impending act of revenge.

"You really don't have to go to the reception, Archbishop," John Krajik said to a preoccupied, flushed Gunnison.

"No, I think it best I make an appearance," Gunnison responded bravely. "The laser dot was probably just a prank by some kid."

A half hour later, Father John Krajik, respected by the priests of the archdiocese and loved by his parishioners, walked a still-shaken archbishop to his car in the church parking lot. Gunnison had insisted Krajik not call the police, but he welcomed the sight of a uniformed off-duty policeman hired for traffic control and security.

Without reason, Krajik felt responsible for the bizarre ending to the confirmation liturgy. "I really regret what happened, Archbishop. I don't know what to think."

"I don't know what to make of this either, John. I still think it was just a prank. Let me know if you hear anything from your parishioners." Before pulling out of the parish parking lot, Gunnison gave Krajik his cell phone number. The pastor stood watching until the archbishop's car was out of sight.

Back in the rectory, Krajik went straight to his phone and punched in the number of Archbishop Charles Cullen. His next call was to Bishop Bryn Martin.

At eight thirty the next morning, Martin, Kempe, and Gunnison were all seated in Archbishop Cullen's office.

"Any idea what this is about, Wilfred?" Cullen began.

"I don't, Charles. It was probably a prank, or a crazy."

Since the clergy abuse scandals in Boston made the national media in 2002, many bishops were wary of the public. Some were more than wary; they were outright paranoid.

Kempe avoided direct eye contact with Gunnison. Both men, in fact, had a very good idea what this was about. And they suspected the other two men in the room did too. Martin caught Cullen's eye, but both churchmen knew how the meeting had to progress. The first concern Cullen raised was for Gunnison's safety. "I'm not going to walk around with a bodyguard at my side," Gunnison said testily. "Let's not overreact here." The second concern, which was really the more important but could not be acknowledged as such, focused on the possibility that the media might hear that the retired archbishop of Baltimore had been the target of a laser beam. As soon as Cullen had addressed Gunnison's safety and well-being, the protocol card had been played. Now it was appropriate to turn the conversation to their real concern—the public relations crisis that the incident at St. Bernardine's might trigger.

"Aidan," Cullen said, "I'd like you to meet with our media director and draft a statement. You'd better get on this right away." Kempe nodded and rose immediately from his chair.

Waiting for the elevator, Kempe felt the adrenaline rush such crises always elicited in him. He believed he knew more about public relations than the overpaid professionals. This was one of his God-given gifts, along with sniffing out bishops who weren't unquestioningly loyal to Rome. Before the elevator door opened on the first floor of the Catholic Center, Kempe had mentally crafted a statement.

Mark Anderlee could be behind this. A bitter wash of phlegm coated his tongue and mouth as he thought of the hundred thousand he had pulled together in a matter of hours. If anything happened to Gunnison—it wasn't the first time an archdiocesan priest had been stalked or threatened by a victim of abuse—or if this became a media circus, the Brotherhood would be put in serious jeopardy. This, Kempe told himself, he would not let happen.

Back in Cullen's office, Gunnison reached for his calendar. He had two more confirmations, one at Immaculate Conception parish in Towson and another at St. Ignatius in Baltimore, before his Jubilee Mass and fundraising dinner.

"The timing of this incident couldn't be worse, with my Mass and dinner just around the corner," he said wearily. "Let's hope it was nothing more than a hoax of some sort."

"Yes, we all hope that's the case, Wilfred," Martin said. "But let's think through the worst possible scenario. What if someone is out to embarrass you and possibly hurt you? Whether or not there was a weapon attached to that laser…we have to consider the possibility."

Cullen remained silent, studying Gunnison.

"We need to consider," Martin went on, "calling in the police, and we need to consider protection for you until we get this cleared up."

"That would only make matters worse," Gunnison said softly. "Let's consider this a prank, at least for now. And I don't think I should ask either of you to take the two confirmations I have. I know we're considering the worst case scenario here, but I've received no threatening calls or messages. I want this to be down-played."

"Bryn, do we have any retired policemen we could ask for some unofficial and private help?" Cullen asked. "Or retired FBI?"

"That might be the way to go," Martin said, leaning forward in his chair. "I know two men who might help us. One is retired FBI and the other was with the Secret Service before the travel and time away from his family got to him. They're Loyola College alums and probably in their late fifties now, but I think they can handle themselves just fine. This would save us, Wilfred, from requesting police protection for you."

They were quiet for a moment.

"The best case scenario," Cullen said, "is that some friend or acquaintance of one of the kids being confirmed got a laser for Christmas or a birthday and was showing off. But Bryn is right, we have to act on the worst case scenario. Wilfred, I'm sure you understand."

Gunnison nodded and whispered a soft, "Yes, you're no doubt right, Charles."

Without knocking, Kempe walked back into Cullen's office with draft copies of a statement. He read it aloud while the three bishops followed along.

"At the conclusion of the Confirmation Mass at St. Bernardine's Church on February 5th, a laser beam was observed focused on Archbishop Wilfred Gunnison, the retired archbishop of Baltimore. Anyone with information concerning this incident is urged to contact the police or the chancellor's office of the Archdiocese of Baltimore."

"Don't you think the statement should say that neither the archbishop nor the archdiocese have any idea what might have motivated this incident?" Gunnison asked expectantly.

There was an awkward silence.

Both Martin and Kempe shook their heads. Kempe said decisively, "We'd be encouraging speculation. If we have to go with a statement, the less said the better." Another brief silence as the three men looked to Charles Cullen.

Cullen nodded his approval. "We'll have it ready should the media want some comment from us. Of course, if we issue the statement, the police will be involved and that means they will have questions we have to be ready to handle. Aidan, you'll be the spokesperson if this gets to the media. And give John Krajik a call. Tell him to direct any media inquiries to you at the Catholic Center. It's important we keep him in the loop as much as we can."

Cullen's "Thank you" signaled the meeting was over.

As Martin moved to the door he turned to Cullen and Gunnison, "I'll make the calls to the retired agents today."

Kempe hid his surprise at the remark. What had he missed while he was drafting the statement? What agents was Martin referring to? He had an idea what Martin had in mind, of course, but especially in the inner workings of the diocese, knowledge, specific knowledge, was power. And in the present crisis mode, his being at the center was critical.

12

Ian Landers' mother phoned a few days after the seminar.

"Ian? It's Mother. How are you?"

"Wonderful. And how are you?" he asked in turn.

"I'm fine, dear. Listen," Ella Landers asked straight out, "can you possibly come to a little dinner party this Friday?"

"Yes, yes I can," Ian responded after a quick look at his calendar.

"I want you to bring your colleague, Nora Martin, the one you've been talking about. I'm not prying, Ian, believe me. I'd just love to meet her. I've invited my high school friend, Margaret Comiskey...she's worked at the Catholic Center for ages and it turns out that she is a good friend of Nora's brother, Bishop Martin. Margaret is driving down with the bishop, who is able to join us."

"I'll call Nora as soon as I get off the phone. I've heard a lot about Bishop Martin from Nora and I'd very much like to meet him."

"Well, Margaret tells me the bishop would like to meet you as well," Ella said, lifting her voice. "It should be a wonderful party, don't you think?"

Before Ian could respond, Ella added, "Around seven then. Call if Nora can't make it. See you this Friday. I can't wait."

"It was clear Bryn liked you, Ian," Nora said on the drive back to Baltimore after the dinner.

"I don't think I've ever met a bishop quite like him. What really struck me about him," Ian responded, "was the way he kept Margaret in the conversation. He treated her like a colleague rather than the chancellor's secretary. It's clear she's an intelligent and capable woman. I'm sure my mother would do anything for her."

"Bryn's told me she's had a tough life," Nora said. "Dropped out of college to take care of her widowed father. Years later when he died, she stayed on at the Catholic Center. Never married. Made working for the church her life. She has a widowed sister, Ann, I believe, who now lives in South Carolina. Ann has a son and Margaret is his godmother. Her sister and her nephew are the only family that's left. The nephew just retired from a career in the army and is back home in Baltimore. Bryn thinks he might be staying with Margaret until he can find a place of his own.

"Your mother and Bryn were both fascinated to hear about the Combier papers. You're obviously absorbed with them."

"I've still got a lot of work to do on them," Ian said. "There must be some reason why Father Combier came to Baltimore when he left the Vatican. Why the States? Why Baltimore? And I'm coming across notes he made on still another secret clerical society—the Brotherhood of the Sacred Purple. Combier believed they were an offshoot of *Fideli d' Amore,* just as the *Fideli* were an offshoot of the Knights Templar."

"Who would've thought the Carmelites were sitting on this little treasure of church history?" Nora said, pleased with Ian's interest in the Combier papers...and pleased with her role in bringing them to his attention.

Less than a mile behind Ian's car, also heading north on Interstate 95, Bishop Martin and Margaret Comiskey drove for the most part in silence.

"Ella Landers is really remarkable, Margaret. How she prepared a meal like that and still found time to be present while we had drinks was quite a trick."

"She's a very capable person, Bryn, and a wonderful friend. She makes everything she does look easy, effortless. Really, her life couldn't be more different than mine—Foreign Service, all those years abroad, meeting Owen, a son like Ian, not to mention her clandestine life with the CIA. But she always stayed in touch. We wrote to each other at least once a month and called on our birthdays and at Christmas."

"I'm not sure there are many friendships like that today," Bryn said. "At least not among men."

"You know I haven't much family. My sister Ann and her husband moved to South Carolina before he died. But my nephew, Mark, is in Baltimore. He just retired from the army and stayed with me for a while until he got his own place. My sister, Mark, and Ella mean the world to me." Comiskey fell silent, starring through the windshield at the soft glow of the taillights in front of them. Her world was so small compared to Ella's.

Martin glanced over at her. "You seem a little tired, Margaret."

"I probably am," she said returning his glance. Then haltingly, "There's something I've been wanting to talk to you about for some time now."

"This might be as good a time as any," Martin said gently.

"It's very delicate, Bryn. I'm sure you know that being secretary to Aidan Kempe is very different from working with you when you were in the chancellor's office."

Martin gave Margaret a guarded yet knowing look.

"It has to do with Kempe. Tonight when Ian was telling us about the Combier papers he's working on and the secret societies of priests Combier had discovered, I decided to say something about what I've noticed since I started working for him. But I need to get my thoughts in order. Tonight's not the right time. When Kempe's out of the office and you've got some time, I'd like to tell you what I've seen and heard."

"Of course, Margaret," Martin said. "But we should talk soon."

"Yes, we should talk soon," Comiskey said with evident fatigue; then she closed her eyes and leaned back against the headrest.

Turning off the lights in her condo, Ella Landers knew that something happened during the evening that she didn't quite understand. Both Margaret and the bishop took more than a casual interest in Ian's discovery of the Combier papers. Something told her that it wasn't just about sixteenth century Italy and the machinations of ambitious bishops. She would have to talk to Margaret—and to Ian.

She let her thoughts turn to Nora Martin and her bachelor son. Might she become a grandmother after all?

13

Mark Anderlee made his way up the open staircase in the back of Immaculate Conception Church. He would remain in the choir loft until the recessional following the Confirmation Mass and then take up a position on one of the lower stairs. The height advantage would be just right for the laser hit on Gunnison's chest as he came toward him down the center aisle. The beam would rest on its target for two seconds. Gunnison would have a restless night. Anderlee wanted the old man to know there was more to come.

There had been nothing in the *Baltimore Sun* about his first hit on Gunnison. Good, Anderlee thought. It would make this second hit easier. The guy had to be nervous after his last confirmation. Tonight might make the bastard a complete nervous wreck. Then, Anderlee mused, he would have the pleasure of ruining the archbishop's big party.

The scent of incense reached the choir loft where Duane Moore, retired FBI special agent, scanned the parishioners gathering below for the Confirmation Mass. He loved the Church of the Immaculate Conception, his boyhood parish, but maybe he loved the elementary school even more. He had been an altar boy here, the first black to serve Mass, and he remembered how he had loved the smell of beeswax candles and the hint of starch in the white surplices. The parish was still mostly white, but blacks and

Hispanics now had their place. He remembered the nuns. Almost all were kind and encouraging. The priests made him nervous.

But tonight was different. He wasn't here to pray or even to remember his boyhood years. He sat close to the west wall of the choir loft. His position put his earpiece out of sight and his whisper into the wrist mike was soft enough not to be overheard.

"Havel? You in place?" George Havel, the retired Secret Service agent, was stationed in the door of the darkened sacristy with a good line of vision to most of the congregation.

"Yeah. Nothing out of the ordinary. It's the recessional I'm worried about."

Moore turned slightly to his right and scanned the dozen or so non-choir members. Five couples who probably were aunts and uncles of the kids being confirmed, an athletic looking man, alone, sitting erect with his shoulders squared, maybe a divorced parent who hadn't been invited to the Mass, and two teenage boys who were busy texting or playing a computer game on their iPods. The ritual seemed interminable, the Confirmation Rite alone taking half an hour. Finally the sign of peace and the hundreds below started moving slowly up to the front of the church for Communion. Only the two teens and the lone male didn't march down the steps into the nave for Communion. Moments later the choir members were climbing back to the choir loft.

"Everything looks good from here," Havel's voice said in Moore's earpiece.

"Same," Moore whispered into his wrist mike. Both men knew the laser dot had hit the archbishop at the end of the Mass as he processed out of St. Bernardine's Church.

Archbishop Gunnison raised his right hand and gave the final blessing, genuflected towards the tabernacle, and took his place at the end of the recessional. The choir, accompanied by two trumpeters and the organ, began the recessional hymn, "Holy God We Praise Thy Name." With his crozier in his left hand, Gunnison carefully took the three steps down from the sanctuary and started down the center aisle. He turned slightly from one side of the aisle to other, blessing the assembly with silent signs of the cross as he moved with episcopal dignity towards the vestibule. He tried hard to project a kindly, fatherly expression, one he had mastered years before. But it didn't work. Tension ballooned in his chest. He couldn't mask the fear in his eyes. Instead of the respectful nods he was used to, the parishioners were staring at him. Impulsively, Gunnison glanced down at the purple-trimmed off-white vestment and the gold-plated pectoral cross that the laser dot had targeted the week before. Just another fifty feet and he would be at the door of the church.

Duane Moore's elbows rested on the choir loft railing as he scanned the assembly below. He saw nothing the least bit suspicious. He leaned back and studied the people in the loft. Each of the choir members held a hymnal, eyes moving from their music to the choir director and back to the hymnal. The two teens were gone—and so was the jock, the man he had pegged as the divorced dad.

"George," Moore said into his wrist mike, "look for a single male, long coat, military bearing, late thirties, early forties. He was up here in the loft a minute ago. I can't find him!"

Mark Anderlee stopped at the third step from the bottom of the open staircase and opened his coat.

Gunnison was just thirty feet from the vestibule when the laser beam hit. It rested steady for two full seconds just above his pectoral cross. He didn't see the red dot, but the surprised and confused expressions on some of the faces he was blessing made Gunnison flinch.

Havel, ten feet behind the archbishop, saw a man in a dark coat dart out of the church. As he rushed to Gunnison's side, he saw Moore moving as quickly as his middle-aged legs would permit down the choir loft steps and out the right front door.

Gunnison was smart enough to keep moving, trying to act as if everything was all right. Havel, now at his side, ushered the red-faced archbishop back to the sacristy by way of the side aisle.

"I don't know what to make of this," Gunnison whispered to Havel, trying to hide and steady his shaking hands. Moore ran into the sacristy, breathing heavily. "Our shooter was male, average height, late thirties, early forties, athletic, and in good shape. He was gone by the time I got outside the church."

Gunnison felt sick. The description fit Anderlee.

"Any idea what this is about, Archbishop?" Moore asked.

"No, no, I don't. It's probably a not-so-funny prank," Gunnison said. At that moment he wanted nothing more than a tumbler of scotch. Then he added, very formally, "Thank you both for giving up your evening."

Havel and Moore exchanged a glance. The archbishop wasn't telling the truth.

Dropped back at his residence by Duane Moore, who secured the premises before leaving, Gunnison poured himself a scotch and called Aidan Kempe. The chancellor listened to Gunnison's shaking voice and incoherent account of the second laser incident without any show of surprise—or of any concern for the archbishop.

"I'm not going to disturb Cullen at this hour. I'll call him first thing in the morning. He'll want to see you, Martin, and me as soon as possible. This is getting out of hand, Wilfred."

Kempe hung up with considerable impatience. Gunnison was a mess—that much was clear. And Kempe was ready to bet the purple purse that Mark Anderlee was behind the laser hits. The hundred grand wasn't enough for the greedy bastard. Whoever was behind this bizarre, sick little game had a plan, a plan that might well culminate at Gunnison's jubilee. Every instinct in his weary body told him this was moving with mounting speed to a public relations disaster. Gunnison, damn him, was putting the Brotherhood of the Sacred Purple at risk.

Gunnison's hand shook as he put down his phone. His rising anger at the outrageous disrespect of Kempe's abrupt termination of their phone call overcame his paralyzing fear for his safety—and for his reputation as the distinguished retired archbishop of Baltimore, the very seat of American Catholicism. Now angry, anxious, and frightened, the old man went back to his liquor cabinet. Scotch and a prescription narcotic were his only hope for the deliverance of sleep.

14

What happened last night at Immaculate Conception, Wilfred?" Charles Cullen asked his tense and drained brother bishop. He listened, along with Bryn Martin and Aidan Kempe, to Gunnison's shaky recollection of the laser spot appearing on his chest as he moved down the center aisle after the Confirmation Mass.

"Bryn," Gunnison said meekly, "thank you for arranging for the two security men. One of them, the one in the choir loft, thinks he saw the man with the laser. He said he was in his late thirties or early forties and rather athletic looking. But he didn't get a good look at his face."

"How are you holding up, Wilfred?" Cullen asked.

"This is rather unsettling, as you can imagine. My anniversary Mass and dinner...I don't want anything to throw that off." Gunnison paused, looking at each of the three men. "And I'm scheduled for another confirmation at St. Ignatius next week."

"Let me take that confirmation for you, Wilfred," Martin offered.

Gunnison nodded his acceptance. "Thank you, Bryn. I'd appreciate that." Another pause. "I still can't figure out what's going on."

Cullen's and Martin's eyes locked in on Gunnison's glassy, dark-circled eyes. Both men thought, *Level with us, Wilfred, level with us.* Kempe's expression remained impenetrable.

"So far there's been nothing in the media at all. Is that right,

Aidan?" Cullen asked, interrupting the awkward silence.

"So far," Kempe added cautiously.

"That's a blessing," Cullen said, trying to offer some comfort to Gunnison. "But let's look ahead to the anniversary Mass and dinner. None of us want anything to mar your jubilee."

Gunnison shook his head, "But what, really, can we do?"

It would help if you'd tell the truth, Martin thought. Instead, hoping to ease Gunnison's anxiety, he said, "The two retired federal agents, Duane Moore and George Havel, who were at Immaculate Conception yesterday, will be at the Mass, the reception, and the dinner."

Martin broke off, realizing Kempe was in the dark about the agents. "They're two friends of mine, Aidan. Moore is former FBI and Havel was with the Secret Service."

Kempe simply looked at Martin, trying to convey indifference to this information, information he should have been privy to from the beginning.

Martin returned his attention to Gunnison. "They'll be meeting with you before your jubilee to go over security procedures. Havel spoke of three cones of protection—I guess that's Secret Service jargon. He'll be as close to you as he can during all three stages of the event—the Mass, the social, and the dinner. The Mass, they think, will be the trickiest, since it's the part of the jubilee that's open to the public. We might have Havel vested in an alb and place him in the sanctuary. He'll be as close to you as possible without creating a distraction."

Cullen and Kempe listened with fascination—as if they were in some kind of situation room of the Secret Service.

Martin continued, "Moore will be the second cone of protection. He'll be off to one side of the Basilica in a position to observe the people in the first twenty or so pews."

Gunnison looked dazed as he wondered whether the "cones of protection" made him feel more secure or more nervous.

"The third cone," Martin said in a tone meant to ease Gunnison's anxiety, "will consist of four uniformed Baltimore police inside the Basilica, two at the side entrances, one in the vestibule, and one in the choir loft. We'll simply tell them that we want a little extra security for your jubilee, Wilfred."

Aidan Kempe sat steaming. He should have been part of this security plan; he should have been its architect, not Martin.

"We'll have another three officers outside stationed at each of the entrances," Martin added.

"Isn't this is a bit over the top, Bryn?" Kempe asked edgily.

"Not really," Martin shot back. "This is just a few more off-duty police than we usually hire for events like this."

"Your plan, Bryn, at least for the present, seems prudent and appropriate," Cullen said definitively. "What about the events at the hotel, the cocktail hour, and the dinner?"

Martin was ready for the question. "The Mass should be over by 6:30 and it's less than a ten-minute drive to the Sheraton.

"Cocktails are from 7:00 to 8:00," Martin said, looking at his notes. "Then we move the guests into the grand ballroom for the dinner. Salads will be on the tables by 8:15. You'll welcome the guests, Charles, introduce the dignitaries, and offer the invocation."

Cullen nodded and said, "I'll be brief."

"The hotel has reserved one of its presidential suites for you, Wilfred," Martin added. "It's quite comfortable—two floors with an imposing spiral staircase and a great view of the harbor. You'll have about thirty minutes to relax before coming down for the last fifteen minutes or so of the reception...unless you want to stay in the suite until the dinner starts at quarter after eight."

"Thank you, Bryn. This seems fine," a tired Wilfred Gunnison whispered.

But Martin wasn't finished. "Havel and Moore will have a car at the Mulberry Street door of the Basilica. I recommend they drive you to the hotel. If you decide to do some mixing during the social, both men will be as close to you as possible without looking like body guards. Otherwise, I suggest you call them when you're ready to come down to the ballroom. I'm hoping the guests will think Havel and Moore are major donors or out-of-town friends. They should be pretty much out of sight during the dinner. They've already contacted the hotel security officer on duty that evening."

"I suppose this is all necessary," Gunnison said, looking at Kempe imploringly.

"After the tributes," Martin continued, "and a pitch from Florence Merriman, the Catholic Charities Board chair—we think around 9:15 or 9:30—you'll speak, Wilfred. The nuncio will offer the benediction. As you proposed, we hope the dinner will be over around ten. Let me know if you plan to have the visiting bishops and your special guests up to your suite. I'll arrange for a bartender and one or two servers with cheese and fruit. You can stay the night at the hotel, of course, but if you return to your residence, I think you should let Havel or Moore drive you home and stake the place out for the evening."

Cullen glanced at his watch. "That's the plan for now. Let's hope the media doesn't pick up on this second incident. I really don't think there's anything else we can do, at least right now." Cullen studied the face of his predecessor. Beneath the stoic expression he saw a man rigid with fear. "Remember, Wilfred, there have been no notes, no phone messages, no threats. Maybe our man with the laser will just go away."

Gunnison and Kempe both knew otherwise.

15

Monsignor Aidan Kempe read for the third time the fax he was about to send to M, the Brotherhood of the Sacred Purple's Vatican protector. Kempe was among a handful of the worldwide Brotherhood who knew that M was Bishop Pietro Gonzaga Montaldo. Montaldo's mother had claimed to be a descendant of the noble ruling family of Mantua that had produced the Jesuit Saint Aloysius Gonzaga. Kempe was more impressed with the other notable sixteenth-century member of the family, Cardinal Ercole Gonzaga, a confidant of popes and kings.

Whatever the bloodlines connecting the two Gonzagas to Montaldo, M was Kempe's link to power. The low-profile Montaldo held the number three spot in the Pontifical Office of Protocol, a visible but minor department in the Vatican's Secretariat of State. Usually the cleric in this post held the rank of monsignor, but Vatican insiders were sure Montaldo held some kind of chip that he had bargained into being named a bishop. His previous assignment was to a modest staff position in the Vatican archives—an appointment that held little status in the eyes of Vatican bureaucrats but paid its holder bonuses in a special kind of currency: information. From that perspective, most members of the pope's Curia considered Bishop Pietro Montaldo a very wealthy man. Kempe was among a handful of American church leaders who understood that M, in spite of his modest status in the eyes of many of his Roman colleagues, was one of the most powerful prelates in Rome.

Kempe smiled. Not even Gunnison knew the identity of M. But Aidan Kempe knew. He read the fax a fourth time. Though it went directly to M's private office, it made no mention of the bishop's name or anyone else's name. Kempe's fax number was the only identification Montaldo would need.

The fax, Kempe thought, conveyed the urgency of the situation concisely. This was another talent of his—saying just what needed to be communicated without compromising the Brotherhood's sacred mission:

Your Excellency,

A situation has developed in my archdiocese that has implications for the well-being of Holy Mother Church and our special interest in preserving her authority and integrity. It is necessary for me to request a meeting with you as soon as possible. The matter in question is both delicate and urgent.

I will arrive in Rome this Friday morning, February 10th, and I trust you will grant me the favor of a private consultation on Friday afternoon or evening. I plan to return to my archdiocese the following day.

Devotedly in Christ and
Kissing the Sacred Purple,
A.K.

Two hours later, Kempe's fax machine hummed into action: *Saturday afternoon, 4:30, Villa Borghese, at the Fountain of the Seahorses.*

A Friday meeting would have been more convenient for the chancellor. His short absence from the archdiocese might have gone unnoticed. Kempe swallowed his irritation with M. He would, after all, get his private meeting. And the meeting would

give him another opportunity to prove his loyalty and compe-
tence—his readiness to do whatever was required to protect the
supreme center.

By the time Kempe left his office for the day, Margaret
Comiskey had booked his flight to Newark's airport and the connecting flight to Rome. Business class, as instructed.

"When the invoice arrives," he had instructed his secretary,
"just put it on my desk. All right?"

So, thought Comiskey, another personal, hush-hush trip to
Rome. And the expenses—business class air fare, luxury class
hotel, meals—would be covered by the chancellor's private fund.
She wondered if anyone at the Catholic Center knew about this
off-the-books account; an account she had overheard Kempe refer to as the "purple purse." Comiskey made a note in her calendar that the chancellor of the Archdiocese of Baltimore would be
out of the office from Thursday evening until Sunday afternoon.

Less than an hour later she was on the phone to Bishop Bryn
Martin's office.

Thursday afternoon, when Aidan Kempe was on his way to the
BWI Airport for his flight to Newark and the connecting flight
to Rome's Fiumicino, Margaret Comiskey walked briskly into
Martin's outer office and smiled at his secretary. Cradled in Margaret's left arm were the folders holding the plans for Archbishop
Gunnison's Jubilee Mass. These included the scripture readings,
the music, the designated homilist, the names of the lectors, the
Prayer of the Faithful—a half dozen or so intercessory prayers
offered by a lay person—and a few other items necessary for a
smooth, devout, and liturgically-correct celebration. Without
stopping, she remarked casually, "Hi, Kathy. Bishop Martin
asked to see the plans for Archbishop Gunnison's anniversary
Mass." Martin waited until Comiskey was seated across from

him. "I see you have the plans for the archbishop's jubilee. We should take a peek at them before you leave."

The folders were never opened.

There weren't many real friendships between the clergy and lay staff of the archdiocese's Catholic Center, but Bryn Martin and Margaret Comiskey were just that—real friends. They instinctively liked each other, and within months of Bryn's arrival at the Catholic Center, they came to trust each other too. Of all the "black suits" Comiskey had worked for, Martin was the least clerical, the least aloof. Among the dozens of secretaries and lay staffers at the archdiocesan headquarters, Martin had come to see Comiskey as bright, competent, and not at all naïve. Nor was she in awe of the archbishops, bishops, and priests she worked for over the years. Both Martin and Comiskey were savvy enough to respect the social formality that controlled the Catholic Center's interactions between the clerical bosses and the lay staff, but that public formality dissolved when they were alone.

"I need to talk to you about something," she said, "something that...doesn't seem right to me."

She took a deep breath and held Bryn's gaze for a moment, as if to say, *Here goes.* "Something's going on in the chancellor's office." She hesitated, but only for a second. "Ian Landers said something at Ella's dinner party the other night that made me think I should talk to you. It had to do with those papers of the Jesuit chaplain to the Carmelites. Didn't Ian say, if I heard him correctly, that the chaplain had come upon priests and bishops who belonged to a group called the Brotherhood of the Sacred Purple?"

"Yes, that's what he seemed most interested in from the Combier papers, as he called them—this Brotherhood of the Sacred Purple."

Margaret steadied her nerves and plunged ahead. "Monsignor Kempe has a file drawer in his desk that he guards with his life. I've seen it open a number of times when he's been working on personnel papers—papers, as far as I can tell, that belong in the clergy personnel files. But I've never been asked to file any of them. There's also a financial account, apparently off the books, that I've heard him call the 'purple purse.' There is no mention of it when he prepares the budget for our office. And I'm sure the auditors know nothing about it. Didn't Kempe himself, as financial vicar, establish a diocesan policy that there were to be no secret or off-the-books accounts anywhere in the Catholic Center?"

Martin didn't respond to her rhetorical question.

"Bryn, the guy's obsessed with purple, with the color purple. Most of his cuff links are purple. The prints in his office are purple or a purplish blue. He'll mention that he loves Rembrandt's *The Apostle Paul* and Winslow Hunter's *Hound and Hunter* because of their deep purple hues. The next time you're in his office say something about the prints. You'll see." Her lips widened in a half-cynical smile. "Sometimes he wears purple socks, for crying out loud."

Martin raised his eyebrows, a patient, attendant expression on his face. "I've noticed Aidan's preference for purple." He had felt strangely uncomfortable with Margaret's visit from the moment she sat down. This kind of office maneuvering could be dangerous. Still, his colleague and friend deserved to be heard.

"And," she continued, "something's going on between Kempe and Archbishop Gunnison. The archbishop came to see Kempe last week. Whatever it was about, it was serious." Margaret paused. "I don't mean to put you into an awkward position, Bryn, but I'm sure there are some folders missing from the clergy personnel files." Another pause. "And then there's that account."

Martin sat thinking for a bit. The silence made Comiskey think she had made a mistake in laying her suspicions on her friend's desk.

Then, to her relief, Bryn said, "There could well be something here, Margaret. But I don't think this is the time to confront Monsignor Kempe or to take this to Archbishop Cullen. The account or purse could turn out to be monetary gifts from Aidan's wealthy friends for Gunnison's jubilee." Martin knew that was a long shot. "And the folders, well, he might ask you to file them on Monday, or whenever he returns."

Comiskey stiffened. She knew what she knew.

"Make a note in your calendar, Margaret, that you met with me today to bring to my attention certain concerns you have about the chancellor's office. I'll make the same kind of note in my calendar. You've been at the Catholic Center long enough to know that if someone on the archbishop's staff isn't playing by the rules, especially if they're clergy, that it's like moving a mountain to do anything about it. An accusation against someone on the archbishop's staff is looked upon by many as an accusation against the archbishop himself. I don't have to tell you about the Catholic Center's culture of silence. This isn't to say we should walk away from what you've seen…what you know. But honestly, Margaret, I'm not sure it's enough to go head to head with Aidan Kempe."

Martin let this settle in. He could see the disappointment in Margaret's expression. "Let's talk again after Gunnison's jubilee extravaganza."

"I know what you're saying, Bryn. And you're probably right about waiting until after the jubilee." Comiskey picked up the plans for Gunnison's jubilee from the corner of Martin's desk.

Glancing at the manila folders, Martin looked up into Comiskey's eyes. "By the way, I'm glad you've agreed to represent the Catholic Center staff and read the Prayer of the Faithful."

"Yes, I was a little surprised that I was asked to offer the intercessory prayers at the archbishop's Mass. After all these years here, I was never sure the archbishop even knew my name."

Comiskey suspected it was Martin who had suggested to Gunnison that she offer the petitions. "Thanks for listening, Bryn. And for your advice," she said with a weak smile.

Bishop Bryn Martin looked at the papers on his desk and the correspondence that required responses, but he didn't move. He leaned back into his chair, thinking about his conversation with Margaret. It unnerved him to realize that she understood the culture of silence at the Catholic Center better than he did. Or the culture of discretion, as he often thought of it, that influenced almost everything that went on here. In spite of the good people who worked here, there was something not quite real, maybe even toxic, about life at the headquarters of the oldest archdiocese in the U.S.

And her mention of Gunnison was all it took to take him back to the night when the archbishop had groped him. A place he didn't want to go…but couldn't help, from time to time, going to nonetheless.

Before he became chancellor, while still a parish priest, Martin had served as Gunnison's master of ceremonies. After a Confirmation Mass, they had stopped for a late, light supper. They each had a scotch before ordering and then sipped Chianti over their split order of spaghetti Bolognese. Gunnison had flattered him, asking his advice on clergy personnel decisions that were none of his business. There were hints, reinforced with warm, approving smiles from the archbishop, that Father Bryn Martin had a bright future in the church.

A half hour later, Martin had turned into the driveway of the archbishop's residence and eased his car to a stop at the side entrance. Leaving the engine running, he had put the car into park position and reached for the door, ready to get out and move to the passenger side of his car to open the door for Gunnison. But

Gunnison had put his left hand on his right arm, holding him in place.

"Let's just sit here for a moment, Bryn," he had said softly. "Let's just sit here for a while in the dark and peace of the moment."

Martin remembered his stomach tightening. It was more than a suggestion, more like a directive—a command—from the man he had solemnly and publicly promised to obey and respect. He had looked straight ahead for as long as he could, then he had turned slightly to his right and saw that the archbishop was gazing into his eyes. Gunnison's eyes had been watery but intense, the eyes of a lonely man hungry for some kind of affection. In spite of his anxiety, Martin remembered feeling sorry for him.

He had fumbled for the handle of the car door, but Gunnison reached over with his left hand, took Martin's hand from the wheel and placed it on his crotch. He remembered feeling the swelling curve of the archbishop's erection. Then, like in a slow-motion film clip, he saw Gunnison placing his right hand over his own right hand, keeping it firmly between his legs. With his free left hand, Gunnison reached across and cupped Martin's genitals. Then neither of them moved. Holding his breath, Martin looked straight ahead, though he felt the archbishop's eyes on him. He remembered being unable to move, unable to utter any word of protest. Then, without a word, Archbishop Gunnison opened the passenger door and got out. Only then had Martin been able to catch his breath. His face, he was sure, had been hot and flushed, yet he found himself shivering. With a conspiratorial smile, Gunnison nodded a silent good night and walked with episcopal dignity to the side entrance of his house.

"Oh God, Oh my God," Martin remembered saying out loud as he put the car in reverse and backed slowly out of the driveway. What in God's name just happened? The archbishop of Baltimore had just groped him!

Over the years, Bryn Martin, perhaps guilty of a small treason, had just let the incident go. He had, again and again, tried to bury it.

Neither Gunnison nor Martin ever referred to the incident again. Nor was it ever repeated. But Father Martin remained the archbishop's favorite master of ceremonies, and two years later he was named chancellor of the archdiocese, the youngest priest ever to hold that important position. And when Archbishop Gunnison retired, he had encouraged his successor, Archbishop Charles Cullen, to retain Martin as his chancellor.

Martin woke from his reverie, reached to turn off his desk lamp, rubbed the back of his neck, and sat back in his swivel chair. On cue, cold confusion and restless anxiety washed over him—as it always did when his mind turned to the archbishop's driveway.

16

M argaret Comiskey picked up the phone on the second ring.

"Aunt Margaret, it's Mark. I'd like to stop over if you don't mind. There's something I'd like to talk to you about. It's kind of important."

A half hour later, Mark Anderlee sat at his aunt's kitchen table with a mug of hot tea in front of him.

"Are you all right, Mark?" Comiskey asked, fully aware this wasn't a casual visit with his favorite aunt.

"Pretty much." Mark sipped his tea, sure that what he was about to say would really upset his aunt. "I know you've worked forever at the Catholic Center."

Margaret nodded, "More than thirty years."

"And when I was staying here a few weeks ago you mentioned you had good friends there, especially Bishop Martin."

"Yes, and with a number of the other secretaries."

Anderlee hesitated. He wasn't really sure why he had decided to tell his aunt about what Father Gunnison had done to him when he was at Camp Carroll. She should know, he had finally concluded, the kind of people she's been working with, the kind of people she'd given her life to.

Margaret got up from the table.

"It's a little chilly. I'll be right back"

A minute later she returned, buttoning the sweater Mark had sent her when his unit was stationed in Germany providing security for the Air Force base in Wiesbaden. She sipped her tea, as if its warmth and the sweater would steel her for what she was about to hear.

"Do you remember when I spent a few summers at Camp Carroll?"

She hesitated, "Hmm…the summers after your seventh and eighth grade, if I'm not mistaken."

Mark nodded. "Well, one of the priests who was at the camp a lot, well…" He paused. "One of the priests sexually abused me. He took me away for a weekend and did some stuff he never should have done." Mark's face was knotted in pain. Or was it shame?

"Oh Mark," is all Margaret could say at first. She had closed her eyes and Mark could sense the pain she felt. When she opened her eyes, they were teary. Then, "I am so terribly sorry."

"I know, Aunt Margaret. I knew you would be."

"All these years, Mark. You've carried this with you all these years."

"I just felt I couldn't tell anyone, not my folks, not you. I was embarrassed. So I just tried to forget about it. And I pretty much did. But I thought about it a lot when you wrote to me about the priests who had abused kids, priests you knew from your work."

Margaret reached over and put her hand on Mark's arm. "I'm so very sorry, my dear Mark."

Their tea went untouched.

Mark sat silent for a moment. "The priest who messed with me isn't really a priest anymore. He's an archbishop. A retired archbishop. Wilfred Gunnison."

Margaret Comiskey looked like she might be sick. But she didn't look surprised, more like she was thinking and trying to stay calm. Mark thought of an expression he couldn't quite recall. It was as if the "penny dropped" or the "dime dropped," something like that, for his Aunt Margaret. He could see that her mind was either racing or shutting down. Some kind of emotion was building in her, the relief of understanding, the numbness of shock, the rage of betrayal—maybe all of these. She couldn't even look at him. She sat perfectly still. After a bit, he went on.

"I was on a night patrol, like countless others. Nothing. Quiet. No incidents whatsoever. On that patrol, like out of nowhere, I knew I had to confront him. It's the reason I decided to return to Baltimore when I got my twenty years in and could retire. I wanted to punish him, Aunt Margaret. I wanted to hurt him. I still do."

"Did you, Mark?" his Aunt Margaret said finally. "Did you confront him?"

"Yes, I went to see him. I just barged in on him one morning. He was scared, really scared. He didn't admit to anything, but he didn't deny it either. He's an old man now, but I keep wondering how many other boys he messed with." Mark had thought he would feel angry telling his aunt what happened. But it wasn't anger he was feeling. It was, inexplicably, guilt. He felt confused, not sure where the guilt was coming from. So, he just went on with his story—his slightly edited story. "He gave me a lot of money," Mark said vaguely. "He said it was to help me get established now that I was out of the army. I could tell he was afraid I was going to go to the papers or sue him."

"He would be afraid of that," Margaret said coolly. "He would be very afraid of that. He's got a big dinner planned to celebrate his fiftieth ordination anniversary and wouldn't want anything to spoil that."

"I know," Mark said. "I've read about it. In fact I know a lot about Gunnison. I know things like his confirmation schedule. I've actually been to two of his confirmations. I don't know what you'd think of this, but I've tried to scare the you-know-what out of him. I hit him with a laser dot as he was leaving the church both times. I wanted him to live scared, like something really bad was going to happen to him."

Margaret seemed not to hear what Mark had just said. Suddenly she seemed even more distant, more distracted.

"Aunt Margaret, what are you thinking?"

"I'm thinking, Mark, of what a fool I've been. What a terrible fool."

Monsignor Aidan Kempe felt his irritation mounting. The flight attendants kept addressing him as "sir." He was traveling, as he always traveled, in a black suit and Roman collar. At least one of the attendants must have had a Catholic background. Where was the respect and deference due to Catholic clergy? As the wheels lifted off the runway of the Newark Airport, Kempe bent down to the leather carry-on bag under the seat in front of him and withdrew his breviary. He would pray vespers as the early evening sky faded into a soft purple—his favorite time of the day—before meeting the merciless darkness that awaited as they climbed above New England and Nova Scotia. Then, after his meal and a single glass of wine, he would say the rosary, a prayer that always eased his anxieties.

An hour later Kempe inserted his ear plugs and placed the band of his eye screen over his head. He had a full day ahead of him. If he could get some sleep, it would make a huge difference. But he was not blessed with sleep this night. Kempe knew when the battle was lost, so he removed the eye screen and pictured his meeting with M and imagined how it might unfold. The conversation would be oblique, indirect, and names would never be mentioned. What might go unsaid could be as significant as what was said, perhaps more significant. He reminded himself not to ask M why he had been passed over for auxiliary bishop of Baltimore. Both he and Bryn Martin had been on the short list.

That he knew from very good authority. M, he finally admitted to himself, had let him down.

The flight attendant approached, ready to ask if he might want something to drink, but catching the sour expression on Kempe's face moved on without a word toward the business class galley.

Kempe's irritation with the flight crew shifted now to M. Being passed over in favor of Bryn Martin still stung. God damn it, he was older than Martin, far more experienced and, God knows, far more loyal to the church. And now his meeting with M was to take place in the Borghese Gardens—like he was some low-level Vatican spy connecting with his undercover controller. Why hadn't M invited him to dinner in one of his favorite restaurants? Was he wary of being seen in public with him? If he hadn't wanted to be seen with him, he could have invited him to his apartment near the Spanish Steps for a private dinner.

Think, man, think, he said to himself. You have always been loyal to the Brotherhood, always discreet, always generous.

Maybe the gifts of money he had sent to M from the purple purse for his birthday, his ordination anniversary, his anniversary of episcopal ordination, for Christmas were not as generous as he had thought. How could he know for sure? If the sixty thousand dollars he had forwarded to M over the years were not sufficient signs of his loyalty and support...was this small change to the leader of the Brotherhood? He repressed a sudden impulse to curse. Never before had he doubted his ability to play the ecclesiastical power game with the best of them. This sudden self-doubt was but a temptation, he told himself, and like all temptations, it must be repressed, it must be buried—like his occasional desires for the company of young, attractive priests.

Kempe was startled back into the moment as the plane, still climbing to its cruising altitude, encountered a bit of turbulence. M must never suspect his disappointment that he was granted only the briefest of meetings with the Brotherhood's Vatican protector, and in the Borghese Gardens of all places.

His thoughts drifted to Gunnison and his mood mirrored the empty darkness outside the window to his left. Kempe had read somewhere that depression was but anger spread thin. Well, he was angry indeed with Wilfred Gunnison. There was the allegation from the career army man, this Anderlee fellow, and the hundred thousand dollar "gift" to keep him quiet. That made him angry. Then there was the laser dot after the confirmation at St. Bernardine's that turned Gunnison into a bag of nerves. That made him angry. His immediate suspicion that Anderlee was behind the laser dots. That made him angry. The real possibility that the media would expose Gunnison's past mistakes. The damn jubilee dinner. What if the man who threatened Gunnison was crazy enough to want to kill him? What if the next laser dot, at the Jubilee Mass or at the dinner, was a silent precursor to an assassin's bullet? Might Gunnison's membership in the Brotherhood of the Sacred Purple be revealed and the Brotherhood's mission endangered?

"Good evening, Reverend," a stewardess said, handing him a menu for the in-flight dinner. *I'm not a "reverend," you idiot. I'm a Catholic priest.* Kempe didn't return her smile. Another flight attendant pushing a wine cart offered him a choice of a red or white. He chose the red.

"Visiting the Vatican?" the attendant asked.

No, he wanted to say, *I'm being called to the Vatican so the pope can appoint me chaplain to Italy's Communist Party.* "Yes. Yes, I guess I am visiting the Vatican," Kempe responded vaguely and with barely a hint of a smile. Yes, he was visiting the Vatican, but not as a tourist. Monsignor Aidan Kempe, chancellor of the Archdiocese of Baltimore, the heart and soul of the Brotherhood of the Sacred Purple, was on a mission to save the supreme center of the Holy Roman Catholic Church.

The wine soothed him a bit. Kempe tried to pray, but was

still too agitated. He put his head back and closed his eyes as a familiar sense of displacement settled over him. Like Christ, he was not of this world. He was indeed a stranger to this world of indulgence and self-idolatry. The church, the church alone, was his world and his home. In this home he had found order and clarity, the beauty of ritual and chant and angelic polyphony. In this home alone he found truth and moral certainty.

Now this household of the Savior was under attack. The list of enemies was long—secularism, materialism, relativism, rationalism, liberalism. Perhaps the most lethal enemy was within the church itself—the dissident theologians, bishops, priests, and know-it-all laity calling for renewal and reform.

17

Nora. It's Bryn. Can you arrange a meeting with Ian—for the three of us?" Nora noted her brother's directness. There was no "How are you?" or "We haven't talked for a while."

"As soon as possible," Bryn added quickly.

At five the next afternoon, Bishop Bryn Martin, dressed in an open-necked shirt, a dark gray sport coat, and black slacks, sat down with his sister in her office at Johns Hopkins University, waiting for Ian Landers to join them. Nora left the door ajar so Ian wouldn't have to knock. It was the first time Bryn had been in Nora's office, but before he could let its ambience settle over him, Ian rapped twice and pushed the door fully open. Bryn stood and the two shook hands warmly. Bryn liked Ian—he liked him very much and wondered if he might be interested in his sister. He assumed so. And he assumed Nora was interested as well.

Nora offered Bryn coffee from a ceramic pot resting on a thermal mat. She poured Ian and herself cups of tea. Smiling at Ian, Bryn said, "I'm glad we had the chance to meet at your mother's dinner party. She's quite a woman."

They had seated themselves at a small round table nestled into a corner of Nora's office. Bryn felt he was in a scholar's study more than the cramped, messy faculty offices he associated with professors from his years of graduate study. Two walls were covered with books from floor to ceiling. A deep red and green oriental rug added warmth to the room. In the opposite corner, on the window side of the office, a healthy ficus tree made his sister's work space rather charming. She had their mother's taste, he thought.

This was Bryn's meeting, and he wouldn't waste anyone's time. "Thanks for meeting with me at such short notice." He paused, then added, "You're both professionals, but I need to say this anyway. What I'm about to tell you needs to stay in this room."

Nora and Ian nodded their understanding. "Of course," Ian said speaking for himself and Nora.

"There is," Bryn paused briefly, "a rather bizarre drama unfolding at the Catholic Center that I'm afraid might mushroom into something serious. Nora, I need your perspective as a psychologist and, Ian, I need to know what you think about it as a church historian. It's a delicate matter concerning our retired archbishop, Wilfred Gunnison. Someone has been harassing him. At the conclusion of his last two confirmations, as he processed out of church, a laser dot hit him square in the chest. If these dots had been bullets, our retired archbishop would be dead."

Nora and Ian listened intently.

"Gunnison claims he has no idea who could be behind the two laser hits. I'm afraid I...we...Archbishop Cullen and I...don't believe he is telling the truth. Before he was named a bishop, there were rumors of accusations of sexual abuse made against Gunnison. Nothing ever came of them, but I am wondering if one of his alleged victims might be responsible."

It crossed Bryn's mind to confide to his sister and Ian that Gunnison had come on to him when he was a young priest. He had thought of telling Nora a number of times in the past about Gunnison groping him. He decided now was not the time.

"And," Bryn continued, "there's a small number of priests, a half dozen or so, who meet regularly with the archbishop." He looked directly at Ian. "I've heard they refer to themselves as the Brotherhood of the Sacred Purple."

Ian sat up in his chair.

"At your mother's dinner party, didn't you mention that you had come across a Brotherhood of the Sacred Purple that was associated with the *Fideli d' Amore?*"

"Yes I did," Landers answered, giving his full attention to Bryn.

Bryn went on, "Our chancellor, Aidan Kempe, is apparently a member of this brotherhood. And they have gone out of their way to keep their association secret. I can't tell you why, but I suspect Gunnison and Kempe are connected with some influential players inside the Curia."

Landers raised his eyebrows as if in sudden awareness.

"This means something to you. You're seeing some connection here." Bryn said.

"It might mean something, but go on. It's best I hear the rest of this."

"There's only one more piece to add, really," Bryn said. "Wilfred Gunnison is going to celebrate his fiftieth ordination anniversary in less than two weeks—the Saturday before Ash Wednesday—with a Mass at the Basilica and a fundraising dinner at a harbor front hotel for major contributors, close friends, and family. If someone wants to embarrass or hurt the archbishop, that would be a choice opportunity."

"Do you think there's anything to the rumors?" Nora asked.

"Yes," Bryn said crisply, "I do. If there were allegations against Gunnison, they weren't followed up on. If there *were* formal allegations, Aidan Kempe or some other chancery pal of Gunnison's saw to it that they were covered up. We know that that kind of thing happened a lot—especially before the Boston abuse scandals broke in 2002. But, yes, I think there was something to the rumors."

"It happened a lot," Ian said echoing Bryn, "from the ninth century on. And all for the 'good of the church.' Once the church came to see herself as a perfect society—a divinely-protected, perfect society—she feared clerical scandal more than the plague. And the church has never been leery of doing whatever is necessary to bury her scandals."

"There hasn't been anything in the media about the laser," Nora said, "unless I've missed it."

"No there hasn't," Bryn confirmed. "We have a statement ready in the event it's picked up. But so far, so good."

"Your archbishop must be one terrified man," Nora said. "Even though he claims not to have a clue, I suspect he has a pretty good idea who's behind this. Maybe a victim riled by the anniversary celebration. The stress he is under has to be enormous. This jubilee is his last hurrah, the capstone of a brilliant career. Any public figure, especially a high-ranking clergyman with a long, distinguished career at risk, is going to be coping with extraordinary pressure. The shame alone can be crippling. A man of his age is at risk for all kinds of trouble."

"And, if Gunnison did abuse minors, he's been living with this fear of exposure for fifty years as a priest and bishop," Bryn added.

"Don't be too sure." Nora responded. "Sexual predators have an uncanny ability to rationalize or repress their seductions. Gunnison may have been a fairly peaceful man until these recent confirmations. What you can be sure of is that the archbishop is a man at risk."

She poured Ian and herself more tea. "Can I get you more coffee, Bryn?"

He shook his head.

"I met Gunnison at your ordination as bishop," Nora said. "What struck me was the complete absence of kindness in his eyes. They had some life in them, but no kindness." Looking straight at her brother, she added, "Gunnison is not a compassionate man. That's the least we should be able to say of a priest or bishop, that he is a man of compassion, a man who projects kindness."

Bryn closed his eyes momentarily. When he opened them he was looking straight at his sister. Yes, a priest must be kind.

He let Nora's insight sink in. Gunnison, and now that he thought of it, Kempe, were men incapable of real kindness. Both were more church bureaucrats than anything else. They thought little of mercy—they were legalists, moralists, building walls of spiritual security around their precious certainties. Their staunch orthodoxy was a cruel perversion of the gospel. They had made dogma the supreme center.

Bryn tried to recover his focus. He had to stay with the moment, with this meeting with Ian and Nora.

Landers sipped his tea, looked at Nora and Bryn, and took a deep breath.

"I've been studying the Combier papers I mentioned the other night, the ones Nora led me to at the Carmelite monastery. I've translated those in Italian and French." Landers paused and lowered his voice. "Bryn, you and Archbishop Cullen should know that the Brotherhood of the Sacred Purple, at least the Brotherhood of the fifteenth and sixteenth centuries, was capable of violence if they believed the church's 'supreme center,' as the Brotherhood put it, was under attack. In fact, they were quite capable of murder."

18

Mark Anderlee stood ramrod straight, as if at attention before roll call, at the picture window of his seventh-floor harbor-front condo. He loved Baltimore's Inner Harbor and living at its edge. Yet giving it up would be but another minor sacrifice. He drew energy from the movement far below of parents pushing their children's trams, of office workers on their lunch breaks. Only in the darkest hours of the night was the harbor really quiet. The dark stillness was his passionate companion, his lover. It was in the dark stillness of a patrol in Iraq that he had come to understand his true mission. He focused his attention on a thirty-something figure in a business suit, the smug financial adviser type, waiting for a client at the door to Phillips Restaurant. It occurred to him how easily he could take him down if he were still a sniper. The suit below, anticipating a midday martini and crab cakes, was but one more anonymous target.

On the coffee table behind him lay two weapons Anderlee had bought just weeks before, a Sig Sauer P226, the standard issue hand weapon of most law enforcement agencies, and a Remington 700 rifle with a Leupold scope mounted on its frame that could take down an elephant at 300 yards. Moments before, he had confirmed the decision made two years ago on the still streets of Tikkrit. It was time. He had teased Gunnison into a state of terror. Now it was time. In a few days he would be out of there. He would move south, maybe find a place in the same city as his mother. Maybe even get married. Anderlee had grown tired of living alone. The loneliness and the decades of anger rose in his chest, threatening to explode. Now that the decision had been made, he might finally find relief.

Anderlee's Aunt Margaret, wrapped in the sweater her godson had given her, stiffened as a damp, ghost-like vein of air crept through the wool of her wrap. The chill, more a dank emptiness, hadn't left her since Mark had told her of his abuse at the hands of Wilfred Gunnison. Not only was she cold night and day, she had no appetite to speak of. And she slept poorly, sometimes lying awake half the night.

She sat in the chair at her front window watching for Ella Landers' car to turn into her driveway. It was less than an hour since she had phoned, asking her best friend to come right away, no questions asked. Before Landers stopped her car in the driveway, Margaret had opened the front door. Getting out of her car, Ella's concern mounted. Margaret looked smaller and older, her eyes watery but focused, her pinkish, Galway skin now gray and drawn.

"Are you all right, Margaret?" Ella asked before unbuttoning her coat.

"Not really, Ella. It's about my godson, Mark."

They sat at the kitchen table, Ella reaching over to hold Margaret's hands as she listened to how the retired archbishop had abused Mark when he was just a boy.

"Mark finally decided to tell me. He knows I know Gunnison, that I'd 'given my life to the church,' as he put it." She was silent for a while. "I saw Gunnison a few days ago—he had a very private meeting with my boss in Kempe's office—just the day before Mark came over to tell me what he'd done to him."

"I'm so very sorry," Ella said in a whisper. The pain in her friend's eyes brought tears to her own. But Landers saw something else in Margaret's eyes, something she had never seen before in the many years of their friendship—a cold emptiness. Or more accurately, perhaps, an empty coldness. Whatever was going on, something had turned in Margaret.

"I feel like such a goddamn fool, Ella." The profanity surprised her friend. "I've given my life to the church," she said, repeating Mark's tribute. "And, believe me, I've been loyal and discreet. The bishops and priests I've worked for are as human as the rest of us." Margaret went silent, then went on, her voice now lowered and her pace sharp, her words sounding like staccato notes. "I've seen arrogance, ambition, envy, jealousy, routine unkindness, ingratitude, addictions of all sorts, including pornography. Even when the abuse scandals broke, I tried not to judge. Most of the priests at the Catholic Center don't seem to be very happy. They seemed rather solemn, lonely men, living for their days off and their vacations. I always tried to see the good most of them do." She paused again, then said in a softer tone, "Bishop Martin is a friend, a dear friend. Bryn is different. And so is Archbishop Cullen. But most of that crowd are ciphers, zeroes—bland company men. And now I know I'm working for a real snake—Monsignor Aidan Kempe, chancellor of the Archdiocese of Baltimore—and that his buddy, Wilfred Gunnison, abused my dear Mark."

Comiskey rose from the kitchen table and went to the thermostat to turn the heat up. She was shivering now with rage. Landers remained at the table, coming to grips with Margaret's inner convulsions.

Returning to her chair, Comiskey said coolly, "Kempe and Gunnison belong to a spooky group of priests that meets monthly. I'm not sure what they're up to, but it's all hush-hush. And they have a budget that seems to be limitless. Ella, listen to this, they call themselves 'The Brotherhood of the Sacred Purple,' for God's sake. And I'm almost certain my boss, the chancellor, not Archbishop Gunnison, is their real leader."

"This sounds like something out of one of Ian's lectures," Ella said, remembering the dinner conversation two weeks earlier.

"Yes," Comiskey said, a weak smile lifting her face, "when Ian told us about the *Fideli d'Amore*, this Brotherhood of the Faithful in Love, the first thing that came to my mind was this Brotherhood of the Sacred Purple. Kempe has a file drawer in his desk that only he has the key to. I've seen it open when he's working on God knows what, but it's definitely top secret. Kempe is the chancery official who has investigated and handled most of the sexual abuse cases in the archdiocese. He's made a lot of them go away quietly. Payoffs mostly. The victims have to sign a letter promising to keep the settlement confidential. And the checks seem to come from some private fund controlled by Kempe. I've overheard him refer to it as the 'purple purse.'"

"That's got to be one of the cheekiest things I've ever heard, Margaret. Not only is it cheeky, it's probably criminal."

"Yes. Criminal," Comiskey said. "And where does the money come from for these payoffs and his trips to Rome and his dinner parties at the best restaurants? But right now I don't give a damn about where the money comes from. I'm convinced he has records and documents in that file drawer relating to sexual abuse—records that show Baltimore's retired archbishop is a child abuser. And this 'Most Reverend' pervert is going to celebrate his fiftieth ordination anniversary next week as if he were Jesus Christ himself."

"I saw something in the papers about his jubilee," Ella said. "It's quite a celebration according to the article. Even the nuncio, Archbishop Tardisconi, is going to attend."

The two women sat without speaking. Finally, Comiskey looked into Ella's eyes and said calmly, "I'm going to ask you to do something outrageous, Ella, something that itself is, quite certainly, criminal."

19

Professor Ian Landers scanned the twelve graduate students seated in leather swivel chairs around the faux mahogany conference table in the Johns Hopkins seminar room. They were all on time, in fact early, in a display of motivation and earnestness. Ellen Stark and John Pointer, the two doctoral students in the seminar, sat at opposite ends of the table. Except for the two seminarians wearing black wash pants, they were all in jeans. Three of the men were clad in well-worn sport coats. Landers, dressed in a dark blue blazer and oxford blue shirt with a paisley maroon tie, sat erect in his usual chair at the center of the table on the side closest to the whiteboard. The British-bred professor was unfailingly both polite and reserved, and no less approachable and generous with his time than his American colleagues in the history department.

"You may pick up your papers on Bishop Barbiano at the end of our session. Barbiano's letter to Cardinal Colonna, a few of you noted in your American vernacular, was blatantly schmoozing. I'm sure you won't use this colorful Americanism in your theses, though it is spot-on accurate. And most of you judged Barbiano's proffer of Ascanio Sforsa for the Cardinal's personal use as a sad case of how far some medieval churchmen would go to satisfy their ambition."

"What I won't forget about the Barbiano letter," John Pointer said cynically, "is the closing: 'kissing the sacred purple.'"

Nolan Connors, one of the seminarians, frowned at the remark.

113

"All right," Landers continued, "today we're going to look at another example of ecclesiastical ambition—the rise of Cardinal Ercole Gonzaga. The English for *Ercole*, as you no doubt assumed, is Hercules. Although historians might judge him a decidedly minor player in the world of ecclesiastical life of the sixteenth century, he managed to live up to his name. Cardinal Gonzaga possessed the strength of will to be a successful reformer of his diocese of Mantua in northern Italy and an effective president or presiding prelate at the Council of Trent. And like Bishop Barbiano, what we know of Cardinal Gonzaga's personal life is drawn primarily from his correspondence. All right, you've read the first five chapters of *Ruling Peacefully*, Paul Murphy's book on Gonzaga—it was originally his doctoral dissertation—what struck you about the man?"

Nolan Connors spoke first, offering a safe question: "Was he related to Saint Aloysius Gonzaga, the Jesuit that the university in Washington is named after?"

"He was," Landers responded crisply. "A distant cousin."

"The whole business," Ellen Stark said, "reminds me of American politics. If you're thinking of running for the presidency you better have a lot of money and a family with political connections. The Gonzaga's had all that. An ambitious family—his mother was something else—noble status, land, an army, and unbelievable wealth. And the family ruled Mantua from the fourteenth century to the beginning of the eighteenth. This was one powerful family."

Before Stark could continue, Pointer cut in, "You mentioned his mother, Isabella Gonzaga. Talk about a pushy mother, on the day of Ercole's birth, she said he would make '*un bella papona*'—a fine pope. Instead of buying an Orioles baseball cap for him, she buys her dear Ercole a cardinal's hat."

"And," Stark said, regaining the floor, "she succeeded in getting him named a cardinal and almost succeeded in buying him

the papacy. He missed being elected pope in the conclave of 1559 by just a few votes."

Landers' mind wandered briefly to Monsignor Aidan Kempe and the Brotherhood of the Sacred Purple. Kempe hadn't the wealth and military strength of Mantua's ruling family but, like the Gonzagas, he had connections at the Vatican, and he had control of the purple purse. "All right," he said coming back to the moment, "we have a snapshot of Gonzaga's social position, his powerful family, and the post-Reformation chaos that his church was struggling with. What surprised you about this medieval prince and churchman?"

"What surprised me," Pointer said, "aside from the fact that Pope Leo X named him administrator of the diocese of Mantua when he was only sixteen, was his apparent sincerity as a reformer of his diocese, especially of his priests and the vowed religious. Murphy gives him credit for cleaning up a lot of corruption in the church and the local government." Pointer paused, glancing at Nolan Connors. "So, how do you figure this good administrator fathered five illegitimate children? This was no big secret. Yet Pope Julius III goes and names him papal legate and president of the Council of Trent. That's a big deal." Pointer looked at his professor, "Didn't the bishops and cardinals of Trent squash proposals to do away with obligatory celibacy?"

"You're right, John. Remember that it wasn't until the Council of Trent that celibacy was generally accepted and practiced by most of the clergy."

Joe Constanza, the other seminarian, blurted, "Wait a minute, Dr. Landers. Celibacy was made universal law for the Latin Church in the twelfth century. Are you saying priests and bishops still didn't practice it a couple centuries later?"

"There's evidence that many, maybe most, didn't honor the law of celibacy, Joe," Landers said gently. Both seminarians tried to hide their disbelief and resentment at such a scandalous notion. The two students from St. Mary's Seminary looked as if Pointer and Landers had slurred the memory of their sainted grandmothers.

Pointer had no patience with Landers' concern for the naïveté of the seminarians. He barreled ahead, "And we can only imagine how Gonzaga felt, what he was thinking, as the bishops at Trent debated celibacy." Pointer paused for effect. "It appears," he said with a smirk, "that Cardinal Gonzaga favored allowing diocesan priests to marry."

"How do you figure?" Ellen Stark asked. "So he reformed his priests, the monks and nuns, and his people, but not himself?"

"That's one of the issues I want us to consider today," Landers said, aware of the tension the two seminarians had stoked. "We're not psychologists, obviously; we're historians. But let me ask, off the record, you might say, how is it this prelate of noble birth, who apparently died a devout and even inspirational death, who was such a reformer of lax clergy and civil magistrates and, as we've seen, a papal legate to the Council of Trent…how could Cardinal Ercole Gonzaga have a private life so at odds with his public life as a prince of the church?"

A jet-lagged Aidan Kempe thought of sinking into the bed in his suite at the Hotel d'Inghilterra, one of Rome's finest, for a siesta. But an odd restlessness broke through his fatigue. His breathing, shallow now, quickened as a familiar heaviness welled up in his chest. He felt hints of this unsettling force when his taxi reached the outlying streets of the Eternal City. The tightening in his chest, his shallow breathing, the blurring of his reason—these symptoms were hardly strangers to the monsignor. They were, he knew well, the familiar precursors of lust, of sexual neediness. And Kempe understood that the urgent ache in his lower stomach for human contact and comfort—he simply couldn't name

116

it sexual desire—would grow more urgent no matter how he tried to distract himself from its unruly heat. At that moment, in spite of his jet lag, Kempe surrendered to the mounting heat. He would visit the little bar where espresso and a knowing look could lead to anonymous, soothing comfort and release of the tension that had been mounting from the moment he unlocked his hotel-room door.

The coffee bar, tucked into one of the side streets off the Via Condotti, had been a favorite haunt during his years of study in Rome. Though he could hardly afford it at the time, Kempe had purchased a black suit from the famed Giorgio Armani's establishment on the Via Condotti. Now he had three Armani suits in his wardrobe. But Kempe wasn't interested in yet another designer suit. Instead, he anticipated the connection, the dark, nervous rush of knowing glances. At the coffee bar, he would find a few young men, unshaven, lean in their tailored suits and open-necked white shirts, sipping espresso, waiting for an early afternoon coupling with a paying gentleman of the city, including on occasion gentlemen from the offices of the Vatican.

Kempe stood at the edge of the canopied bed, slowly raised his hands to the back of his neck and unsnapped his Roman collar, placed it over the back of one of the chairs, and walked, trance-like, into the bathroom. After using the toilet, he washed his face, lathered, shaved with a safety razor, and applied a modest amount of cologne. The steadfast man of the cloth, the defender of the supreme center, the leader of the Brotherhood of the Sacred Purple had disappeared. In his place was but another lonely middle-aged man seeking the temporary pleasures of anonymous sex. Moments later, dressed in a black suit and a white silk shirt, the two top buttons unfastened, he walked past the floor-length mirror in the sitting room of his suite, permitting himself a quick, approving glance. In spite of his fatigue, the imperious, purple drug of Eros was now in control. Aidan

117

Kempe gently closed the door to his hotel room, tried the handle to make sure it was locked, and headed for the elevator. A coffee would do him good.

20

Ella Landers couldn't remember being so upset with her life-long friend. Margaret should never have asked her to do something so outlandish—and so dangerous to both their good names. But it was clear that Margaret was now indifferent to her own good name and life-long standing at the Catholic Center. Not only had her nephew's abuse severely shaken Margaret's faith, she was no longer at home in her Catholic world, the only world she had ever known.

But how could she refuse Margaret's request? She had never really asked Ella for anything. But breaking into the private file drawer of the chancellor of the Archdiocese of Baltimore was hardly a small favor. She knew she shouldn't do it. But Ella Landers also knew she *could* do it. The months of training at Langley and at the other operations facilities for field agents came back to her. *And the rush.* Landers remembered the adrenalin rush—the challenge, the danger, the exquisite planning and preparation of her few field assignments many, many years ago. Yes, she could do this. And, yes, her months of CIA training had converted her to the secular belief that the end can indeed justify the means.

Tucked away in the back of a bedroom drawer was a now outdated but serviceable document camera the agency had allowed her to keep. She would need it. Then, true to her training, she began rehearsing what she would do if things went wrong. From an operational standpoint, this would be relatively easy. But would she be as good with locks as she had been so long ago?

At six p.m., Margaret Comiskey sat still at her desk in the Catholic Center, hands folded tight on its blotter. With Monsignor Kempe in Rome, this was the perfect time for the "operation," as Ella had called it. The fluorescent ceiling lights were off, and a low wattage table lamp resting on one of the filing cabinets softened the hard edges of her office, anteroom to Kempe's inner sanctum. She remained motionless at her desk with her coat on, strangely cold—shivering from nerves rather than the temperature. Never in her life had she been party to anything close to what was about to happen. A cup of tea might have calmed her nerves, but she remained still, staring into the shadows of her office. She could still call this off. Ella would be relieved. *No, she would go through with this.* She turned to the credenza behind her desk and picked up the photograph of her smiling nephew and godson, Mark. *No,* she thought, *we're going to do this.*

It was a Friday night and only a few of the staffers hadn't left for the weekend. In a short while the building would be empty except for the security guard in the lobby. Kempe's office was dark, and Comiskey checked again to make sure both his door and the outer office door were unlocked. She moved quietly to the copy machine. It was turned on, the office code entered, and ready for use, the paper drawer filled. Comiskey returned to her desk. She had another twenty minutes before going down the back stairs to let Ella Landers into the Catholic Center. Nothing, she understood with absolute clarity, would ever be the same.

Their plan was simple. Once Ella was inside, Margaret would go directly to her car and drive straight home. Ella was emphatic about this. She wanted her friend home and on the phone with someone who might testify to her whereabouts should she ever need an alibi. Margaret had provided Ella with precise directions up the back stairs to the third floor of the Catholic Center. At the top of the stairwell, Landers would turn right and move down the carpeted hallway to the last door on the right, the corner office of Monsignor Aidan Kempe. The door to Kempe's outer office, Margaret's office, would be open and so would the door to Kempe's inner office. Landers had memorized the floor map Margaret had drawn up. She would move silently and quickly to his desk and, in a matter of minutes, if her long-untested skills didn't let her down, carefully open his private file drawer.

Ella estimated her time in the chancellor's office, if all went according to plan, at less than thirty minutes. It all depended, she had explained to Margaret, on the amount of material that needed to be photographed or photocopied. And—she had decided not to trouble Margaret with this piece of the operation—on how much time she needed to open the chancellor's private file drawer without leaving any betraying sign of forcible entry.

At six-twenty-five, Margaret Comiskey rose from her chair, her eyes moving slowly over the few remaining personal items in her office—the photo of Mark, and a framed picture of herself with Pope John Paul and Bishop Martin taken during the pope's visit to Baltimore. She had always thought it a privilege to work at the headquarters of the archdiocese. There were people she would miss. Bryn Martin in particular. He made her feel more like a colleague than a secretary. And Archbishop Cullen—always courteous, always a gentleman. Both were churchmen, but they remained down to earth and easy to approach, never stuffy or taken with their own importance, unlike more than a few of the priests who worked at the Catholic Center. And without question, she would miss the other secretaries who worked in the various archdiocesan offices. Most were underpaid and underappreciated. But the quiet pride she had taken in working at the Catholic Center guttered now like a sanctuary lamp caught in a mysterious draft. It was all a sham. Gunnison, and Kempe, so prissy and pious, were criminals in Roman collars. This long chapter in Margaret's life was drawing to an end. She put on her coat and hat and went downstairs to let Ella in.

At exactly six thirty, she leaned her hip against the panic bar to the back door of the Catholic Center. Ella Landers, dressed in dark slacks, a hip-length charcoal coat, and wearing Latex gloves, slipped inside. "I left my car on Park Avenue," she whispered. "You were right. It's less than a three-minute walk." On her left arm she carried a large cloth tote bag with twin arm straps. Margaret mouthed a "thank you" to her friend. They stood for a moment in the semi-darkness, bathed in the red glow of the exit sign, holding each other's gaze. Ella gave Margaret a confident nod, indicating she should go. Both women understood they would remember this moment of truth for the rest of their lives.

Carefully, quietly, Comiskey pushed the door's panic bar with her gloved hand and stepped out into the chill of the mid-February air. It stung her cheeks. She found her eyes watering. She was shaking now, more from nerves than the cold. She closed the door as silently as she could and half walked, half ran to her car. The Catholic Center's parking garage was nearly empty. As far as she could tell, no one had seen Ella Landers enter the Catholic Center. If all was going as planned, Ella had silently climbed the back stairs to the third floor and slipped unnoticed into Kempe's darkened office.

21

Wearing a black cashmere coat with a dark maroon scarf high around his neck, Monsignor Aidan Kempe walked out the main entrance of the Hotel d'Inghilterra at precisely three thirty. It would take no more than twenty minutes to walk to the Borghese Gardens for his four-thirty rendezvous. He might stop for another coffee in the Piazza del Popolo and rehearse, yet again, his report to M, the very private yet powerful Bishop Pietro Montaldo. This would be only his second meeting with the Brotherhood's Vatican protector and he hoped they would speak, as they had earlier, in English. Montaldo was fluent in Spanish and Italian, but his English, like his French, while passable, was somewhat halting. Still, Montaldo's accented, deliberate English was better than Kempe's Italian.

It was four-twenty when Kempe reached the Gardens. A few minutes later he stood in front of the Fountain of the Seahorses. There was no sign of M, so he walked slowly down the Via dei Pupazzi toward the Temple of Diana, stopping every few steps to discreetly check for a figure that could be M. At four-twenty-five he turned and strolled back to the fountain. Kempe stood off to the right pretending to admire the sculpture, which had never really captured his imagination. Tourists were sparse this time of the year, particularly at this hour. The late afternoon light faded into a purple and gold dusk. Save for the rumbling of the cascading waters of the fountain and the distant, muted sounds of Rome's traffic, a chapel-like quiet fell over the Gardens of the Villa Borghese.

"It's quite exquisite, don't you agree?"

Kempe had not heard him approach, but there was no doubting the voice—refined but not quite effete. He turned to find M just a few feet behind him. His eyes, he had forgotten, were dark and searing, almost cruel in their intelligence. M, a good four inches shorter than the monsignor, was wearing a black cashmere coat similar to Kempe's, a Greek fisherman's cap, and a black silk scarf worn high to hide his Roman collar. He was, Kempe knew, in his late sixties. And while not slim, M carried only a few extra pounds at his waist.

"Excellency," Kempe said with a nod that M could read as a discreet bow. "Yes, the fountain is quite extraordinary."

"Shall we walk?" Bishop Pietro Montaldo suggested. "It's too chilly to sit on a bench." The two clerics turned and walked slowly down the tree-canopied stone path of the Via di Valle Giulia, with Kempe at M's right elbow. The long shadows cast by the early evening light suggested two cloistered monks taking a prayer walk.

But the two were far from sharing a moment of prayer.

Though they had the path to themselves, Kempe spoke softly. "Our brother Wilfred has decided to mark his fiftieth ordination anniversary with a Jubilee Mass at the Basilica of the Assumption, followed by a fundraising dinner for close friends and major benefactors. He hopes to raise a hundred thousand dollars—for our Catholic Charities." Kempe's slight pause was enough to inform M that a portion of the gifts would be directed to the archbishop's personal retirement needs—perhaps a generous portion.

"Hadn't we expected him to retire quietly?" M asked.

"Yes, Excellency. But he has opted for what he believes is a modest celebration. Even though we know that the archbishop at times may have been…imprudent…with young men."

"Those lapses in judgment," Kempe felt a need to emphasize, "occurred before he was named to the episcopacy." Kempe hesitated, glancing at M's silhouette in the descending darkness. "He doesn't see the public celebration of his jubilee as ill-advised."

Kempe paused briefly to see if he could catch M's expression. He couldn't. The bishop's face was turned to the trees and shrubs that lined the Via di Valle Giulia.

Kempe knew he had to get to the heart of the matter or M would dismiss him as a fool wasting his time. "The Mass and dinner represent a risk to our Brotherhood, and possibly an embarrassment to the archbishop and to Holy Mother Church," Kempe said in the argot of church-speak.

Montaldo, for the first time, turned to search the face of his American counterpart.

Kempe cut straight to the heart of the matter. "A short time ago a man confronted the archbishop with an allegation that he abused him when was a boy. The accuser is now in his late thirties, and recently retired from the army." Kempe paused. M's eyes were now fixed on him. "I have used the Brotherhood's purse to help this accuser get on with his life." Still, M remained silent. "The archbishop is gambling that this accuser, this army veteran, will remain discreet. We can only hope."

Kempe's stomach dropped. M had listened without so much as a word, his face expressionless in the declining light. Coming to report personally to M was a mistake, a terrible mistake.

Kempe hesitated, then, in spite of his mounting panic, plunged ahead. "Then something quite bizarre happened, Excellency," his voice betraying his anxiety. "After a Confirmation Mass, during the recessional, a number of the priests and the laity saw a laser beam resting squarely on the archbishop's chest. The red dot disappeared almost immediately. But not before Wilfred noticed it. I've been told it shook him to his core."

M paused as if thinking, and then turned to Kempe. Finally, he seemed to grasp the seriousness of the situation. "Go on," M said returning to his slow pace.

Kempe's composure returned. "The same thing happened at the archbishop's next confirmation. You can understand, I'm sure, that our brother is quite anxious, quite fearful. I'm afraid, Excellency, he is so unnerved that he is, as we say in America, close to the edge."

As if in support of Kempe's shaky but growing confidence, M nodded.

"*Fragile,*" he said quietly.

The two members of the Brotherhood of the Sacred Purple walked on in silence.

M, at last, spoke, "What do you make of these events, Aidan?" His voice, like his expression, was flat, impatient for the complete assessment of the situation that had brought Kempe to Rome.

"So far there has been nothing in our media. That is a blessing. But this business with the laser makes me think the archbishop, and the Brotherhood, are in danger. Something is brewing." Kempe immediately regretted the expression. M would have no idea of its meaning. "I fear something is developing. I fear something terrible might happen at his jubilee celebration."

M stopped a second time and turned his shoulders toward the American. "And?" he said coolly.

"I fear, your Excellency, that the archbishop is likely to expose and embarrass us.

"There are a few, perhaps four individuals," Kempe continued awkwardly, "who have accused the archbishop of inappropriate behavior when they were boys. Thank God, the allegations were brought to my attention. I was able to defuse each situation discreetly, thanks in no small part to the purple purse. Again, thank God, the families of the alleged victims agreed to spare the church scandal."

M already knew from his own sources that Kempe, as financial secretary of the archdiocese, had protected the church from scandal with his adroit handling of Wilfred Gunnison's indiscretions. "And we know, Aidan," he said, "how the media in your country enjoy sensationalizing questionable allegations of misconduct by a few priests—and sometimes by our brothers wearing the sacred purple."

Kempe heard a hiss of air part the lips of M—like a sigh. But it wasn't a sigh at all. On the short rush of air from M's lips floated a hint of garlic. What he had just heard wasn't a sigh at all. It was, Kempe now understood, a guttural "ugh" of contempt.

"We know only too well how your secular legal system allows greedy attorneys and so-called victims to sue our holy church for millions of dollars. We in the Vatican see your legal system and your media as enemies of our church. Your culture, dear Aidan, I mean no offense, is simply corrupt."

Kempe could not allow himself to take offense. "Sadly, Excellency, we have liberals controlling our government, our media, our education system—and they are intent on subduing and humiliating our church." They walked in silence for a few minutes, hands deep in their coat pockets.

"I've asked the archbishop," Kempe went on, "to consider postponing the jubilee celebration. I suggested he could claim illness. He wouldn't hear of it." Kempe knew he must be careful here. He was close to condemning a fellow brother of the Sacred Purple. "I fear Gunnison is out of control, Excellency. Even on the verge of a breakdown. And I suspect the public adulation that will accompany his jubilee might be the prod that motivates one or more of his alleged victims to go public. The archbishop seems to think that the brotherhood's purse will make his problems go away, that it can buy the silence he desires."

127

Kempe paused, giving M an opportunity to comment. He didn't.

Knowing his words were hammering the final nails into Gunnison's coffin, Kempe said, "Wilfred moves from paranoia to denial and from denial to supreme confidence that nothing can possibly go wrong." He paused again, glancing down at the little Italian bishop on his left.

"What do you think would be best for Holy Mother Church, Aidan?"

And for the Brotherhood, Kempe thought to himself.

"It would be best, Excellency, for Archbishop Gunnison to relocate his residence outside the United States, as soon as possible after his jubilee. His presence in Baltimore puts the church at great risk of scandal."

M's silence gave Kempe hope. The bishop was considering his advice. M led his friend toward the Garden entrance closest to the Fountain of the Tortoises. "Yes, yes, Aidan," he said, "we have reason to be concerned."

Outside the Garden, M approached a black Audi sedan parked at the curb with a driver at the wheel. Kempe hesitated briefly, then followed. At the door of the car, M said thoughtfully, "I will send my personal representative to the archbishop's Jubilee Mass and dinner. I ask you, Aidan, to arrange to have him meet with our brother Wilfred as soon as possible after the celebration to convey my personal congratulations, and to persuade him to relocate outside the archdiocese. My envoy will identify himself to you as Monsignor Giancarlo Foscari. He will not, however, vest to concelebrate the Mass and he is not to be introduced to any of the bishops or guests at either the Mass or the dinner. In particular, do not introduce him to Archbishop Cullen or to the nuncio." M paused to let his instructions sink in. "And do not mention his presence even to the priests of the Brotherhood," he added. "Monsignor Foscari's short visit is to go unnoticed. Do you understand, Aidan?"

"Yes, Excellency," Kempe responded quickly. "I understand."

M padded Kempe's forearm. "You were correct to bring this situation to my attention." At these few words from the mysterious and powerful M, Kempe regained his confidence, embarrassed now at his momentary pangs of self-doubt.

Aidan opened the right rear door of the Audi and M slowly backed his small frame on to the seat, lifting his legs in after him. Before allowing Aidan to close the door, he looked up at him and asked, "When do you return to Baltimore?"

"I leave tomorrow morning."

"Then let me drive you to your hotel. You will be rising early," M said as he slid over to the left side of the back seat.

"Thank you, Excellency, that is very kind of you." The driver, a large, dark figure, didn't turn to inspect his new passenger, though he did steal a glance at Kempe in the rearview mirror.

"*Andiamo*, Giorgio," M said, with a flutter of his hand.

The driver nodded, and put the Audi in gear. He appeared to Kempe to be a muscular man, and tall for an Italian. Kempe and M sat in silence during the kilometer or so drive to his hotel.

"*Grazie, Eccellenza*," Kempe said as the car pulled up to the hotel's entrance.

But as Kempe reached for the door handle, M reached out and took hold of his left arm, holding him in his seat.

"Let me take this opportunity to offer you a fraternal word of counsel, Monsignor."

Kempe, suddenly on guard at the formality of M's address, braced himself.

"Your visit to a certain coffee bar this afternoon was ill-considered. And your weekend escapades in Chicago have not gone unnoticed. I refer to the bars on Division Street, the bars that cater to men with special interests. *Prudenza*, Monsignor, *prudenza*." He patted Kempe's arm and added in a paternal, unctuous tone, "*Discrezione.*"

Kempe raised his eyes, sure that his dismayed expression, even in the darkened car, betrayed him. He was searching for some word or gesture that said, *This is not a serious matter.* But M's dark eyes said only that he knew too well the weaknesses of the flesh. Then Kempe caught the driver's eyes fixed on him in the rearview mirror. They were ice cold and unblinking. "Yes, yes, of course, Excellency," he said softly, unable to hide his humiliation.

"Good evening, Aidan," M said abruptly.

"Good evening, Excellency," Kempe whispered as he opened the door and stepped out of the car. The Audi moved slowly from the curb into the dark night of the Eternal City.

For a moment, Kempe lingered at the foot of the marble steps leading to the grand entrance to the d'Inghilterra. As he climbed the few steps he almost lost his balance, then forced himself to walk with dignity into the high-ceilinged lobby and, without the slightest hesitation, straight to the hotel's bar. He ordered a double scotch at the bar and took his drink to a high-backed, brocaded chair where he sat in shock and silence. He winced at his afternoon indiscretion. M must have had him under surveillance since he arrived in Rome. But how could M possibly know about Chicago? And, a thought that made him almost sick to his stomach, who else knew? Kempe replayed as many of his Chicago weekends as he could, trying to remember the priests he had seen, especially those with Roman connections. He enjoyed more than a few assignations, but those men were now faces without names. His anxiety rose as it dawned on him that a few of his encounters had been with seminarians—seminarians home on vacation from studies in Rome. God, this was awful. He glanced around the softly lit bar distractedly, barely noticing the piped-in coronation anthem of Handel's *Zadok the Priest*, one of his favorites. Now, he thought, I might never be named a bishop. Did this explain why Bryn Martin was elevated in his place?

What else did M know about him? Kempe replayed the conversation in the back seat of the Audi. He closed his eyes, straining for every nuance. The warning was paternal, without moralistic overtones, but that was the Roman way. That this Giorgio knew his hotel without him mentioning it was disturbing in itself, but that M had spoken to him of such delicate matters in the driver's hearing was unforgivable. Giorgio, obviously, was more than Bishop Montaldo's driver.

Kempe flagged a server and ordered another scotch. As he sipped it, his anxiety and confusion slowly morphed into a constricting anger. "*Prudenza*, Aidan, *prudenza*." The hypocrite. Did M think he hadn't heard about M's own frolicking on the beaches of Mykonos with the island's party girls? And all of this, Kempe was sure, was paid for with euros from the purple purse. With a little digging, he was sure he could find other examples of Montaldo's own lack of prudence. He took a deep swallow of his scotch. He was prudent, he told himself. He was prudent *and* discreet.

Aidan Kempe sank exhausted into seat 3-A in the first class cabin of Continental Flight 15 to Newark. He would have a glass of red wine and then find, surely, blessed sleep. It would be at least another half hour before the passengers in coach were boarded and the doors of the 757 were closed. He hated this interminable period of pre-flight jostling and settling in, the repeated announcements from the crew about the proper stowing of luggage.

"Would you like something to drink, sir?" the flight attendant asked.

"Red wine, please," he said without making eye contact. She returned with two bottles in hand, a Cabernet and a Pinot Noir. "The Pinot Noir," Kempe said curtly. He sipped the wine when she poured it and tried to relax.

He instinctively opened his eyes at the shuffle of another first class passenger finding his seat. A tall, thick-set man in black placed a bag in the overhead compartment and settled into seat 2-A. Kempe was ready to close his eyes after this interruption when he suddenly found himself fully awake. The last-minute arrival had the same muscular neck and shape of head and shoulders as M's driver. Kempe's blood went cold as a blanket of fear slapped his face.

The man in the seat directly in front of him was Giorgio.

22

A pot of herbal tea rested innocently on the dining room table next to three neatly stacked piles of documents.

"I'll never forget what you did for me, Ella," Margaret said, shaking her head. "I can't believe we did it. *You* did it." The two women looked at each other the way underground operatives might after a successful mission—silently proud of their own audacity. "Ella," Margaret said with teary eyes, "Thank you, thank you for the risk you took for me, thank you for having the copies made. Most of all, thank you for being such a dear friend over these many years."

Ella smiled a wordless *You're welcome.* "Once I got a look at all this, I felt much better about our little operation." Landers' "look" had taken three full hours.

Margaret blinked, then squeezed her eyes tight. She would not cry. And now Ella's endorsement of the operation, light as it was, softened the guilt she felt about asking her friend to commit larceny.

"Your boss had good reason to keep his drawer under lock and key. From what I've seen, your Monsignor Kempe could well go to jail."

"I knew it. I just knew it," Margaret said, more self-righteously than she intended.

"Let's begin with the finances, the ledgers and records relating to Kempe's purple purse," Ella suggested. "It provides context for the rest of the file. I found records relating to a group of priests Kempe referred to as the Brotherhood," she said, gesturing towards a second pile, "and the third set of copies are his notes on allegations of sexual abuse. Kempe appears to have handled a number of those cases on his own, without taking them to the archbishop, much less the police."

Ella wanted to begin their reading with the first two categories, knowing the last group of papers, the one's Margaret would be most interested in, described how Kempe and Gunnison plotted their handling of Mark Anderlee's charge that the archbishop had abused him. Once Margaret read those notes and records, her focus would be shattered and her judgment compromised.

"All right." Margaret said. "I knew he had control of some off-the-books funds, but I never had any idea how much money was involved," Margaret said.

"About half a million dollars," Ella said. "Almost half of that comes from just two pastors in the Brotherhood. Didn't Ian suggest some kind of group or society of priests like this when we had dinner last week? Apparently, the pastors of the Brotherhood make monthly cash payments of one thousand dollars each to the purse. Two of the pastors have been doing this for years. The rest of the money seems to be contributions or gifts from Kempe's friends and from companies doing business with the archdiocese—contractors, builders, suppliers, accounting firms, PR firms, law firms, and the like. There was even a contribution from a private detective agency. Some of the contributions were clearly personal gifts to Kempe."

"I bet," Margaret said shrewdly, "the donors made sure they were able to claim them as tax-deductible contributions to the church."

Ella nodded. "Most likely," she said. "As financial vicar, Kempe was in a position to influence the awarding of contracts to firms doing business with the archdiocese. And he still has considerable influence in the awarding of contracts as chancellor."

"And all of this was happening right under my nose," Margaret said, as if kicking herself. She couldn't wait to get this evidence to Bryn Martin and Archbishop Cullen. She sat still for a minute, finally wondering out loud, "Do you think all this might be technically legal?"

"I'm not sure. Probably much of it is, or maybe border-line. It seems to me that at least some of this falls into the category of kickbacks. If that's the case, considering the sums of money Kempe was managing, it's not only illegal, it's probably a felony."

Ella reached for the documents dealing with clergy abuse. Why wait? After all, this was the driving force behind Margaret's passion to have Gunnison exposed. The pile on the Brotherhood could wait.

"You should look at these, Margaret. Mark is mentioned. It's the last entry Kempe made."

Margaret took the copies from Ella. She read silently, her breathing now deep and slow.

Ella said evenly, dispassionately, "Kempe's notes indicate several other priests were accused of abusing boys. And Gunnison, you will see, was accused by at least four other individuals or their families." She went silent as she noticed Margaret's hands shaking, then went on, "Mark wasn't the only boy abused, and he probably wasn't the last."

The tea went cold in their cups.

"He's going to pay for this," Margaret muttered. "He's going to pay for this."

Ella turned to look at her old friend, alarmed at the transformation unfolding before her very eyes. "You'll see," Ella said, deciding not to respond to Margaret's implied threat, "that the allegations against Gunnison go back to his days when he was in the Education Department of the archdiocese—before he was named a bishop."

Margaret was familiar with the archdiocesan attorneys walking the halls of the Catholic Center, with their strategy meetings with the archbishop's top advisors to counter the law suits mounting against the archdiocese. "You can imagine how the victims' lawyers would love to get their hands on these papers," she said more to herself than to Ella.

"Your boss was very shrewd. Somehow he managed to keep the allegations from getting to the police and to the media. In most cases he promised the victims' parents that the priest would get professional help and the archbishop would make sure he didn't abuse again. In every case, Kempe offered counseling to the victim and his family."

"How compassionate," Margaret said sarcastically.

"This certainly won't surprise you, Margaret. Kempe also offered every one of the victims' parents money to help them get on with their lives. According to his notes, there must be an archdiocesan fund, a discretionary fund, that he had access to as financial vicar and now as chancellor. Most of the payments came from this fund. But not all. Sometimes the money, especially in the cases involving Gunnison, came from something called 'the purse.'"

Margaret said knowingly, "That would be the purple purse."

Ella pointed to a line entry and said, as gently as possible, "A hundred thousand went to Mark."

"Oh God," Margaret said, "I wondered how Mark was able to buy the condo at the harbor. He told me Gunnison had given him some money, but…" She sat back in her chair, silent and sad, more troubled, more confused than ever.

"Ella," she said, the tone in her voice signaling a new resolve and strength, "you know that just two weeks ago Mark sat at my kitchen table and told me what Gunnison did to him. I saw tears in his eyes. And I had worked for this guy! I was his goddamn secretary for a few years."

Ella placed her hand on Margaret's and squeezed.

Margaret went back to her conversation with Mark in her kitchen. "He said he told two friends from high school who I don't remember, Dan Barrett and Paul Kline. He said with pride, and with a determination that must have come from his years in the army, that he confronted Gunnison and told him he was going to pay, and pay dearly."

For more than a dozen of her years at the Catholic Center, Comiskey had seen Gunnison almost daily. And for the last month and a half she had spent much of her time working on preparations for his Golden Jubilee Mass and dinner—supervising the invitation list, the mailings and response cards, the dinner, the hotel arrangements for the visiting bishops. Every courtesy was to be extended to the bishops. God damn them all now, she thought.

Ella now laid a hand on the arm of her old friend. "Are you okay, Margaret?"

"Yes, just a little cold." She rose from the table. "Let me get a sweater."

A few minutes later, a fresh pot of tea on the table, the two women sat back down to their task. Deliberately, carefully, they studied each and every entry, each and every page of documentation snatched from Aidan Kempe's personal and private file drawer.

An hour later, their necks stiff and achy, they stood and stretched. Margaret looked at Ella. "Something snapped in me when Mark told me what Gunnison did to him. I've never thought of myself as a mean person. But now I know something about myself I never suspected. I'm capable of great meanness after all." She looked into Ella's eyes and held her glance. "I hate Gunnison, I hate this man."

Ella put her arm around her friend, feeling the tightness in her shoulders and back. "Gunnison is all Cary Grant good looks and clerical charm, but he's a snake," Margaret said.

"One other thing you should know," Ella said, stroking Margaret's hair, "Kempe wrote in one of the journal entries we didn't get to that he saw Bryn Martin leaving the Catholic Center late one evening dressed in jeans and a dark leather coat. He implied that Martin was on his way out cruising or something like that. The entry was underlined. It looked to me like your boss believed he had something on Bryn."

"Was the entry date a Wednesday?" Margaret asked.

Ella paged through the stack of documents until she found the entry. "Yes, as a matter of fact, it was a Wednesday."

"Kempe is *so* sick, Ella. Bryn told me in confidence that on some Wednesday evenings he and Archbishop Cullen accompany Loyola College students taking food and clothing to inner city homeless. Of course he's not going to be dressed as a priest."

Ella shook her head in simultaneous relief and disbelief. She stood and walked to the closet next to the front door for her coat. "I need to get home before it gets too late."

"I know. You have an hour's drive ahead of you, and in rush hour traffic. But there is something else I want you to think about," Margaret said. "I want to get into Kempe's personal computer. He's extremely careful about guarding the password. Can you give me some help with that? There's more to this. I can just feel it."

Ella raised her eyebrows. "We've got to assume Kempe is too smart to use a password that someone might guess at. Birthday, address...." She thought for a moment. "I'd look at words related to his fixation with purple. Google the German, Italian, and Latin words for purple. See if that might work."

"Good idea. I know Kempe's mother was Irish. She was born in Cork. And she spoke Irish. I'll Google the Gaelic for purple as well. And when I know it's safe at the office, I'm going to make duplicates of the copies you made," Margaret said, glancing at the papers spread over her dining room table.

Before her eyes, Ella saw her friend committing irretrievably to a mission. It unnerved her to realize that it was not admiration she felt for Margaret's fierce and focused will. What she felt for her friend was fear.

23

The too-familiar fog of travel settled over Monsignor Aidan Kempe, now made thicker and more disorienting by Giorgio's presence on his trans-Atlantic flight. On numb legs, Kempe moved with the herd from the arrival gate to the customs area of the Newark-Liberty Airport.

"Monsignor Kempe," a voice said softly into his ear in accented English, "just keep walking and look straight ahead."

Kempe didn't turn his head, but his peripheral vision confirmed that Giorgio was at his side, walking in step with him.

"Allow me to introduce myself. I am Monsignor Giancarlo Foscari." He handed Kempe a Vatican diplomatic passport with the picture of a man in a Roman collar. The passport bore the name, "Monsignor Giancarlo Foscari." But Kempe was certain the man at his side was M's driver, Giorgio. He permitted Kempe but a moment's glance before abruptly taking the passport from him and placing it in an inside pocket of his overcoat.

The anxiety Kempe felt the moment Giorgio boarded the plane had only grown through the nine-hour flight. Now his stomach was queasy and his breathing came in shallow gulps. What was M up to? They stood stiffly at the baggage claim, having passed through customs without incident. The impostor, Foscari, had even won a respectful nod from the uniformed agent.

"We will not meet again until after the archbishop's celebration. I will contact you on your mobile phone for the information I need to meet privately with the archbishop. Your only task is to arrange for this private meeting and to do so with the greatest discretion. Is that clear?"

Kempe felt his blood rising. He was not accustomed to taking orders, especially from a chauffeur with a doctored passport. He nodded, spitting a "Yes" through his teeth.

"I will be in the back of the Basilica for the Jubilee Mass," Foscari continued. "You are to ignore my presence. As you have been instructed, I am to be introduced to no one. Do you understand?"

Kempe's face burned red. "I understand, *Monsignor*," he said emphasizing Foscari's phony title. Foscari, *Giorgio*, this chauffeur was treating him like some idiot acolyte.

"During the dinner for the archbishop, I will be in the lobby of the hotel."

The two men stood shoulder to shoulder at the baggage carousel, speaking softly but emphatically avoiding eye contact.

"As his Excellency instructed," Foscari said with his eyes scanning the bags now moving slowly on the carousel, "you are to mention my presence only to Archbishop Gunnison, telling him I am here to extend the personal greetings of his friend from the Vatican." Foscari paused to underscore his next directive. "No one but the archbishop, Monsignor Kempe, is to know of my presence as his Excellency's special envoy." Yet again Kempe was asked, "Is that clear?"

Kempe nodded, straining to keep his composure.

"In case of necessity," Foscari said handing Kempe a piece of cream-colored, stiff paper bordered in deep purple, "this is my international mobile number. Use it only if necessary. Please arrange for my private meeting with Archbishop Gunnison on the Monday morning following his jubilee dinner."

Kempe thought he would have screamed if Foscari had added another, "Is that clear?"

"You are to wait for my call for the time of my meeting

with his Excellency. I have your mobile number." Without another word, Foscari, his carry-on bag over his shoulder, lifted a checked bag from the carousel, extended the collapsed handle, and walked like an Italian gentleman of the Vatican court toward the final customs checkpoint.

Kempe, humiliated and frightened, stood frozen in place next to his own bag until Foscari was out of sight.

The chancellor of the Archdiocese of Baltimore would have been even more distressed had he known how Giorgio Grotti had come to the personal service of Bishop Pietro Montaldo. Grotti had been a pious but sensual young boy, dreaming one day of the priesthood and the very next day of the *dolce vita* of an Italian playboy. To his mother's great—and tearful—delight, the boy entered the seminary when he turned eighteen. But three years later, to her tearful disappointment, Giorgio was expelled for nearly beating to death a fellow seminarian who had made sexual advances. For a short time Giorgio worked as a waiter, earning enough money to indulge—as a veritable prodigal son— in Rome's vibrant night life. But his sense of vocation, to Grotti's surprise, welled up once again. He wanted to do something useful, even meaningful, with his life. If he couldn't save souls, he could save lives. Giorgio Grotti would be a policeman. Without as much as a second thought, he joined the Carabinieri. His superiors soon enough noted his intelligence and toughness, but missed the violent vein in his temperament. Less than two years later, Grotti was promoted to the Carabinieri's Special Forces Group, the GIS. The GIS, some one hundred or so troops trained in counter-terrorism, were the Carabinieri's elite unit, superbly conditioned, highly disciplined, multilingual—and renowned for their marksmanship. Grotti's file indicated he was fluent in English and Arabic.

That Grotti was one of the best of the best became clear when he was chosen for a high-priority, top-secret mission. He was to eliminate a suspected terrorist linked to al'Qaeda who was, according to hard intelligence, recruiting and training a network of subversives in a suburb of Naples. The assignment was Grotti's alone. No backup, no tactical support if he botched the kill. Moreover, there would be absolute deniability from the Italian Ministry of the Interior if things went wrong.

The terrorist, Grotti reported to his superiors, never knew what hit him—two shots, the first to his chest, the second to his head. Grotti was almost in his car as the target hit the sidewalk, he said, trying not to sound boastful.

Grotti felt the warrior's satisfaction of a mission accomplished—and a strange, surprising sensual pleasure that baffled him. But he hadn't slept well the night he brought down the terrorist. Nor did he sleep well in the weeks that followed. And worse, his sex life had turned decidedly weird. He now could have sex only if it was rough, punishing, and bordering on violence. The word soon spread among the circle of women who regularly shared his bed. For the first time in his life, Grotti had to pay for it. And getting rough with prostitutes could be dangerous.

"I can't sleep. I don't have much of an appetite," was all Grotti said to the Carabinieri's psychiatrist. He left with prescriptions for sleeping pills and anti-anxiety meds, which he refused to fill. Finally, the Carabinieri's *capo* granted him a three month leave of absence with pay. It changed little of his inner misery. "The assignment," as he referred to his assassination mission, was justifiable. He had done nothing wrong, but something *was* wrong. Something was wrong with everything.

His mother, finally over her disappointment in not having a priest for a son, now took pride in Giorgio's status as a member of the Carabinieri's elite Special Forces Unit. Still, her smothering attention irritated him, and his visits home became more irregular. In fact, Grotti found most people irritating. What made him morose, he had to admit, was the sad truth that there was no longer any easy pleasure, any easy laughter, only a ready-to-erupt restless anger—and a disturbing inclination to inflict pain.

One morning, sitting under the awning of a trattoria watching women his mother's age buying their groceries and cuts of veal at Rome's ancient market, the Campo de' Fiori, Giorgio found himself praying to the Virgin. *Holy Mother of God, please help this dumb ass. I am so screwed up.* He opened his eyes and looked again at the women in the market place. They were doing what women do at market—visiting with friends, whispering gossip, haggling with the merchants—and often laughing. Giorgio couldn't remember the last time he had laughed. He wanted to be happy again, like the ordinary people across the street shopping at the Campo de' Fiori.

Perhaps the idea came from the Virgin. But soon after his prayer, Giorgio Grotti made up his mind to go to confession. His confessor, he would soon discover, was a bishop—Bishop Pietro Montaldo. He had been kind and had tried to assure Giorgio that he had not sinned against the fifth commandment—he had not committed murder.

"Sometimes, my son, sometimes it is necessary to take drastic action for the good of Italy—and sometimes for the good of Holy Mother Church," Montaldo told him. "Action that only the most loyal of believers understand."

Grotti nodded in the dark of the confessional. He waited, not sure if his confessor expected a response. Then in a hushed voice Montaldo prayed the prayer of absolution, *"Ego te absolvo in nomine Patris, et Filii, et Spiritus Sancti."* Giorgio started to rise from the weathered leather of the padded kneeler when he heard his confessor say, "I believe you are the last penitent, my son. Would you mind walking with me for a while?"

Two weeks later Giorgio Grotti resigned from the Carabin-

ieri and entered the personal employ of Bishop Pietro Montaldo at almost twice his GIS salary—a salary that came from
Montaldo's *viola borsa,* his purple purse. The first lesson Giorgio
learned from his new boss was surprising—and yet not really
new. Bishop Montaldo now said aloud and with conviction the
words he had whispered to him in the confessional. "Sometimes
it is necessary to take drastic action for the good of the church."
Grotti soon learned that the good of the church always included
the good of an organization he had never heard of, the Brotherhood of the Sacred Purple.

24

The modest black on white sign said simply, "Carmelite Monastery." Bryn Martin turned left off Dulaney Valley Road onto a rolling tree-lined half-mile drive that led to the monastery's main entrance. Although the monastery was well out of sight, the road itself seemed to share in the spirit of the cloister. Martin invariably felt drawn into the contemplative world of the nuns every time he turned onto the monastery property. Ninety-foot-high red maples, their shorn winter branches now offering a broken yet stately gothic canopy, stood guard as silent porters.

To his right, the decks of the up-scale homes of the Meadowcroft development were visible in the gray February light. The homes, little more than a decade old, always distracted Martin from the spirit of solitude he felt whenever he approached the monastery.

He imagined young professionals and rising execs sitting with their neighbors under table umbrellas, sipping white wine before grilling salmon steaks. Even with the houses' facades out of sight, the landscaped back yards told Martin they were striking. A few of the homes had floor-to-ceiling windows revealing spacious family rooms with two-storied fire places. When he visited the monastery during the summer months, Martin had seen children playing on the manicured lawns. He moved deliberately down the drive, no more than ten miles an hour. Out of the blue, he felt a twinge of guilt—the guilt of a voyeur. No, it wasn't guilt.

There was nothing prurient in his scanning—he was searching for sights of something he would never have. He was looking for glimpses of ordinary family life. If the monastery had its pull for him, so did the homes of the Meadowcroft development. He had idealized these families snuggled into their village-like community, with their suburban comforts and happy children. He knew there is no home, anywhere, without its problems, without its secrets. There were infidelities, divorces, addictions, financial crises, violent arguments. But he was feeling a little regret, a disguised grief. Martin winced at his own attempts to assuage his envy of family life. He knew well that the married bore their own crosses. But he knew even better the crosses of celibate life.

During his first assignment as a parish priest, Martin had regularly come to the monastery to visit his sister, Nora, a novice at the time. The simplicity and peace of the place, the unpretentious intelligence and welcoming spirit of the nuns, struck a chord with his own natural bent for contemplative spirituality. For more than a decade now, even though Nora had since left, Martin had been coming to the monastery for a retreat day each month.

A week earlier, Martin had called Sister Miriam, the prioress, and arranged for a half-day visit to the monastery. Gunnison's jubilee celebration was now just a few days away and the quiet time would prepare him, he reasoned, for the added stress of protecting an archbishop under threat who was intent on forging ahead with his fundraising Mass and dinner. Martin was relieved to hear that a guest room was available, and he smiled when Sister Miriam mentioned that John Krajik, the pastor of St. Bernardine's, would also be there, making a week-long retreat. Martin and Krajik had telephoned each other a number of times since the first laser hit on Gunnison. As far as Krajik could tell, the incident at the Confirmation Mass had ceased to be a point of conversation among the relatively few parishioners who had seen the red dot rest momentarily on the chest of the archbishop.

Krajik had been two years ahead of Martin in the seminary. He was a good student, athletic, with a lively sense of humor. Some thought Krajik looked like a young John Paul II. So did Martin. But he knew Krajik's theology and vision of the church were more nuanced than those of JP II.

Martin looked forward to talking to the priest for two reasons—he wanted an update on the incident at the Confirmation Mass and he knew Krajik would have a good reading on the morale of archdiocesan priests. Moreover, John Krajik was one of the few Baltimore priests who appreciated the spiritual resource of the Baltimore Carmelites. Martin could never figure out why more priests didn't spend some time at the monastery.

The sister on phone duty rose from the reception desk to let Martin into the monastery. "Bishop Martin, welcome. Sister Miriam asked me to ring her when you arrived."

Martin smiled, "Thanks, Sister. I'll wait in the parlor." He moved across the hall to a tastefully appointed sitting room, with French doors facing onto the cloister, and sat down on a brocaded love seat facing a framed print of Teresa of Avila in prayer. But the Carmel's monastic tranquility didn't hold. The Gunnison affair distracted him. Maybe a few hours at the monastery would give him some perspective. He reminded himself he had taken reasonable and discreet security measures for the Mass and dinner. Additional Baltimore policemen had been hired for security and traffic control outside the Basilica, and the hotel security chief had been directed to pay special attention to the well-being of the archbishop during the jubilee dinner. Still, the laser dots, Margaret Comiskey's suspicions about Kempe's special account, the rumors of Gunnison's messing with young boys, and his own embarrassing encounter decades ago all left him on edge.

"Bryn, how are you?" Sister Miriam said as she entered.

"I'm fine, Miriam."

The anxiety in his eyes and the tightness around his mouth gave a different response. They exchanged a brief hug. "A little time here will do me good. Things are hectic at the Catholic Center these days. It's Archbishop Gunnison's jubilee celebration."

"I can imagine," Sr. Miriam said with a slight raising of her brow. "Let me take you upstairs to your room. John is in the retreatant's suite just down the hall from you. I told him you'd be here for part of the day. He was happy to hear that."

Before leaving Martin to get settled, she added, "Nora was here not long ago with a colleague from the university, a history professor who was quite interested in our archives, especially the papers of one of our earliest chaplains, a Jesuit named Gilbert Combier."

"Nora told me. And I've met him." Martin hesitated. "I don't mean Gilbert Combier," he said with a grin. "Her colleague's British and a specialist in medieval church history. A very interesting man."

Miriam smiled, glad to confirm her impression that Nora seemed to find the Englishman very interesting indeed.

An hour before vespers, bundled in coat, scarf, and gloves, John Krajik closed the door to his room and headed for the staircase down to the main entrance as Martin reached the top of the stairs leading to his room.

"John," Martin said in greeting. "Sister Miriam told me you were here on retreat." The two shook hands warmly.

"She mentioned after Mass this morning that you'd be here for part of the day. It's good to see you. I'm just on my way out for a walk. Care to join me?"

"Yeah, I would. Let me grab my coat."

Like the monks they so admired, the two clergymen, their

collars turned up and chins nestled into their coats, walked in measured steps down the asphalt drive leading to Dulaney Valley Road. Martin was reminded of their silent, solitary walks as seminarians when they prayed the rosary before the evening study period.

"Bryn," Krajik said looking straight ahead, "I appreciated your calls after what happened at our Confirmation Mass. Knowing that Gunnison had a similar experience at Immaculate Conception was somehow comforting, realizing it wasn't a St. Bernardine thing."

"The laser scared the old man, that's for sure, but he's hell bent on going ahead with his jubilee. You may have heard that I took Gunnison's confirmation at St. Ignatius last week. Nothing at all out of the ordinary. Two friends from my parish days, retired FBI and Secret Service agents, were in the congregation, but the confirmation came off without a hitch. Gunnison seems to be banking on the fact that there haven't been any threatening calls or letters to the Catholic Center and nothing in the media."

"You probably can't say anything, Bryn, but a couple of things make me wonder about Gunnison. There are persistent rumors that he was pretty randy with some of our school boys before he was named a bishop. I wonder if one of his victims might have something to do with this."

Martin and Krajik moved to the side of the narrow drive as a car passed heading toward the monastery, the woman driver offering a smile and waving amicably. In a voice close to a whisper, Martin conceded, "I've wondered the same thing. And if somebody wants to embarrass or hurt Wilfred, his jubilee celebration would be pretty tempting. It would be far more public than a Confirmation Mass. We're gonna be as careful as we can be without allowing too obvious a police presence at the Mass or the dinner."

Krajik nodded, "Not much else you can do if he is determined to go ahead with it." The two men moved to the edge of the drive as another car, its headlights winking on in the muted purple dusk, approached the monastery's main entrance. "There is something else that makes me uneasy about Gunnison," Krajik continued. "It's this priest group he's part of. A number of priests know about it. Kempe, Tom Fenton, Herm Volker, and a couple of the younger pastors meet with Gunnison once a month or so. What bothers me, Bryn, is if you ask any of those guys about it they act as if they don't know what you're talking about. It's not only private, it's, like, secret."

"Yeah, I've heard of it too." Martin said. "Cullen isn't bothered by it. When he hears of priests getting together he assumes it's some fraternal support group. But this group is not only private, it's exclusive. And I think you're right, there is something furtive about their meetings. Cullen knows that his predecessor and his chancellor are at the center of it. But he's trying to think of it as just another support group for priests."

"Whether most priests know about the group or not," Krajik said firmly, "it's not good for our morale."

Martin, again almost in a whisper, said, "I know, I know." What Martin couldn't tell Krajik was the group's possible link to the Brotherhood of the Sacred Purple.

They turned back toward the monastery when the harsh hum of Dulaney Valley rush hour traffic began to drown their conversation. Lights were now on in the family rooms and kitchens of the homes of the Meadowcroft development. Martin caught the movement of a woman busy, he thought, preparing supper. The two walked in silence for a bit as Krajik noticed his companion's interest in the houses to their right. "Those are really nice homes," he observed casually, "must be close to a million each. Maybe more."

Martin, recalling his earlier examination of conscience, nodded. "They fascinate me, John. Not so much the homes, but the family life I imagine going on inside." Bryn realized this was the most personal revelation he had made to a brother priest since he had been named a bishop. And then, with a hint of embarrassment, "I get a little sentimental every time I walk by them."

"I know what you mean, Bryn." Krajik paused and repeated, "I know what you mean."

It was the way priests spoke of celibacy and the absence of a family life—indirectly and by inference. Neither man could say out loud that from time to time each grieved the absence of a family—and sexual intimacy. Nor was it easy to talk about the loneliness that was part and parcel of their celibate lives. It was part of the clerical code. A priest just didn't talk about loneliness or sexual neediness. And when those thorny realities were from time to time approached, even peripherally, it was more often than not with locker room humor or an adolescent curiosity.

When they were less than fifty yards from the monastery, Krajik asked Martin, "You've been a bishop now for a few years. What's it been like?"

"Like being an acolyte with a miter and crozier," Bryn replied. "You learn right away there really is only one bishop in a diocese. If you're an auxiliary, you really are a helper, a minor helper, prelate to the Lord of the Manor. You take your share of the confirmations, maybe take responsibility for a region of the archdiocese as we do here in Baltimore, and do what you can to make the archbishop's life manageable. And if the boss isn't insecure, you might be something like an adviser." Martin paused and looked at Krajik. The glance said, *This is between you and me.*

"We're fortunate to have an archbishop like Cullen. He knows who he is, he's open-minded, and he's pastoral. I'm not sure I could manage being an auxiliary bishop to Gunnison."

"An honest answer, Bryn. I appreciate your trust," Krajik said softly.

They were back at the monastery now but neither man wanted to end their conversation—rare among Catholic clergy for its frankness. So they walked slowly around the oval drive in front of the main entrance. Neither priest took much note of the life-sized stone statue of the Sacred Heart meant to catch the eye of visitors to the monastery. It represented another time, another church in fact. Martin then added, "I don't feel as close to the people in the pews now. I miss that. And my work now isn't too different from my time in the chancellor's office—except for the confirmations and parish anniversaries that call for the presence of a bishop." Martin went silent for a bit. "I'm still adjusting."

They began their second slow turn around the oval.

"Bryn, I hope you know how happy most of the priests were when you were named auxiliary. We were afraid the appointment would go in another direction." Krajik swallowed. He didn't have to mention that he was referring to Aidan Kempe.

"Thanks, John," was all that Martin could say. But what Krajik said touched him.

"How are things at St. Bernardine's?" Bryn asked, afraid that the emotion rising in his chest might show. "And how are you doing?" Martin felt stupid. His second question sounded lame, like *How's the family?*

"Things are more or less okay at the parish. Really good people, and I'm working with a good staff." But Krajik picked up on Bryn's awkward personal question. "These are not the best of times for me."

Martin said nothing but his silence said, *Go on. I'm listening.*

"I think I'm just tired, Bryn. And a little lonely." His voice halted—and then John Krajik found the courage to say, "Celibacy's never been easy for me. I'm not sleeping around or anything; it's just the loneliness of it. I thought it would get easier as I got older. So far, it hasn't."

Martin nodded a silent *I understand.* He understood very

153

well, for Bishop Bryn Martin was drinking from the same well of discouragement. "Years ago, when I was chancellor, I asked one of our oldest priests, he was in his nineties, what he thought of celibacy. The old man was quiet for a moment, then he said with a twinkle in his eyes, 'Bryn, it's okay...during the day.'"

Both men smiled at the half truth. Martin continued, "We both love the priesthood, John. It's the Vatican's drive to control that makes me crazy. And celibacy, among other things, is a means of control."

"Yes," Krajik said simply, "and if you control a man's sexuality, you really control him."

"There is pressure on us bishops to pretend everything is more or less okay, more or less under control. There are huge problems, of course, like the abuse scandals, the drop in Mass attendance, empty seminaries, and now the financial scandals. But we bishops simply deny these realities. We can't let ourselves look at these problems too closely. They might point to flaws in the institution. We just won't let ourselves do that, so we write it off to human nature, like people cheating on their income tax returns or not going to Mass on Sunday."

"God, Bryn," Krajik said, "how do you cope with all the crap, all the institutional politics?"

"A couple of ways. I try to remember the history of the church. These are not the worst of times. And it's not just the Catholic Church that's in trouble. All of the mainline churches are in trouble, serious trouble."

"I know," John agreed.

"One of my favorite theologians is a married Orthodox priest. Reflecting on the state of Christianity, he said something like 'all of us have to cope with corners of weakness and corruption, of self-satisfaction and triumphalism that bring us close to despair.' I copied that into my journal. Maybe misery loves company, but I took some comfort from that."

They had been outside for more than half an hour now and the cold was getting to them.

"Do you know what I find myself doing, Bryn? Counting the years until I can retire. That's not good. It's one of the reasons I'm here on retreat."

They stood for a moment at the door of the monastery.

"Once we get through Gunnison's jubilee event, I'm going to call you for dinner, John. I want to continue this conversation."

They entered the monastery chapel and sat in the back as the nuns chanted vespers. It was already dark and the light was subtle and calming. The thin but prayerful chant somehow lifted the priests above the hard realities they had confronted only minutes before.

At the end of the liturgy, the priests turned with the sisters to face the icon of the Virgin as the nuns intoned the *Salve Regina*.

This, Martin said to himself, *is real*. He remembered reading somewhere that a mystic's name for God is…reality.

25

Margaret Comiskey stood at her front-room window and watched as Ella Landers got out of her car and headed for her front porch.

"Ella," Comiskey said opening the door, "I got it. I got into Kempe's PC!" Margaret took Ella's coat and almost ran into her bedroom where she dropped it onto her bed. Then taking Ella by the arm, she led her to the dining room table.

"Too bad you're not thirty years younger. The NSA might have a place for you." But Landers' feelings didn't really match her light tone. She immediately regretted her remark.

"The foreign words for purple didn't work," Margaret said, "But 'Daniel 5:7' did. 'You shall be clothed in purple.'"

"Very nice work. And…?"

"Concerning Gunnison and Mark and the other abuse cover-ups, nothing came close to what you found in his private drawer. What I did find was a list of priests who have been vetted for appointment as bishops. Kempe also has a list of U.S. bishops being considered for promotions to a bigger diocese and a list of auxiliary bishops who are likely to be named to head their own diocese."

Landers didn't see the significance of the lists and her expression showed it.

"Ella, nobody's supposed to know that. Only the papal nuncio and the two American cardinals on the Congregation for Bishops and maybe a handful or so of U.S. archbishops. Those lists are like top-secret—what the chancery suits call a 'papal secret.' Break a papal secret, the priests say, and you're in big spiritual trouble. So, how did Kempe get this information? I don't even think Archbishop Cullen has those names."

"It appears," Landers said evenly, "that Monsignor Kempe hasn't been wasting his time on his trips to the Vatican. The corridors of church power aren't that different from most governments—or the Foreign Service."

"God, Ella," Margaret closed her eyes, "I've been so naïve."

"If you have the right sources," Ella went on, "and the money and the know-how to work the system, that kind of information is not impossible to come by."

"Kempe has all that," Comiskey said. "He has all kinds of connections with Vatican officials and with dozens of American bishops. Almost half his day is spent on the phone with church higher-ups, both here and in Rome. And he has control of his purple purse. And, believe me—I've seen him in operation—he knows how to work the system."

"He's a careerist, Margaret, a climber. But he appears to be more crass than most and more dishonest." Ella hesitated. "And more ruthless."

Comiskey shook her head. "I am so damn naïve, Ella, I could scream. I've sensed for some time now that something didn't smell right in the chancellor's office. But I never suspected Kempe was outright corrupt."

Ella looked at her, sad at her friend's self-tormenting rant.

Margaret took a deep breath, trying to compose herself. "What I found on Kempe's computer is interesting, but none of it is what I was looking for. There's nothing more about Mark or any of the other victims than we already have. Or about Gunnison. Unless, of course, he's hidden it under a file name no one would suspect. I even looked at the 'sent' folder in his email. Looked like ordinary chancery business."

"I need to say something, Margaret. I'm actually glad you didn't find anything relating to Mark and Gunnison." Landers placed her hand on Comiskey's forearm and said gently but firmly, "I don't think you should dig anymore. Aidan Kempe is a powerful man. Be careful. He's covered up for Gunnison and other priests and that's wrong. But if you try to expose Gunnison, Kempe could hurt you. The system could hurt you. Do you know what I'm saying?"

Comiskey turned to face Ella and nodded a silent yes. But the resolve in her eyes was unchanged.

They took their tea into the dining room. Margaret pointed to the sideboard where three pocket-style manila folders were placed side by side. "I made two more duplicates of the documents from Kempe's drawer. I'm going to give a set to Bryn Martin. I'm sure he will take it to Archbishop Cullen. I'm going to keep a set. Maybe I'll turn it over to the media, but I'll have to talk to Mark about that first."

"Oh Margaret," Ella said, a concerned look on her face, "be careful."

"Would you hold on to the third set for me?" Margaret asked. "Just in case."

"Just in case of what?"

"Just in case," Margaret said looking away.

"Do you have a minute?"

Bryn Martin turned from his computer screen to see Archbishop Charles Cullen standing at his open door. Unlike many bishops, Cullen didn't hesitate going to the offices of his staff if he had something on his mind. Still, Martin was surprised.

"Sure. Come in." Martin got up from his desk and moved to the corner of his office where two leather club chairs were angled for easy conversation. Between the chairs, a silver-framed picture of Bryn's parents and a black-shaded table lamp rested on an oval end table.

"I've just had a call from the nuncio. Tardisconi is driving up from D.C. for Wilfred's Mass and dinner. I thought he might come, but since this isn't the official archdiocesan celebration of his jubilee, the nuncio is doing Wilfred a favor."

Martin wondered where Cullen was going.

"This is an opportunity for the nuncio to get to know you, Bryn. I think you should seize it."

Now Martin knew—and he was uncomfortable.

"You've been a bishop almost three years. Not that long, but long enough for me to see that you're too talented to remain an auxiliary. The church would benefit if you had a diocese of your own. And, I think, the sooner the better. I'm going to arrange to have you seated next to Tardisconi at the dinner."

"Charles…" is all Martin could manage to utter, his discomfort at Cullen's suggestion unmistakable.

"Bryn," Cullen said looking straight into Martin's eyes, "this isn't about you. It's about the church. What's good for the church." The archbishop lowered his eyes and sat without speaking for a moment. When he finally spoke, his voice was soft and sad, "We're a rather sorry lot these days. Our botched handling of the abuse scandals seemed to shatter our credibility. I can't blame them, but I think a lot of Catholics think all we bishops care about is protecting the institution and covering our episcopal behinds. Some want us skinned alive for moving abuser priests around without calling the cops. I understand all that."

It was almost four in the afternoon and Cullen looked tired and drawn. He closed his eyes, giving Martin a moment to study his features. His smile was his best feature, really, but today he didn't wear even the hint of a smile—and his color was bad. The faded pink flesh of his throat and jowls rolled over the top of his Roman collar, hiding completely its white plastic band. He opened his eyes and looked at Martin.

"I'm not flattering you, Bryn. You know that."

"Charles, I know you mean well and I'm grateful for your confidence. And for your friendship. But I'm happy to be your auxiliary and I'd prefer to just let things take their natural course."

Martin thought of Ken Untener, the late bishop of Saginaw, Michigan. When a reporter asked him why he'd become a priest, Untener said, "It wasn't my idea." Bryn liked to think of his vocation that way. *It wasn't my idea.* Nor was it his idea to become a bishop. And he didn't think he was kidding himself.

"I'll sit wherever you think I should sit at the dinner, Charles. But I would just like to let things unfold as they are meant to."

Then, as if Cullen hadn't heard a word Martin had said, the archbishop perked up and said, "Here's what you need to consider saying to Tardisconi. He'll probably ask you as a relatively new bishop about what committees you're interested in being appointed to at the Bishops' Conference. The preferred responses, Bryn, are the Bishop's Committee on Pro-Life and the Committee on Clergy, Consecrated Life, and Vocations."

Martin remained silent. He felt a wave of alarm, a slap in the face alerting him to moral danger. He wanted to move, he wanted to stand and walk out of the room; he wanted to suck fresh air into his lungs. The silence was uncomfortable for both men, but Martin didn't know what to say. What he did know, from the heaviness in his stomach and the confusion in his chest, was that he didn't want to play this game. But Bryn Martin didn't stand up. He didn't walk out of the room.

Cullen took Martin's silence as a rebuke.

"Bryn, please listen to me. Don't say anything about the role of women in the church, about celibacy or the shortage of priests, or the role of the laity. And of course you can't say anything about the abuse scandals. Until you get your own diocese you need to—pardon my directness—keep your mouth shut."

Martin knew he should say something like "thanks for the savvy advice" or "I'll think about this." Instead he remained silent.

"This is the way things get done in the church. You know that. We're a human institution, guaranteed the guidance of the Holy Spirit to be sure, but we are a human institution. The 'positioning' I'm proposing to you is going on all the time. It's just the way things are. It's the way most appointments are made."

Martin's mood darkened as he realized his own complicity in the system. Hadn't Gunnison engineered his appointment as an auxiliary bishop?

Cullen continued, "If Kempe and his friends are actually part of some ancient brotherhood, you can be damn sure they are 'positioning' as we speak. Brotherhood or no brotherhood, they've made an art out of 'positioning.' And they're masters of that art."

"Isn't this 'positioning' you're referring to just another name for church politics?" Bryn asked.

"Of course it is," Cullen responded with a hint of impatience. "But there's politics and then there's politics. There's human politics and there's demonic, crass politics, no-holds-barred politics. What we've been talking about here is the human kind. At least I hope it is."

With that, Cullen rose from his chair a bit unsteadily. Martin accompanied him to the door of his office.

"You'll have some time with Archbishop Tardisconi, Bryn. All I'm suggesting is that you *carpe diem.*"

Bryn Martin went back to his desk and mindlessly started to shut down his computer, too upset to get any work done. Cullen was a good man. But Martin didn't much relish the game he had proposed. Like it or not, Cullen had reminded him that he was in the game. If he was, Martin wanted to play by *his* rules, not the ingratiating, please-notice-me rules of the clerical boys' club. Archbishop Jean Jadot, who served for several years as the papal nuncio to the U.S., was once asked how he liked living in Rome after his U.S. diplomatic appointment was over. Without missing a beat, Jadot quoted the nineteenth century theologian, John Henry Newman, who had been asked the same question after being named a cardinal and called to Rome: "Nowhere have I found more courtesy and less friendship."

That pretty much summed up Bryn Martin's first few years as a bishop—an abundance of courtesy and a dearth of friendship. *No,* he thought, *that's not quite true.* He knew he had real friends—and a family—that kept him grounded. But the clerical circles he moved in fit Newman's somber insight.

For some of the bishops and priests, he knew, that was precisely how they wanted it. Courtesy and deference, yes, but friendship, at least authentic friendship, required at least some self-disclosure and a certain vulnerability. These traits were alien to clerical culture, especially to episcopal clerical culture. Martin's mind drifted back to his recent conversation with John Krajik at the monastery. John would have smiled at Newman's honest answer.

In her third floor Catholic Center office, Margaret Comiskey sat nervously checking the RSVP's to Archbishop Gunnison's dinner. Her boss, hiding any signs of jet-lag from his short trip to Rome, gave no indication he suspected his private files had been compromised. Comiskey exhaled, thinking, *So far so good.* She told herself to focus, and just before five o'clock she completed the tally of the dinner responses—there were fewer than a dozen regrets. Before leaving for the day, she would inform the other members of the dinner committee to plan for two hundred and eighty guests for the banquet scheduled for the last Saturday before Lent.

Comiskey decided to ignore standing instructions about the checks tucked neatly into the response envelopes; she sent them immediately and without tallying to the Catholic Charities offices. She was painfully aware of the irony that on her last days at the Catholic Center she was spending most of her time on her godson's abuser's jubilee—arranging for the printing of programs for the Mass and dinner, processing the guest responses, confirming hotel arrangements for the visiting bishops.

Until Mark told her of Gunnison's abuse, she had been proud to work for the archdiocese and had considered it an honor to be in the daily presence of archbishops, bishops, and some fine chancery priests—especially Bishop Bryn Martin. Not anymore. Now, in spite of the many good people she knew and cared about, in spite of all the good work done by the church—the schools, financial support for the poor, shelters for the homeless and for battered women, and all the rest—now she was aware of a corruption that spoiled it all. And she didn't give a damn about the consequences her plan would certainly bring raining down on her. Margaret Comiskey, with care and new-found cunning, formulated some plans for next Saturday night that were all her own.

In the chancellor's inner office, fewer than thirty feet from Margaret's desk, Aidan Kempe's cell phone rang.

"Is this Monsignor Aidan Kempe?" He recognized the accented voice immediately.

"Yes," Kempe said softly.

"You are, I remind you, to arrange for me to meet privately with Archbishop Gunnison after his anniversary dinner. Early next week, Monday morning to be precise, I will meet with the archbishop at ten o'clock at his residence, his humble little house next to your humble little Basilica."

Kempe imagined Foscari's smirk at the implied comparison of Baltimore's Basilica of the Assumption to the grand basilicas of Rome. His dislike of Foscari, of Giorgio, was echoed by his mounting fear of him.

"As I informed you earlier, Monsignor, I will be in the back of the Basilica for the Mass and in the lobby of the Sheraton Hotel during the reception and dinner. Do not approach me under any circumstances. You have my mobile number in case of an emergency. I repeat, Monsignor, no one save Archbishop Gunnison is to know of my presence."

Kempe's face reddened at the arrogance in Foscari's voice.

Then, in an ominous, unctuous tone, Foscari added, "His Excellency would be most disappointed if these instructions were not followed, as you say in your country, 'to the letter.'" Foscari abruptly ended the call.

26

Bishop Bryn Martin walked quickly through the lobby of the Catholic Center, raising the collar of his lined, black raincoat while pushing open the main door with his left hip. He headed across Cathedral Street then waited impatiently, his hands stuck deep in the pockets of his coat, for the light to change. A minute later the tiny white pedestrian icon started flashing and he crossed Mulberry. It was a windless but cold Wednesday in February, and the archbishop's jubilee celebration was set to begin with the 5:00 p.m. vigil Mass on Saturday. The clock was ticking. Diagonally across from the archdiocese's Catholic Center, the Basilica of Our Lady of the Assumption stood fortress-like in the late afternoon's unflattering gray light. The renovation completed the year before had left the neoclassic landmark cathedral with an impressive facelift. Still, Martin had mixed feelings about the old building. It had the dignity of a Greek temple, he conceded, but also communicated the abstract, passionless rationality of a Greek temple.

Martin jogged up the steps to the Basilica's portico, guarded by eight Corinthian columns, and moved directly to the main entrance. Duane Moore and George Havel were waiting inside.

Martin managed a brief business-like smile as he shook their hands. "Thanks for coming down. I'm sorry about the timing. You'll probably get caught in rush hour traffic going home."

"No problem, Bishop," Moore said quickly. "We need this on-site meeting."

Havel took in the renovated Basilica. "It's been quite a few years since I've been here. It really has a nice new look. My family and I were here for Pope John Paul's visit." Havel nodded a thank you to Martin, who had provided the tickets.

Martin wasted no time. "In addition to a handful of auxiliary police handling the traffic, we've hired five uniformed police, three more than usual for an event like this. Three will be outside, one at each of the doors, and two will be inside, but at the back of the Basilica," Martin said. "What do you think?"

"Sounds reasonable," Moore responded. Havel nodded in agreement.

The three stood with their coats on at the foot of the center aisle scanning the back pews and the side aisles looking for likely places someone might claim who was intent on disrupting the Mass with a laser—or worse.

"We won't have to worry about the choir loft," Martin said glancing upward. "It will be closed off to all but the musicians and choir members. I'll have one of the uniforms stationed at the staircase leading to the loft. Any trouble would likely come from the floor of the Basilica."

"Bishop," Moore proposed, "I'll take a position in the vestibule until the Mass begins and then stay in the back area of the Basilica. I'll be looking for a match to the profile I got at Immaculate Conception."

They turned and walked slowly up the center aisle, each looking for locations that would provide good angles for a shooter.

"George," Martin said looking at Havel, "I'd like you to vest in an alb and take a position in the sanctuary—like you were one of the chaplains to Archbishop Tardisconi, the papal nuncio. You won't have to do anything except to try and look like a priest."

Moore couldn't resist, "That's asking a lot, Bishop."

Havel grimaced at the crack. But keeping one of them in close proximity to Archbishop Gunnison was a good idea.

166

They stood on the first step of the sanctuary looking like building inspectors. "I'll have a chair for you in a position that'll give you a good view of the entire assembly. In addition to Archbishop Tardisconi, there will be four or five other bishops in the sanctuary and at least the same number of seminarians who will be serving, so you won't stick out."

"Will the sacristy be secured?" Havel asked.

Martin hadn't thought of that. "I'll make sure it is, George."

Martin led them out of the sanctuary towards the first two rows of the north side aisle pews. Havel and Moore slipped into the second pew and Martin sat sideways in the first pew so he could speak quietly to his two friends. The Basilica was empty except for a matronly docent and a gray-haired male volunteer wearing a tie and a blue blazer he had grown out of years ago. They spoke softly to each other, as if wondering what Bishop Martin and the two middle-aged men were up to.

"It seems to me," Martin said with his right arm over the back of his pew, "if our laser-man is going to be here and if he follows the pattern he set at St. Bernardine's and at Immaculate Conception, the recessional will be the time for us to be most alert. But you two are the professionals."

Havel took the cue, "We're operating under the assumption that someone might want to embarrass or scare or harm Archbishop Gunnison. And we don't know why."

Both he and Moore held Bishop Martin's eyes for a moment. Their looks said what neither man could say: *You haven't told us of any motive, but we're damn sure there's something unspoken behind all this.* At the same time, Havel and Moore understood that Bishop Martin might not be able to disclose anything more than he had already.

"Let's go over what we do know," Havel said, breaking the awkward silence. "We know our man with the laser, thanks to the glimpse Duane got of him, is on the tall side, maybe six foot.

He moves quickly, like a man in shape. We believe he operates alone. There haven't been any threatening calls or messages to the archbishop. If that's the case, if the laser hits are meant to shake him up, then we're taking all reasonable precautions."

"But," Moore added, "if someone really wants to hurt Archbishop Gunnison and the laser hits were designed to be tormenting signals that something really harmful was to follow, then it's a different game altogether." Duane looked at the bishop and then at George, then back at Martin. "If that's the case, Bishop, you need more than two retired, past-their-prime federal agents."

Martin nodded, hesitating for a moment to let Moore's warning sink in. He had avoided giving serious thought to that possibility. If there is a remnant of the Brotherhood of the Sacred Purple embedded in the archdiocese, then, as unthinkable as it was, Bryn Martin needed to consider a much darker scenario. Coming back to the moment, he said abruptly, "Let's go over the cocktail hour and dinner."

This was former Secret Service Agent George Havel's turf. "In fluid situations like the drinks before dinner," he began, "one of us should be as close to the archbishop as possible without causing too much of a distraction."

Both Martin and Moore understood that would be Havel's role.

"Duane," Havel continued, "you need to find a vantage point that allows you to scan the crowd. We also need to have the hotel's security people check out the kitchen and serving areas."

"Actually," Martin added, "the archbishop will spend as little time schmoozing his guests during the cocktail period as possible. The Mass will have taken a good deal out of him. He'll make a brief appearance and slip out to go up to his suite to rest a bit and freshen up. He'll return when the guests move into the banquet hall."

"During the dinner," Havel proposed, "Duane and I should

be seated up front on opposite sides of the dais." He looked to Martin and Moore for approval. Both men nodded their agreement.

"I'll arrange to have name tags for you, so that you'll blend in with the guests," Martin said.

"What about the hotel's security people?" Moore asked.

"The only thing we've told the hotel people," Martin answered, "is that they should be alert to anyone who might try to disrupt the reception or banquet. They need to be alerted about the kitchen area, though."

"Well, this is your ballgame, Bishop," Havel said, signaling his concern.

"George, it's the *archbishop's* ballgame. So, we're doing what we can," Martin said revealing his own unease. He looked at Moore, "Duane, what do you think?"

"George is right. There are holes in our game-plan, but there always are," Moore replied.

The three sat thinking for a moment. Then Duane asked, "How will Archbishop Gunnison get from the Basilica to the hotel?"

"I'd like you two to drive the archbishop and Monsignor Kempe—he's the chancellor and a good friend of the archbishop—to the Sheraton. I'll take Archbishop Cullen and the nuncio in my car. Is there anything else you can think of?"

Havel and Moore shook their heads and started to rise from the pew when Martin waved them back down. Reaching into the inside breast pocket of his suit coat, he removed two envelopes. Each held a thank you note from Martin and a check for five hundred dollars.

"You two have been great. You're helping us deal with a delicate matter and you're giving us a big chunk of your time. Archbishop Gunnison and Archbishop Cullen are very grateful. And so am I."

George and Duane shook their heads to indicate, *This isn't necessary or expected.*

"Please, please," is all Martin could say.

27

Wilfred Gunnison, his nerves ready to crack since the laser incidents and Mark Anderlee's wild allegation, had decided to make a one-day retreat—a fitting and hopefully comforting prelude to his Jubilee Mass and dinner. His decision to make the easy drive north on Route 140 to Mount Saint Mary Seminary in Emmitsburg had already brought a shallow peace, a slight semblance of inner calm. Even a one-day break from the immediate preparations for his jubilee would settle him, he had reasoned. Again and again, Gunnison squashed his doubts about his decision to go forward with the celebration. No weirdo with a laser was going to keep him from marking fifty years as a priest. And this Anderlee character should get on with his life, grateful for the extremely generous check he had placed in his greedy hands. But he still shivered when he thought of Anderlee's threat to attack him. He thought with no small comfort of Kempe's track record of making people like Anderlee go away.

Gunnison was approaching Westminster, Maryland, the halfway point in the two-hour drive to the seminary. Getting out of the city was definitely a good idea. Gunnison leaned back into his seat and relaxed his grip on the wheel. Both as a priest and bishop, he had been faithful in the things that really mattered, he told himself. He possessed a certain vanity perhaps, but the archbishop of the oldest diocese in the country had to think of his appearance. He was not, he admitted, a particularly gifted preacher. But he thought himself a very good administrator who had left his successor a well-organized, education-focused, and financially-sound church to govern and shepherd.

Gunnison reached to turn on the car radio but then resisted the impulse. Instead, he decided that a little time reviewing his fifty years as a priest and bishop was more appropriate. He wasn't an Archbishop John Carroll or a Cardinal James Gibbons. But he knew he had played a bigger role in protecting the American Catholic Church from liberal secularists than history would ever recognize. Kempe might be the leader of the Brotherhood of the Sacred Purple, but it was Gunnison's influence that brought it back to life in Baltimore, and the Brotherhood was playing a critical role in keeping the church faithful and strong. Without the efforts of bishops like him, the U.S. Catholic hierarchy would be weak and accommodating. It would be, in a word he detested, liberal. Yes, the church needed bishops like Wilfred Gunnison. God needed bishops like Wilfred Gunnison.

For the most part, he believed himself chaste—especially over the last twenty years or so. And he had little compassion for priests who got entangled with women. Didn't they know how controlling women were, how much attention they demanded, how seductive they were? A married priesthood would be a disaster. He, on the other hand, had aligned himself with the classical poets and philosophers of Greece and Rome. Men like himself understood what most people of pious bent could not— that these giants of Western civilization found inspiration and emotional fulfillment in the company of young men. And these same young men needed tutoring in the art of male friendship.

He, Wilfred Gunnison, by the grace of God, retired archbishop of Baltimore, was a part of this noble tradition of men of letters and refinement. Moreover, their physical expressions of affection with young men of intellect and breeding could hardly be thought of as harmful.

Yes, there had been times long ago when he, too, needed the

urgent, erotic delight found only in the company of young men. And yes, there had been a few mistakes when he was a priest. Yet he had always been gentle, never rough or crude. And he had never crossed the line—he had never sodomized anyone.

Gunnison's mind wandered for a bit and then, out of nowhere, he thought of his one awkward moment with his master of ceremonies, young Father Bryn Martin. It was at the end of a long day, he told himself, and he had been quite tired. It was just too insignificant to be concerned about. In fact, he hadn't thought about it in years. And he shouldn't be thinking about it now.

He lowered the heat in the car and scanned the long stretches of barren farm land that reached to the horizon. There was something pristine and pure about the country, even in the gray of February. Yes, a day and night at the seminary would be good for him—body and soul. He would be back home on Thursday in time for lunch and have the whole day Friday off to make sure all was ready for his jubilee. Archbishop Wilfred Gunnison would give thanks to God for his fifty years of ordained ministry with the unmatched ritual and majesty of the full Roman Catholic liturgy. He could hardly wait.

Later that day, now settled in the guest room reserved for visiting bishops and cardinals, Gunnison told himself to relax. He stood in the center of the room, however, not sure what to do with himself now that he was here. On the small writing desk, under a clear plastic protector, lay an alphabetical listing of seminary faculty and their phone numbers. Third on the list was Father Joseph Donlon, the seminary's retired spiritual director, a priest with a reputation for being an exceptionally wise and caring confessor. Two years earlier, Joe Donlon had celebrated his own fiftieth ordination anniversary. Gunnison prided himself in being uncompromisingly loyal to the teachings and disciplines of the church—a staunch conservative. Donlon, on the other hand, was theologically progressive. Gunnison liked him too much to think of him as a liberal. But both men shared the easy cordiality of priests who had more or less weathered the same rigorous seminary formation program of the pre-Vatican II years. To Gunnison, those were the good old days when priests knew who they were—God's chosen and anointed pastors charged with governing their parishes, and the laity knew who they were—the docile flock obedient to God's own bishops and priests.

There was yet another difference between the two churchmen that Gunnison would not allow himself to consider. Joe Donlon's only ambition had been to be a good priest and a kind pastor. Wilfred Gunnison's ambition, almost from the beginning, had been to one day vest himself in the sacred purple.

Seeing Donlon's name on the faculty list triggered an old, deeply embedded association. Gunnison thought he would go to confession. For priests of his era, retreats and confession went hand in hand. Not even his rationalizing of the pederasty of the poets and philosophers of antiquity could smother his Catholic moral conscience. Wilfred reached for the phone.

"Hello. Is this Joe Donlon?"

"Speaking."

"Joe, this is Wilfred Gunnison."

"Well, this is a surprise, Wilfred. How are you?"

Gunnison ignored the priest's light banter. "I'm here for a retreat day before a little celebration I've planned for my golden jubilee. Can we meet in the chapel? I'd like to go to confession."

A few minutes later, the two met in the seminary's reconciliation room just outside the entrance to the chapel. A stained glass window of the Good Shepherd, vivid in the late afternoon sunlight, dominated the small room. Earth-tones had been chosen for the walls and carpeting—a much more inviting space than

174

the dark, stale-aired, box-like confessionals still pressed against the walls of many Catholic churches. The room itself, uncluttered and airy, elicited a sense of peace and order. The furniture was Spartan but tasteful: two comfortable upholstered armchairs and a table with a lamp, a Bible, and a box of tissues on it. An over-sized crucifix hung on one wall and a reproduction of Rembrandt's *Prodigal Son* was mounted behind the confessor's chair in easy sight of the penitent.

Father Donlon reached for the purple stole draped over the back of the confessor's chair, kissed it, and placed the vestment over his shoulders.

"Bless me, Father, for I have sinned," Wilfred began while making the sign of the cross. "This will be a kind of a general confession, a review of my half century as a priest and bishop." Joe Donlon smiled at Wilfred, then lowered his eyes.

"First the usual suspects. I've been uncharitable in my speech and in judging others. I've been impatient with the chancery staff and I haven't always been faithful to prayer. A few times, not often, I've had a little too much to drink." Wilfred went still—the silence confessors know often signals what's really on a penitent's mind.

"But what I really want to bring to the sacrament is some unseemly behavior," Gunnison cleared his throat, mustarded his resolve, then pushed out the words through the thin slit between his lips, "with teen-age boys."

Donlon squeezed his eyes shut, then raised them to Gunnison's bowed head.

"This goes back decades, Joe. I may be rationalizing, but most of the time it was just fooling around, wrestling with some boys in a swimming pool and things like that. A couple of times it went further than that. But there never was any kind of penetration." Wilfred hesitated, then heard himself say, "I never, ever, sodomized any of them."

Joe Donlon had heard thousands of confessions during his years as a priest and thought he had heard everything there was to hear. But Gunnison's confession stunned him. He knew better than to ask the question that rose up from his tightened throat, but he couldn't swallow it. "Wilfred, I need to ask. Did you ever speak to the boys? Did you ever tell them you were sorry?"

"Well, yes. A few of the boys told their parents, and when they asked to meet with me I did apologize if I had upset their sons. Some of boys didn't seem bothered by it." Gunnison blocked out the memory of the parents, who had been furious. "They were offered counseling and the financial vicar was able to come up with some cash for most of them. None of them, thank God, sued or went to the police or to the media."

The penitent archbishop searched Donlon's eyes for some flicker, some hint of understanding. Instead he saw the pain in his confessor's face.

"I'm not a pedophile, Joe. No one's at risk. It wasn't anything like what you read in the papers these days. This hasn't been a problem for a very long time now."

"It's very good that you're here, Wilfred."

Both men took deep breaths. They released soft whooshes of air that loosened the tensions draining the confessional room of oxygen. Joe Donlon reached over and put his hand on Gunnison's arm. Wilfred teared up at the gesture. The simple kindness prompted the archbishop to say softly, "I'm a lonely old man, Joe—a man with lots of friends who are really acquaintances. Not many friends at all." The words wouldn't come, but Wilfred Gunnison whispered to himself, *I really can't think of even one.*

"I think it's hard for priests to develop and sustain real friendships, Wilfred. And I think it's especially hard for bishops. You bishops seem like a pretty self-reliant lot. Your priests are very aware of the power you have over them. Friendship requires a certain common ground where people are equals. Bishops don't have that. Sometimes I think wealthy laity who like to entertain bishops make up most of your social life."

"You're pretty much on target, Joe." Wilfred paused. "There's something else I want to tell you. It could be the reason why I'm going to confession. At my last two confirmations, as I was processing out, a red dot, a laser dot, hit me in the chest. It was gone the instant I noticed it. I've been afraid that it has something to do with what happened years ago. I've been rather nervous, thinking that something will go wrong at the Mass or dinner."

Stay focused on the sacrament, Donlon told himself. "Let's talk about the laser incidents and your anniversary celebration later, if you want. We both believe Christ is present in this room. And his presence is healing."

Wilfred said a silent yes.

"As a penance, I want you to make a holy hour in the chapel this evening praying for the boys, the men now, who you abused."

Wilfred tensed at the word "abused." He never used that word himself.

There was nothing more to say except what Father Joe Donlon always said at this point when celebrating the Sacrament of Reconciliation. "Let's be still for a little while, then I'll offer the prayer of absolution."

Wilfred made his Act of Contrition.

In words just above a whisper, Joe Donlon prayed:

God, the Father of mercies,
through the death and resurrection of his Son
has reconciled the world to himself
and sent the Holy Spirit among us
for the forgiveness of sins;
through the ministry of the Church
may God give you pardon and peace,
and I absolve you from your sins

in the name of the Father, and of the Son,
and of the Holy Spirit.

Eyes welling with tears, Wilfred Gunnison, the emeritus archbishop of Baltimore, whispered the word believers throughout the ages have uttered when they sense the mysterious presence of God: *Amen. I believe.*

He met Joe Donlon's eyes. If he had been a little less self-absorbed, he would have caught the unspeakable sadness there.

"Go in peace, Wilfred."

Father Joe Donlon knew he couldn't return to his room. Perhaps some fresh air and some late winter sun might lift the sadness and confusion that hearing Wilfred Gunnison's confession had roused. The wind made the relatively mild day uncomfortable. He lifted the collar of his coat and pulled up the folds of his scarf, taking slow but steady steps in the direction of Mount St. Mary University, whose campus abutted the seminary's property. College students, he knew well, were hardly a virginal lot, but they bore a freshness and innocence that always lifted his spirits. The ones he had gotten to know were hardly promiscuous—they didn't hesitate to tell the old priest they found casual sexual hook-ups repugnant. On the other hand, Donlon learned that some—many—of these same students had little difficulty believing sex before marriage was okay if they were in a relationship. Still, he had to admit that a number of the students he knew seemed more sexually mature than the majority of the priests and seminarians who sought him out for spiritual direction and counseling.

Donlon turned and headed back to the seminary thinking of the blur of seminarians who had sat rather stiffly in his office, confiding to him their struggles to be celibate. They were the normal struggles of young men living exclusively with men. In their naïveté, they seemed to think that with enough prayer and will power they could learn to live like angels. For many, accepting the rule of celibacy made them feel they were doing something heroic. Some indeed appeared to have the aptitude and temperament for celibate living—what the church called the "gift of celibacy." Most did not.

A good number of the men seemed to possess the qualities necessary for priestly ministry—they were generous and caring and idealistic. Others, it was clear, were in love with an idealized and romantic notion of priesthood that was captured in films like *The Bells of Saint Mary* and *Going My Way*. They could hardly wait to don Roman collars, cassocks, birettas, and the other accoutrements of the clergy.

His troubled thoughts returned to Wilfred Gunnison. He wondered how many boys the archbishop had hurt and damaged over the years. Maybe he had been sexually abused himself. Donlon had read that more than half of priest abusers were. Yet over the years he had never once heard a priest confess to abusing minors. Donlon wanted nothing more than to relax in the warmth of the seminary, but he left his coat on and walked toward the refectory for something hot to drink. It was only then that he realized what was gnawing at him. Wilfred Gunnison had shown little concern, in fact, no concern at all, for the spiritual and emotional well-being of the boys he had abused. He would pray for him.

28

Monsignor Aidan Kempe, and Fathers Tom Fenton and Herm Volker had secured a window table at the Prime Rib, a favorite restaurant of the priests who worked at the Catholic Center. Kempe had seated himself facing the window so that he could watch the chilling rain that began as if on cue with the rush hour traffic. As long as he could remember, rainy nights had given Kempe a sense of emotional security, a feeling that somehow everything would work out. He attributed this romantic streak to his Irish mother and was stubbornly convinced that the wind and rain and the low, brooding blue-black clouds of western Ireland had shaped his intense loyalty to the Catholic Church.

For a moment or so, Kempe, ignoring Fenton and Volker, sat still, as if in prayer, drawing on the familiar comfort of the red, rain-muted taillights of the cars moving north on Calvert Street. Perhaps, other than the Basilica's sacristy with its air of beeswax and redolence of incense, no room evoked a better sense of place and identity than this five-star restaurant. Good dining and good wine were, after all, sacraments in their own right, and modest enough entitlements for faithful priests. But Kempe had more than good dining on a rainy night in Baltimore on his mind.

"Very soon after Wilfred's jubilee," Kempe began, speaking so softly that Fenton and Volker had to lean over the table, "he will take up residence a good distance from the archdiocese—

perhaps even out of the country. It's best for the Brotherhood." Kempe sipped his drink and took pleasure that his little announcement had caught Fenton and Volker off guard.

"Is it the allegation you told us about?" Fenton asked.

"Yes, that's at the heart of it," Kempe responded, "but there are other factors."

"How do you know this?" Volker demanded. He was closer to Gunnison than Fenton or Kempe, and certainly closer than Eric St. John or Paul Carafa.

"Last week I flew to Rome to brief M on Wilfred's situation. He thinks it best that Wilfred should move his residence as soon as possible after his jubilee celebration. This is M's decision—for the good of the Brotherhood."

"But Aidan, you said the allegation against Wilfred was false. That the man had exaggerated a back rub into abuse," Volker said, his color rising.

Fenton, looking at Volker rather than Kempe, said, "I think M is sacrificing Wilfred to protect the Brotherhood. This isn't right."

"It might be for the best," Kempe said solemnly, "both for Wilfred and the Brotherhood. Something quite strange—and ominous—occurred at Wilfred's last two confirmations. As he processed to the back of the church, he was struck with a laser dot square in the middle of his chest. The dot disappeared after just a few seconds and it seems only a few parishioners noticed it."

Volker and Fenton looked confused.

"I take it neither of you heard about this?" Kempe asked.

"Of course not," Volker said, obviously irritated. "I would have called you if I had."

"I didn't hear anything either, Aidan," Fenton added.

"That's good. Wilfred is damn lucky this didn't get picked up by the media," Kempe said sternly. "And so are we. M believes— and so do I—that it would be best for Wilfred to move a good distance away as soon as possible.

The three men sat still for a while, Volker and Fenton quietly processing Kempe's announcement. Kempe stared out the restaurant's window, watching the evening traffic thin. *Get over it, boys,* he said to himself, and then opened his menu.

"How's Wilfred holding up?" Volker asked.

"Not as well as he thinks he is," Kempe answered abruptly. "Beneath the bluster, he's actually quite fragile."

"He loves this city," Fenton said. "How does he feel about moving?"

Kempe sipped his Johnny Walker Black Label and carefully lowered his glass. "He doesn't know yet."

"He doesn't know?" Volker said sharply.

"He'll be informed," Kempe said with a hint of sarcasm, "after his little celebration. M thought it best this way." Aidan Kempe always enjoyed playing the M card. It reinforced his authority as the Brotherhood's leader. "And another thing," he continued, "it's prudent that we suspend our monthly meetings—indefinitely."

Fenton and Volker sat stunned. They glanced at each other. *What could this mean?*

"Of course," Kempe added before either priest could speak, "I expect you to make the usual monthly contribution to the purse."

Fenton and Volker remained silent, suddenly not quite as smugly confident in the mission of the Brotherhood as they were when they sat down at their corner table at the Prime Rib.

Kempe turned to Fenton, "Tom, call St. John and Carafa and tell them we won't be meeting until they hear from you. And let them know their monthly offering to the purse is not suspended. Don't say anything about Wilfred's move. They don't need to know that now." Kempe looked out the window to see the rain had stopped. Frowning, he returned to scanning his menu. The server approached to take their orders. Only Kempe felt like eating.

With military efficiency, Mark Anderlee detached the Leupold scope from his Remington 700. He wouldn't need the scope. He wrapped the rifle in an oversized bath towel, holding the towel in place with strips of duct tape stretched around the barrel, the chamber, and the stock. He set the rifle aside and proceeded to fold a hand towel around the Sig P226. Anderlee picked up both weapons, walked into his bedroom and placed the rifle in the back of the closet and the Sig on the closet's shelf. They had to be close at hand.

The decision he had come to just days ago made his chest swell. His abuser's anniversary Mass and dinner were just two days away—the Mass at five o'clock in the Basilica of the Assumption and the dinner at the Sheraton at eight. He knew the schedule down to the minute. And he knew where he would be stationed. "You won't see me, Archbishop," he said out loud, "but I'll be there. I will be at the Basilica. I will be there for my Aunt Margaret and for all the boys you messed with."

29

Nora Martin, suddenly aware of her shallow breathing, walked with a business-like stride down the carpeted hall to Ian Lander's office. Two of Ian's colleagues nodded as they passed her. Nora managed a slight smile, feeling her neck blotch as she approached Landers' office.

"Got a minute?" she asked with two light knocks on Ian's half-open door.

Landers pulled his half-lens reading glasses from his nose. "Actually, I have quite a few minutes...for you anyway."

"Thanks to my brother, we're in a reserved pew, along with your mother, at the big Mass tomorrow. Are you driving?"

"I am. Can I pick you up?"

"I'd like that," Nora said, wondering what it might be like to be at Mass with this very reserved, very interesting Englishman.

"My mother's driving up to my place around four. I've talked her in to staying over rather than driving back to Silver Spring. She wouldn't get home until almost midnight. I offered to pick Margaret up, but she has a role in the liturgy—I think she's doing the Prayer of the Faithful as I recall—and has to be in the Basilica sacristy a half hour before the Mass begins."

"Bryn has us seated at the same table," Nora said casually, "The reception and dinner should be quite nice. No long speeches, or so he promised."

"Really, Nora, I'm sure the dinner will be quite nice indeed, but I don't feel good about the archbishop's decision to go ahead with his jubilee celebration." He had more reason to be concerned than Nora knew, but he hesitated to tell her so.

"Bryn doesn't feel good about it either. He can't wait until it's over." Nora got up to leave. "I think he's more worried than he lets on."

Landers frowned at the possibility of something going amiss but didn't know what to say. He went on, a bit dismissively, "Mother and I will pick you up around four thirty then."

"Great," Nora said at the door. "Okay."

Tell her, Landers said to himself. "Do you have another minute, Nora?"

"Sure," she responded, coming back to her chair.

Landers got up deliberately from his desk chair and closed the door to his office. "My mother is hardly an alarmist, but she's really worried about Margaret. To be honest with you, Nora, 'worried' is too weak a word. She told me Comiskey believes she knows why Archbishop Gunnison was struck by those laser dots."

"I'm not sure I get this," Nora said.

"Apparently, the rumors about Gunnison and young boys are more than rumors. It appears one of Gunnison's victims was Margaret's nephew and godson."

"Dear God," Nora whispered. "If that's true, Margaret's inner world, all that's given her life a sense of coherence and meaning...all that's been destroyed."

"I know my mother's concerned. No," Landers corrected himself, "my mother's really worried about Margaret's state of mind. I'm worried about her myself."

Monsignor Giancarlo Foscari took a room at the Mount Vernon Hotel, within walking distance of both the Basilica and the Sheraton. At ten each morning he called Bishop Montaldo, reaching him before he left his Vatican office for the day. From his daily reports to M, Giorgio saw how little respect his boss had for Monsignor Kempe. Yes, it had been a note of contempt he had caught in Bishop Montaldo's eyes the night he had returned the arrogant American to the Inghileterra. Still, M treated Kempe with formal courtesy. Giorgio smiled. Of course M would treat Kempe with a certain respect. The Baltimore Brotherhood of the Sacred Purple remained a major source of income for Bishop Pietro Montaldo's behind-the-scenes work at the Vatican.

For the past two mornings, Giorgio had walked to Baltimore's Inner Harbor. He imagined himself an officer on the sloop of war, the USS *Constellation*, and the retired submarine, the USS *Torsk*. But his service to Bishop Montaldo had awakened this former policeman to the more refined pleasures of art and architecture, so he visited the Walter's Art Gallery. It was hardly Rome, but he liked this American city. This morning, wearing a black leather jacket over a silk Armani shirt, Giorgio found the winter day mild enough to sit at an outside table at an Inner Harbor Starbucks. He propped his designer sunglasses on the top of his head and thought of the international call he was about to make. The espresso was good enough, but he missed the pastries he enjoyed at the coffee bars of Rome's piazzas. A copy of the *Baltimore Sun*, his phone, a double espresso, and a raisin scone were spread before him. He ate his light breakfast while scanning the major stories in the *Sun*. Because of the past few mornings with the paper, his English had improved. Thirty minutes later, staring at the crumbs from the too-heavy scone, Giorgio saw it was time to complete his only assigned task of the day. From his inside pocket, he pulled out an oversized leather wallet. Slipped into the narrow pocket facing his Vatican passport was a folded piece of note paper. Giorgio withdrew it carefully, replaced the wallet in the inside pocket of his jacket, and reached for his cell phone. The tables around him were empty, and it was chilly enough for the Starbucks employees to remain inside.

Written on the paper before him, in the hand of Bishop Montaldo, was a name, Mother Francesca, and a phone number followed by the word *privato*. Below the number M had scrawled, Convent of the Immaculate Heart of Mary, Bogotá, Colombia. He touched in the international code and then the number. It was picked up after five rings.

"Mother Francesca?" he asked in English.

"Yes, this is Mother Francesca."

"Let me say that I am calling on behalf of Murex." Giorgio waited for the correct response.

"May you be clothed in purple," Mother Francesca said softly.

Satisfied he was speaking with the right *Mater Francesca*, he said deliberately and slowly, "M believes it best that I do not tell you my name. I trust you understand."

"Yes, I understand."

"M asks if you and your sisters might be so kind as to provide lodging and care for a retired American archbishop." Then he added, "I am unable to say how long his Excellency will be your guest."

Mother Francesca remained silent. Then she said evenly, "I believe we can find a suite here in our convent for the archbishop. He will be most welcome."

"M will be most grateful," Giorgio responded, sounding to himself more like a diplomat than a former policeman. "His name is Archbishop Wilfred Gunnison. Once your guest is settled, a monthly stipend will be wired to your convent's bank in Bogotá from the Banca D'Italia in Rome."

"That would be most appreciated," she said as if she had expected nothing less.

"Archbishop Gunnison will be arriving soon. Perhaps in a week or two," Giorgio said. "Once his travel plans are confirmed,

I will call you at this number with the date and time of his arrival. It would be most kind of you to arrange for a car to meet the archbishop at the airport."

"Of course," she responded. "And perhaps you might assure Murex that the archbishop is welcome to stay with us as long as his Excellency wishes."

"I will, Mother. *Ciao.*" Then Giorgio added a more formal, "Good-bye, Mother Francesca."

Giorgio placed his mobile phone in his pocket and thought about his conversation with the nun. She had asked no questions. And she made a point of saying the archbishop could stay as long as he wanted to stay. M must be quite generous with the monthly stipends. Yes, of course. Hadn't his boss been generous with him, very generous? Giorgio looked thoughtfully at the soaring masts of the dock-bound *Constellation*. Then, with a slight turn of his head, to the *Torsk's* iron-gray shell. Both in their time had been proud ships of war. M had taught him to see that the church was at war with the forces of darkness—with heretics and radicals and liberals. And worse, much of the swirling darkness spewed up from within the church herself, from arrogant reformers and dissidents. Defending the church from its internal and external enemies, his confessor had told him, required, from time to time, drastic action that many of the faithful would not be able to understand. And he, Giorgio, aka Monsignor Giancarlo Foscari, was M's secret agent, like an unseen submarine commander trolling enemy waters. Even better, he was now a secret agent with a mission. He had been so naïve to think as a boy that he wanted to be a priest. Giorgio was no priest. He was no policeman. He was a sacred warrior with a license to do whatever was necessary for the good of the church.

Giorgio's thoughts returned to the nun. His thin lips tightened in a smirk. This was not the first time *Mater Francesca* had been of assistance to the Brotherhood. Giorgio never imagined

that going to work for Bishop Montaldo would prove so interesting, so fulfilling.

30

Bishop Martin, there's a call for you on line one. It's an Ella Landers and she said it was important."

"Yes, put her through." Martin said to his secretary.

"Bishop Martin?" she began. "This is Ella Landers, Ian's mother."

"Of course, Ella. And it's 'Bryn,' if you don't mind."

Landers didn't respond.

"Thank you again for the wonderful dinner party," Martin said trying to strike a familiar tone. "I had the feeling that Ian and my sister, Nora, are perhaps more than just colleagues."

Landers also let this remark pass. "I'm calling about Margaret Comiskey." Ella hesitated but a few seconds, but the pause and the tightness in her voice were enough to tell Martin the call was awkward for her. He waited for her to go on.

"I'm worried about her. And why I'm worried about her must remain between you and me. I'm walking a fine line here in talking with you, but I'm going to tell you what I believe I can tell you without betraying her trust."

Bryn wanted to say something assuring, but was at a loss.

"Margaret," Landers said gravely, "has good reason to believe that Archbishop Gunnison once sexually abused her nephew and godson."

Bryn was quiet while he absorbed what Landers was telling him. Did Margaret know this when she had come to his office last week? Did Kempe know this? *Of course he does, you idiot.*

Landers stammered, "And she's very fond of him. Loves him like a son. Margaret has a picture of him in her office. She's crazy about him. She had the Catholic Center staff praying for him for years when he was in Iraq and Afghanistan. You probably know he was in the army for twenty years."

Bryn shook his head, reprimanding himself. Ella Landers knew more about Mark Anderlee than he did.

"Bishop," Ella said in a measured tone, "Margaret hasn't been herself since she discovered Mark's abuse, by a man she felt honored to work for most of her life." She paused, but Martin could still discern the concern in her silence.

"I'm worried about her, too," Bryn said. "She seems at the edge, so to speak."

"I'm very worried about her, Bishop. And I'm afraid for her." Ella knew she could say no more. She had to leave Kempe out of this, even though his protection of Gunnison had deepened Margaret's already dark mood. Nor could she tell Martin about the other allegations against Gunnison, or the secret funds that Kempe controlled, or his journal entries, including those about Martin himself.

"Margaret's a life-long, dear friend, Bishop, and I know she's a friend of yours. I'm afraid something has hardened inside of her and she won't talk to me about it. And believe me, we can talk about anything. I'm afraid she's going to do something she'll regret."

"I've seen a difference in her, too, Ella." Martin thought he finally understood the weight Margaret was working under. "I'm worried too."

Neither said a word. Finally, Ella broke the silence. "I'm not sure there is anything either of us can do, but I thought I should speak to you in confidence. I wouldn't have called if I didn't think our friend really needed help."

Martin half rose from his chair, only to ease back down.

He had to think. How did Margaret learn about her nephew? He must have told her he was abused by Gunnison—and must have told her rather recently. Why had he waited so long? Maybe Gunnison's jubilee prompted him to tell his aunt? And what if the man with the laser was Mark Anderlee? What if Margaret suspected—or knew—that her nephew was going to take some kind of revenge? He remembered Margaret mentioning that Mark was an army sharp-shooter and head of an elite sniper unit. He swore a decidedly unpriestly oath.

Martin looked at his calendar: lunch with John Krajik. He reached for his phone to cancel and it rang in his hand. *Damn, it was Kempe.*

"Do you mind if I come over for a minute?

"Sure. Fine."

"Good. I'll be right there."

Kempe walked into Martin's office without knocking. Bryn pointed to one of the two chairs in front of his desk. Kempe remained standing.

"I just wanted see how security was shaping up. Is there anything I can do to help?"

Martin didn't answer his question. "George Havel and Duane Moore will be with us at the Mass and at the Sheraton for the reception and dinner. We'll have a few extra off-duty police at the Basilica and the hotel security has been alerted. I didn't want to overplay this with the hotel staff."

"You're probably right," Kempe agreed.

"How's Wilfred doing now that his big day is here?" Martin asked.

"His big day won't be what he hoped for. The laser incidents really dampened his spirits. But he's determined to make the most of it. Earlier this week he drove up to Emmitsburg for a retreat."

"Might calm him down a bit," Martin said.

"He did seem more relaxed when we spoke this morning. I tried to assure him that the man with the laser would hardly try anything at the Basilica. Most people know there are police around at archdiocesan events like this. But he's uneasy."

"I've heard he's hosting a little dinner tonight for some of his out-of-town guests," Martin said. "That might take his mind off the confirmation incidents."

"I hope so," Kempe replied. "The nuncio is driving up early tomorrow afternoon. His secretary said they would leave right after lunch. Wilfred is honored that he's coming, of course, but it's adding to his nerves. If there is another laser incident it would be all the more embarrassing with Tardisconi here."

There was an awkward pause. Then Kempe continued, "By the way, I'm a little concerned about Margaret Comiskey. She's not quite herself. Hasn't been for a week or so. Have you noticed anything?"

"Not really," Martin lied. "She's been working rather hard on the jubilee. We're all a little overwrought."

"Yes," Kempe said moving toward the door. "It could be the strain of Wilfred's anniversary."

Martin caught a hint of disappointment in his voice. Kempe had gotten nothing out of his visit.

"Thank you," he muttered as he turned and walked out of Martin's office.

Martin remained motionless in his chair, staring at the door Kempe had just closed. It was unusual for Kempe to come to his office. When the two needed to communicate, it was almost always by phone or email. And while he outranked Kempe in the church's hierarchy, the chancellor, as the *de facto* chief operating officer of the archdiocese, had a broader sphere of executive power. And Kempe knew it. His brief visit was an attempt to display this power. He had staged and scripted his little visit—a mini-drama in clerical theater and clerical power. He had raised the curtain by refusing to take a chair, by remaining standing. On the surface, it could have been interpreted as a signal that Kempe didn't want to take any more of Martin's time than was necessary, but Martin knew better. It was a subtle discourtesy aimed at gaining control of the meeting.

The visit had nothing to do with the security preparations for the jubilee.

Aidan Kempe had come to his office to find out what he might know about Margaret Comiskey. And he wanted to read Martin's expression and body language when he brought it up— casually, almost as an afterthought.

So Kempe had noticed a change in Margaret too.

Now it was Martin's turn to visit Kempe's office, actually to Kempe's outer office, the office of Margaret Comiskey. He walked slowly down the third-floor hall, past the portraits of the last three archbishops of Baltimore, past the bust of John Carroll, Baltimore's first archbishop and the first Catholic bishop of the newly established United States of America. Martin knew he had to be careful here. He stopped just outside Margaret's open door. As he had anticipated, the door to Kempe's inner office was closed. Margaret sat facing her computer screen but glanced over her right shoulder as she sensed the presence of someone standing in her door.

"Margaret," Martin said by way of a greeting.

"Hello, Bishop." Her tone was flat and there was no hint of the smile that almost always accompanied her greetings.

"You look hard at work." Martin said lightly, glancing at the door to Kempe's office, a door the chancellor might open at any moment. "I know getting ready for the archbishop's jubilee hasn't been easy. How are you doing?"

"Most everything is ready," she said deflecting his question. Comiskey barely glanced at him. "The Mass booklets were the last major concern. But the printer delivered them this morning. There's a box of them on the chair. They look pretty good. The archbishop's coat-of-arms came out particularly well. Take one if you like."

Her office seemed sparser than Martin remembered it. And the picture of her nephew Mark had been removed.

"Can I speak directly, Margaret?"

Margaret didn't respond but simply held his gaze.

"You haven't been yourself since we had our little talk. I know we can't talk here but would you mind stopping by my office before you leave?"

"All right. I'll stop by when I close up here." Still, not even a hint of a smile.

Precisely at five o'clock, Margaret stuck her head in Bryn Martin's office. He waved her in and they both moved to the conversation chairs to the right of his desk.

"There's still coffee on…"

"No, thank you." The tension in the room was palpable.

"I feel something's really bothering you, Margaret, and I don't think it's just the strange goings on we talked about or the extra work connected with tomorrow's celebration. Is it anything I might be able to help with?"

Comiskey realized she looked at priests differently now that she knew what was in Kempe's private file drawer and on his personal computer, now that she knew Gunnison had abused her nephew and a number of other boys. *Was Bryn Martin guilty by association? Could she even trust him?*

The thought made her look away. Gunnison and Kempe were only two of the dozens of priests she had come to know while working at the Catholic Center. Some had problems. You couldn't work in the chancellor's office for all the years she had without coming to see priests as human beings who struggled like everyone else. Of all the priests she had come to know, she realized she had liked most of them. But now she felt neither affection nor respect for priests and bishops. With Wilfred Gunnison it wasn't a question of respect. Margaret Comiskey hated the man. And the force of the hatred had shocked her. She had never hated anyone before Gunnison—and hating, she had discovered, changed everything.

Margaret broke the silence. "Recently, my life has taken a turn. I'm afraid that's putting it mildly." Another pause. "I'm not ready to share what this turn is with anyone. Not Ella Landers, my best friend, and not with you. I've had to do some digging, and I've learned things that have made me sick."

Martin listened without moving but felt the heat rising in his face.

"I really can't talk about it now." Then Margaret said, almost in a whisper, "Maybe in a few weeks when things are…are a little quieter."

"That's okay. That's okay," Bryn said softly. "We'll talk when the time is right… But if you hold this in too long, it can really do you harm. And maybe cause you to do something you may wish you hadn't."

Martin fell silent. Comiskey lowered her eyes looking exhausted and every bit like a woman betrayed.

"Sometimes, Margaret, you can tell a counselor things you can't tell a friend."

Comiskey nodded, but the resolve in her eyes deepened.

"It's really important you talk to a therapist…and soon. Please think about this."

Margaret stood to leave. "Thank you for your concern. I'll be all right, Bishop."

Margaret Comiskey sat at her kitchen table with a manila folder squarely in front of her. It held her letter of resignation as secretary to the chancellor of the Archdiocese of Baltimore. It was late. She usually was in bed by this time. Tomorrow's anniversary for Gunnison would change absolutely everything, and she had resisted going upstairs to bed knowing she wouldn't be able to sleep. Margaret had lied to Ella and Bryn when she said she couldn't tell anyone what was going on inside her. She had told her nephew, Mark, sitting at this kitchen table just two nights ago.

Mark had listened in disbelief.

"Are you sure you want to do this, Aunt Margaret?" he had asked. She remembered how he had then taken her hand and whispered, "I've made a decision, too." Half an hour later they got up from the table with the resolve of co-conspirators.

Margaret strained to read the wall clock in the darkened kitchen. It was almost midnight. She opened the folder and stared at the letter, reviewing her plans for the next day.

Before going to the Basilica for tomorrow night's Jubilee Mass she would stop at the Catholic Center. It would be deserted. She would place her letter on Kempe's desk—where he would find it Monday morning. Then she would clear out her desk and put her remaining personal belongings in a banker's box, carry it down the back stairs and place it in the back of Mark's SUV, parked on Mulberry Street across from the side entrance to the Basilica. She would cross Mulberry and proceed to the sacristy for the final instructions from the master of ceremonies. Margaret read the short, curt letter one more time before going to bed.

Monsignor Kempe,

I hereby resign from my employment at the Catholic Center of the Archdiocese of Baltimore.

By the time you read this letter, my reasons for terminating my association with the archdiocese will be clear to you.

Instead of Daniel 5:7, you might read Luke 14:11.

Margaret Comiskey

If Kempe checked the reference to Luke 14:11, he would read, "For all who exalt themselves will be humbled, and those who humble themselves will be exalted."

What Margaret Comiskey didn't understand sitting at her kitchen table late that Friday evening was that her short letter of resignation was not short enough.

31

On the eve of Archbishop Wilfred Gunnison's jubilee, the cathedral rectory was wrapped in a monastic silence as eerie as the empty and darkened Basilica of the Assumption. Lights remained on, however, in the suites of Bryn Martin and Aidan Kempe.

Martin thought of watching the late news before taking a Tylenol PM and turning in. Two concerns would likely keep him awake—a mysterious man with a laser and a badly shaken Margaret Comiskey, a good friend and long-time employee of the archdiocese whose nephew and godson, he had just discovered, had been sexually abused by the retired archbishop of Baltimore. She had to be devastated. What compounded his anxiety and concern was Margaret's determination to keep this information from him.

Martin opened his briefcase and took out the Mass booklet that ushers would distribute at the doors of the Basilica. The irony of it all caught him—Margaret had been placed in charge of drafting the booklet and having it printed. In fact, she had done much of the planning and organizing that went into Gunnison's golden jubilee. Martin thought the Mass booklet rather striking—premium cream vellum stock that worked nicely with the Century Gothic font. The cover, bordered in a rich maroon, consisted of a color photograph of the still-handsome Gunnison in his episcopal robes. The practiced smile, cordial but hardly warm, was aimed to project intelligence and pastoral solicitude.

Martin never thought it worked. Maybe it was the vacuous gray eyes. The frontal page, again in color, featured Gunnison's coat of arms and his motto: *God is my rock and fortress.* A short paragraph under the arms and motto listed the significant dates—ordination to the priesthood, ordination as bishop, his taking charge of the Archdiocese of Baltimore, and finally the month and year of his retirement.

The processional hymn, to Martin's surprise, was *Confitemini Domino,* "Let us praise the Lord," a popular hymn from an ecumenical community of Christians in Taizé, France. Bryn loved the piece—it was prayerful, contemplative, and inclusive. He had expected something triumphal, something with trumpets and drum rolls. The humble, contemplative tone of the Taizé piece disarmed him.

The back of the second page, under the heading *Liturgy of the Word,* listed the scriptural readings of the Mass and the names of the lectors. The first reading was the well-known Isaiah passage from Chapter 61, "The spirit of the Lord is upon me, because the Lord has anointed me; He has sent me to bring glad tidings to the lowly, to heal the brokenhearted..." Appropriately, the lector was Florence Merriman, chair of the Catholic Charities Board of Trustees. Gunnison had been a champion of Catholic Charities, and Catholic Charities in turn provided care and shelter for boys and girls in need of special help. Good for Gunnison. But Bryn thought of the boys abused by Gunnison. There would be a certain irony if some of them had received help from Catholic Charities agencies.

Lately, whenever Martin had a chance to speak to Baltimore's priests, he liked to remind them of the maxim embraced by the medical profession: "First, do no harm." He turned to the next page and saw The Reverend Monsignor Aidan Kempe, JCD, listed as the homilist. No surprise here. Kempe would pull it off, but it would be a challenge. He would have to be careful. He had to avoid damning Gunnison with faint praise or showering him with effusive plaudits. Martin returned his attention to the booklet and found that The Reverend Eric St. John was the master of ceremonies for the Mass. Again, no surprise. St. John was part of Gunnison's priest support group and an expert liturgist.

Martin's eyes rested on Margaret's name next to the heading: Prayer of the Faithful. He wondered if she would even show up now that she believed Gunnison had abused her nephew, and he made a mental note to tell St. John to arrange a backup. Her name was listed again on the last page under Acknowledgements where Gunnison thanked by name the Catholic Center staff who did the real work on the planning committee.

Just down the hall from Bryn Martin's cathedral rectory suite, Monsignor Aidan Kempe rested the four-page text of his homily on his lap. The chancellor sipped mineral water and stared into the flames of his gas fire. Better than no fire at all, but he wanted to hear the crackling snaps of dry wood and to inhale the smoky smell of a wood-burning fire. The room was dark, save for the patterned flames of his faux fire, the lit candles on the mantle, and the reading light next to his chair. Kempe took several deep breaths and closed his eyes. Could it not be that the breath filling his lungs and swelling his chest was the very breath of the Holy Spirit? His mission, the mission of the Brotherhood of the Sacred Purple, was, beyond question, critical to the very survival of the Roman Catholic Church. If poor Wilfred Gunnison could dodge one more bullet and then move far away, the Brotherhood would be safe. The odds, he felt, were in his favor.

Kempe paged through his homily. His theme was God's grace, especially God's grace in the life of Archbishop Wilfred Gunnison and God's grace in the glorious history of the Archdiocese of Baltimore. A rather clever way, he thought, to dance around Wilfred's secret past. Gunnison's strong suit was his un-wavering, uncritical loyalty to the Roman Catholic Church, his unfailing support of Catholic Charities and Catholic education, and, unknown to the Catholics of Baltimore, his loyalty to the Brotherhood of the Sacred Purple. Kempe smiled. Of course Wilfred was loyal to the Brotherhood; he wouldn't have reached his high station without the influence of M's secret society. And it certainly hadn't hurt his career that Wilfred Gunnison came from a Baltimore family with money. Even as a young priest, he had moved easily in the upper circles of the city's civic and busi-ness elite.

Early on, Kempe would emphasize the archbishop's long-standing commitment to Catholic Charities and Catholic edu-cation, mentioning a few examples, including the fundraising dinner that would follow the Jubilee Mass. "On so many levels," he would say with ringing sincerity, "Archbishop Gunnison was a good and faithful priest and bishop to the people of Baltimore." Here his homily would make a turn from praising Gunnison, *God knows he's not a candidate for sainthood*, which should draw a laugh, to the glories of the archdiocese, especially its Basilica. This second part was little more than a brief history of the Ba-silica. But what else could he do? It was simply too risky to praise the man further.

Then Kempe would deftly turn to the archdiocese's first bishop, John Carroll, a cousin, he would note in passing, of Charles Carroll, a signer of the Declaration of Independence. "It was John Carroll's collaboration with Benjamin Latrobe, the foremost American architect of the period and the first architect of the U.S. Capitol, that led to the construction of this historic house of God." Kempe reread the last sentence and penciled out "and the first architect of the U.S. Capitol."

"Together," he would say, "Bishop Carroll and Benjamin Latrobe fashioned our historic and majestic cathedral, now graced with the title, *Basilica*, in which his Holiness, Pope John Paul II prayed during his 1995 visit to Baltimore. In this Basilica of the Assumption, the Holy Father saw an expression of 'the sanctuary of conscience, the very heart of all authentic freedom.'" Nice, Kempe thought. But the next two sentences might have to go. "Perhaps even long-time Baltimore Catholics might be unaware that when nearby Fort McHenry was being bombarded during the War of 1812, our cathedral was a part of the strategy of defense against the British. The Cathedral of the Assumption was constructed on the highest point in Baltimore, and had Fort McHenry fallen the walls of the cathedral were to be manned as the last line of defense against the British." Interesting enough, he told himself, but too disconnected from Gunnison's anniversary. He penciled them out.

At this point he would return to Gunnison and the reading from Isaiah. "Today we give thanks to God for our brother Wilfred, for 'The spirit of the Lord is upon him, for the Lord has anointed Archbishop Gunnison to bring glad tidings to the lowly, to heal the brokenhearted, to proclaim liberty to the captives...to announce a year of favor from the Lord.' On this occasion of the fiftieth anniversary of your ordination to the priesthood and in the name of all gathered here in this historic Basilica, may I say...*Congratulations Archbishop Gunnison!*" Here he would pause and turn respectfully towards Gunnison, seated on his throne-like chair. The pause, he had no doubt, would lead to a standing ovation, an ovation that might hold for a full minute or more. Wilfred would be in his glory, failing to recognize it as vainglory. Then as the applause died and the assembly sat down, he would close with, "May God bless you, Archbishop Gunnison, and give you many years of favor from the Lord."

It would do quite nicely. In fact, a second standing ovation might follow.

Dan Barrett and Paul Kline sat high up in the seats of the Loyola Blakefield gym watching the boys varsity basketball team play Towson Catholic.

"He hasn't returned one of my calls." Barrett said. "Not one."

"I've tried, too," Kline added. "Haven't heard from him either."

Neither one of them paid much attention to the game.

"Do you think we should go to Gunnison's big Mass tomorrow? If Mark's going to do something stupid, the Mass might be…like…the perfect place to get even with him."

Kline nodded. "Yeah, that's a good idea. We should go. The Mass would be something he'd find tempting. If he's there, we could just sit next to him or close enough to keep him from doing something he would regret."

"I was thinking, Paul, if he's at the Mass we might not see him."

"What the hell are you talkin' about? Kline asked sharply.

"Mark was a sniper, for Christ's sake. Think about it. If he doesn't want to be seen, we won't see him."

"Maybe," is all Kline could say.

"The Mass is at five," Barrett said. "I'll pick you up at four. We oughta get there early." Then he added, "And wear a sport coat."

With Blakefield up by twelve, they left at half time.

32

Thirty minutes before the start of Gunnison's Jubilee Mass, Bishop Bryn Martin stood at the entrance to the sacristy of the Basilica, flanked by Duane Moore and George Havel. Each of the men scanned the half-empty pews trying to anticipate where a man with a rifle might station himself.

Martin broke the silence. "Archbishop Gunnison and Monsignor Kempe understand you will drive them to the Sheraton directly after the Mass. Meet them here in the sacristy and take them to your car." Moore and Havel nodded.

Martin reached into his pocket, "I have an usher's badge for you, Duane," Martin said, handing him a blue plastic lapel tag that read "Usher" over "Basilica of the Assumption" printed in smaller type. Moore clipped it over the pocket edge of his suit coat.

"Good idea," he said. "I can move up and down the aisles without drawing too much attention."

"We're expecting around three hundred guests at the dinner," Martin reminded them. "Probably a third of them will come to the Mass. They should be easy to identify in their business-formal dress. The ushers will encourage them to move to the front pews. The rest of the worshipers will be parishioners. Around two hundred or so. It's hard to say. It's likely the Basilica will be two-thirds full."

"The only thing I can tell you two," Moore said, "is that the guy I got a glimpse of is about six foot, athletic build but trim, built more like a tennis player than a football player."

Havel and Martin nodded.

"We can expect one or two of the local TV stations to send a camera crew to film a bit of the Mass. Once they get a little action footage of the archbishop," Martin said with the hint of a smile, "they'll be out of here. Probably WBAL will show up and maybe WJZ. And we've hired a photographer. He'll be shooting discretely throughout the Mass and he'll also be at the reception and dinner."

"I think Duane and I should separate, move down the side aisles and check out the vestibule," Havel suggested. "We'll meet back here in ten minutes."

"That should work," Martin said. "I'll have a cassock and surplice ready for you, George. Some of our seminarians will be serving the Mass, but I've asked another senior server, a man about your age, to serve so you won't stand out."

"Very kind of you, Bishop," Havel said.

"The master of ceremonies is Father St. John, a friend of the archbishop's. I've informed him that you would be seated in the sanctuary. He seemed a little puzzled," Bryn added, "but didn't ask any questions."

At four forty-five, Bishop Martin made his way into the nave and slid into the pew next to his sister Nora, Ian, and Ian's mother. "Hope this goes well," Nora said to her brother. Ian simply put an encouraging hand on Bryn's arm. But it was Ella's tense shoulders and alert eyes that ratcheted up his own mounting anxiety.

"I'll meet you at the reception," Bryn said matter-of-factly. "I'd much rather be at your table for the dinner, but Archbishop Cullen has seated me next to the nuncio."

"Of course, Bryn," Nora said. "We never thought you'd be at our table."

"I made sure Margaret would be at your table," Bryn added quickly. "She's really pulled this whole celebration together."

"Yes, I know," Ella said, holding Bryn's gaze. *And that's why I'm so worried*, she wanted to say.

Ian squeezed Nora's hand as Bryn gave his sister a quick hug.

"Time for me to get vested," Bryn said, trying to sound hopeful. "I'll see you at the reception."

At four-fifty, Moore and Havel stood at the outside door of the sacristy, trying to catch Bryn Martin's eye. The large, high-ceilinged vesting area and the robed and mitered bishops made them both feel out of place. Martin waved them in and motioned them to a corner of the sacristy next to the vestment closets.

"Anything out of the ordinary?" Bryn asked.

Moore spoke first. "A few minutes ago two men entered the main door, stood in the vestibule for a while apparently looking for someone. But then they split and seated themselves on opposite sides of the Basilica. Both were close to the height of our man with the laser."

"And they seemed to be in their late thirties, early forties," Havel added. "Why didn't they sit together?"

"I'll be keeping an eye on them from the back, and George from the sanctuary, The only other person of interest is a man seated in the last pew. He's dressed in black and at first I thought he was a priest. But he's not the man I saw at Immaculate Conception...too heavy set," Moore added.

"During the procession, point them out to me if you can."

It was almost five o'clock.

"George," Martin said, too sharply, "You need to put on the cassock and surplice that's on the vestment case behind you."

Havel slipped off his suit coat and self-consciously started dressing like a senior acolyte. "By the way," he said offhandedly, "I spoke with both photographers and checked their IDs."

"George," Martin said with alarm, "We hired only one photographer."

Duane Moore looked from Havel to Martin. "I'm on it," he said and hurried out of the sacristy and down the side aisle of the nave.

The only women among the bishops, priests, and seminarians in the Basilica's sacristy sat on folding chairs near the door leading out to the sanctuary.

"I'm Father St. John, the master of ceremonies," the young priest said, bending slightly as if he were speaking to two deaf old ladies.

Margaret Comiskey and Florence Merriman looked up at the officious priest and waited for him to go on.

"When the procession leaves the sacristy, that will be your cue to take the two chairs in the sanctuary I pointed out to you earlier. They're on the same side as the ambo."

Comiskey said nothing. Merriman nodded and St. John noticed her forbearance.

"After you do the first scripture reading, Mrs. Merriman, you simply leave the ambo and return to your chair." Then he turned to Comiskey. "Margaret, after you complete the Prayer of the Faithful, remain at the ambo while Archbishop Gunnison says the concluding prayer, and only then do you return to your chair. Are we clear, ladies?"

The president of the Board of Catholic Charities and the secretary to the chancellor held the gaze of the master of ceremonies.

Finally, Merriman said coolly, "Perfectly." Then under her breath, *You little....* She rose and went to the water cooler. It seemed strangely out of place in the Basilica's clerical dressing room.

Martin, now vested, took the opportunity for a last word with Comiskey. Even a longtime chancery staffer could be a little nervous if given an active part in a major Mass in the Basilica, especially with a sanctuary full of bishops. He sensed that only a month ago Margaret would have been thrilled and honored to have a role in this kind of high-church liturgy. Now he could only guess at the emotions swirling inside her.

"Are you okay, Margaret?"

Comiskey remained seated, her eyes distant but clear. She nodded.

In spite of the flattering dark blue, ankle-length dress she was wearing, Margaret Comiskey looked anything but okay to Bishop Martin. Her abrupt response was close to rude. Bryn mustered a brief smile and walked back to the vestment case where Gunnison and Cullen made awkward attempts at small talk.

She could do this, Comiskey told herself. The Prayer of the Faithful, a series of prayer petitions, approved by Wilfred Gunnison himself, were in place on the shelf of the ambo from where she would offer them. After Kempe's homily and the assembly's recitation of the Nicene Creed, she would move from her chair, bow to the altar, and walk slowly, like a nun in a monastery, to the ambo. The officious master of ceremonies would be pleased. Margaret glanced down at the Mass booklet in her lap below her folded hands.

"Archbishops, Bishops, Fathers, may I have your attention please?" Eric St. John intoned a bit too formally. "Please take your places for the processional."

Joseph Constanza, one of four seminarians recruited for the Mass, would lead the procession, carrying the smoking censer with burning charcoal already layered with incense, followed by the cross-bearer, two lay servers—including a self-conscious George Havel—and the priests assigned to the Catholic Center staff. The only archdiocesan parish priests in the procession were Fathers Paul Carafa, Herm Volker, and Tom Fenton. Monsignor Aidan Kempe, as homilist, took his place immediately in front of Bishop Martin and the few visiting bishops. Last in line came Archbishop Cullen followed by Archbishop Gunnison, wearing a jeweled miter and carrying a brushed silver crozier. Archbishop Tardisconi, as the presiding prelate, had already taken his place in the sanctuary, flanked by two seminarians serving as his chaplains.

Father St. John, with a nod to Archbishop Gunnison, picked up the intercom and told the choir director they were ready. It was two minutes after five o'clock.

The assembly rose as the first strains of the contemplative and soothing "*Confitemini Domino*" filled the Basilica. "Let us praise the Lord, for he is good and merciful." Some of the older benefactors looked puzzled. They had expected trumpets and "*Ecce Sacerdos Magnus*." Behold the High Priest.

Martin scanned the backs of the assembly as the procession turned and made its way up the center aisle. He found the man in black standing stiffly in the last pew. His scarf had opened, revealing a Roman collar. Bryn was puzzled. He wasn't a priest of the archdiocese. Martin knew them all. And if he were a priest friend of Wilfred's he certainly would have been vested and in the procession.

Bryn caught Moore's eye. Standing next to one of the real ushers, Moore shook his head, signaling the second photographer was not a problem. So far, so good.

Dan Barrett looked across the nave at Paul Kline. Both men shrugged. There was no sign of Mark Anderlee.

Margaret Comiskey sat stiffly in her chair, her stomach tight, breathing through her nose, pretending to listen to Florence Merriman read the scripture passage from Isaiah. She had forced herself not to look out at the assembly. She couldn't risk meeting Ella's glance. She rehearsed again what was only now minutes away. She saw herself moving without wavering, steady and sure, to the ambo for the Prayer of the Faithful. She would walk deliberately—most eyes would be on her—make the head and shoulder bow to the altar, and then move with eyes down, to the ambo. The master of ceremonies would have placed the prepared prayer intentions on the ambo for her.

The cantor and choir began the responsorial psalm, "Here I am Lord; I come to do your will." Margaret thought it would never end. There would follow a second reading from the New Testament and finally a passage from the sixteenth chapter of Matthew's Gospel, "I for my part declare to you, you are 'Rock,' and on this rock I will build my church.... I will entrust to you the keys of the kingdom of heaven. Whatever you declare bound on earth shall be bound in heaven; whatever you declare loosed on earth shall be loosed in heaven."

Margaret would have to suffer through Kempe's homily. After the homily and profession of faith, it would be time.

Kempe's homily didn't surprise her. Phony praise for a pervert bishop and a mini-lecture on the Basilica's historic past. Margaret had expected nothing more. But the applause for Gunnison unsettled her. When Kempe finally finished, Gunnison let the assembly sit in silence for a short while before rising to begin the Creed. Comiskey stood with everyone else. *You can do this*, she told herself, *you can do this*. It was time. She had rehearsed this act of retribution over and over. She would do this for Mark...and for the others.

As if from nowhere, the master of ceremonies was standing before her. He gave her the slightest of nods, her signal to walk to the altar, bow, and move to the ambo. Ten seconds later Margaret was at the ambo. She had done it. She had walked steadily enough, made the ritual bow, and stepped up on the ambo's platform. Then, discreetly, she placed her Mass booklet over the typed prayer petitions so carefully prepared for her. She waited for Gunnison to give the customary invitation to the Prayer of the Faithful.

"Grateful for God's many blessings and confident in his abiding goodness," Gunnison proclaimed with exaggerated diction, "we now lift up our hearts in prayer."

Martin and Kempe both sensed something wrong. Comiskey had carried her Mass booklet to the ambo and taken a folded piece of paper from it. Kempe took a half step toward Margaret, intending to tell her to sit down. He would do the prayers himself. But it was too late. She had already started.

Comiskey spoke softly but the Basilica's sound system carried her steady voice throughout the nave.

"For our Holy Father, the bishop of Rome, that he might lead the church with wisdom and govern God's holy people with prudence, we pray to the Lord."

The assembly responded, "Lord, hear our prayer."

"For our Holy Catholic Church," Margaret continued, "that we might be light to the world and hope for the hopeless and lost, we pray to the Lord."

"Lord, hear our prayer," the people responded.

"For the shepherds of our church, especially for Archbishop Gunnison and for all who preach the gospel of Christ, that they may be faithful to the Word of God, we pray to the Lord."

"Lord, hear our prayer."

Martin thought Kempe's tightened jaw seemed to relax a bit. Margaret was reading the prepared and approved prayers. But

Bryn's stomach remained knotted. He searched for Ella Landers. When he found her she looked pale. Bryn was certain she was thinking what he was thinking. *Don't do this, Margaret.*

"For the victims of violence and all forms of injustice," Comiskey continued, "we pray to the Lord."

"Lord, hear our prayer."

Margaret grasped the side edges of the ambo shelf trying to steady her hands.

"For Archbishop Wilfred Gunnison, celebrating his fiftieth ordination anniversary, that he may know God's mercy, we pray to the Lord."

"Lord, hear our prayer."

Kempe stood rigid with anger. Margaret had altered the last petition.

"For the victim-survivors of clergy sexual abuse, that they may find healing and peace, we pray to the Lord."

"Lord, hear our prayer."

Kempe shot a glance at Gunnison, who looked confused.

Margaret paused, now squeezing the sides of the ambo shelf. She took two shallow breaths and searched for Ella in the assembly. But Ella's eyes were shut tight.

Then in a voice slightly louder, "For the young people sexually abused by Archbishop Wilfred Gunnison—for Mark...for David...for Larry...for Sean...for Matthew. And for all the victims of abuse who have suffered at the hands of clergy and religious, we pray to the Lord."

The assembly, held in a communion of confusion, seemed to hold its breath. Many thought they had misheard. Some whispered, "What did she just say?" Others simply hadn't been paying attention and were startled into awareness by the sudden electric silence. In the sanctuary, Gunnison turned instinctively to Kempe. Both men were white with anger and shock. The nuncio stared at Cullen, his eyes demanding an explanation.

213

Then, in the steely silence that lasted no more than seconds, the Catholic instinct, forged in ritual prayer, kicked in. A weak but audible, "Lord hear our prayer," broke above the whispers of the benefactors and regular worshipers.

Margaret Comiskey, as if in slow motion, folded the paper that had just shredded the reputation of Archbishop Wilfred Gunnison forever, and placed it inside the Mass booklet. She walked deliberately down the steps of the sanctuary, turned to her left and moved with perfect poise to the Basilica's side exit onto Mulberry Street. The early evening cold gusted and caught her by surprise, blurring her vision. Her left hand grasped the railing as she moved down the steps to the sidewalk and onto the curb, where Mark Anderlee stood next to his Ford Explorer holding the passenger door open. Exhausted and shaken, Margaret Comiskey closed her eyes and said simply, "It's done. Let's go."

As Comiskey escaped through the side door, two men bolted from their pews and ran to the Basilica's front portico in time to memorize the license plate of the dark suburban as it turned onto Cathedral Street. Monsignor Giancarlo Foscari and former agent Duane Moore watched for a moment as the Explorer's taillights blended into the wavering red ribbon of traffic heading out of the city.

Inside the Basilica, Kempe almost ran to the ambo.

"Please be seated," he began. "Margaret Comiskey has worked at the Catholic Center for a very long time, most recently as my secretary. Lately she has been under considerable stress due to personal and family problems. She is clearly disoriented and confused. I ask that we all keep her in our prayers."

Kempe's ploy seemed to work for most of the assembly. His deflection restored some calm and order, but the whispering continued. Yes, the reader of the Prayer of the Faithful was distraught, and her bizarre final petition should be understood—and dismissed—in that light.

Gunnison, in shock and disbelief, sat slumped in his episcopal chair while the altar was prepared for the offertory of the Mass. Beads of perspiration dotted the lower part of his ashen forehead and upper lip. His dry tongue pushed through his lips in a futile effort to moisten them. He felt the nuncio's eyes on him—he felt everyone's eyes on him. He had been afraid of another laser hit. But not this. Not this! Worse, far worse than the ruined jubilee was the shattered reputation of the eighteenth archbishop of Baltimore. This was not right. He was no pedophile. Why would this woman do something like this? His horrible confrontation with Mark Anderlee flashed before him. Is there a link between Anderlee and Comiskey? The thought made him dizzy and nauseous. And how could she possibly know about the others?

The presider, Eric St. John, approached the archbishop and bowed his head, as if all were well, indicating to Gunnison it was time to move to the foot of the sanctuary to receive the large plate of hosts and carafes of altar wine. Kempe walked at his elbow, steadying him. Somehow, Gunnison knew he had to get through the rest of the Mass. It would be an agony. But he did it—and it was.

Finally, back in the security of the Basilica's sacristy, Wilfred Gunnison leaned against one of the vestment cases, too shaken to unvest. Around him, bishops and priests disrobed without looking at one another. The few that spoke did so in whispers. No one knew what to say or where to look. Eric St. John was suddenly at Gunnison's side with a glass of water. As soon as he had taken a sip, Kempe took his arm and led him to the chairs that Comiskey and Florence Merriman had occupied earlier. Charles Cullen sat down next to him and put his hand on Gunnison's arm. Bryn Martin and Aidan Kempe stood in front of the two archbishops, both men waiting for Cullen to speak. The nuncio remained on the other side of the sacristy, trying to avoid being contaminated by the scandalous melodrama he had just witnessed.

"Wilfred," Cullen said gently, "You have a decision to make. Do you want to cancel the dinner? Your guests will understand."

"That would only make matters worse, Wilfred," Kempe said too quickly. "You'd be giving credence to Comiskey's accusation."

"You don't have to go," Martin said supporting Cullen's position. "Charles is right, your guests will understand."

Gunnison sat still for a minute, then looked up at Kempe, the leader of the Brotherhood of the Sacred Purple, the fixer. Kempe knew what the archbishop couldn't say: *Tell me what to do, Aidan.*

"Wilfred, listen to me," Kempe said sternly. "If you attend the dinner you will help erase the doubt that is now planted in people's minds. Your guests will give you the benefit of the doubt. Right now most of your guests believe Comiskey is a confused and emotionally unstable woman. And you, Wilfred, are the retired *Archbishop of Baltimore!*"

33

Giorgio Grotti sat stiffly in the lobby of the Sheraton Hotel as far from the main entrance as possible. M had to be informed of the debacle in the Basilica, but it was nearly two o'clock in the morning in Rome. He pulled his scarf over his collar and tried to stay out of the line of vision of the dinner guests moving through the lobby to the second floor reception area and ballroom. For a moment he considered calling Kempe. No, better to call M first. He stood slowly and made his way out of the hotel onto South Charles Street and walked in the direction of the Inner Harbor, hoping for a good connection as he pulled out his mobile phone.

"Excuse me, Excellency, for calling at this hour, but I need to inform you of something most strange that occurred at the Jubilee Mass for our friend."

"What is it?" M demanded curtly.

A few minutes later, M had an accurate, if abbreviated, account of what transpired at the Basilica. He paused briefly, calculating the risk Gunnison now presented to the Brotherhood of the Sacred Purple.

"Excellency?" Grotti said wondering if he had lost the connection.

"Let me think," M snapped as he recalled Kempe's recent visit and his assessment of Gunnison's fragile emotional state.

Grotti pressed his lips tight.

Then in a soft but decisive voice, M described precisely to

217

Giorgio Grotti, aka Monsignor Giancarlo Foscari, what he must do—and do as quickly as possible.

"Do you understand?"

"Yes, Excellency, I understand."

"For the good of the church," M added piously just before ending the call.

Grotti's next call was to Kempe. "I realize I am to meet with our friend Monday morning, but in light of what has happened at the Mass, I need to see him immediately."

A moment of silence passed.

"*Pronto!*" Foscari barked.

"Archbishop Gunnison is resting in the presidential suite until the start of the dinner. He insisted on some time alone. He's feeling very hurt, of course, very embarrassed. Can't this wait?"

Grotti ignored the question. "Put a key card to his room in an envelope and leave it at the registration desk. Address the envelope to 'Father Peters.' Am I clear?"

"Yes," Kempe replied curtly, irritated at the question. But the chancellor of the Archdiocese of Baltimore and the leader of the Baltimore cell of the Brotherhood had no choice but to follow the orders of this chauffer, this bogus priest, this *Monsignor* Foscari.

"Do it immediately. I will pick the envelope up in five minutes."

Bryn Martin huddled once again with Duane Moore and George Havel—this time in the hotel's hallway outside the reception room reserved for Wilfred Gunnison's guests.

"Archbishop Gunnison wants some time alone," Martin informed them. "To be honest, the man's a wreck. He was sipping a stiff scotch when I left him."

Both Moore and Havel repressed the questions uppermost

in their minds—who is this Margaret Comiskey? Has Wilfred Gunnison really abused minors?

"I've told Archbishop Cullen and Monsignor Kempe," Martin continued, "that you two would go up to get the archbishop when the guests move into the ballroom for the dinner. I'll let you know when I hear from the kitchen that they're ready to serve."

Moore and Havel nodded in agreement.

"What a turn," Havel said more to himself than to either Bryn or Duane.

Without saying it, all three felt the threat of a targeting beam had greatly diminished. Comiskey's words had wounded Wilfred Gunnison far more seriously than any laser might, save a laser mounted on a gun. Still, they couldn't relax their guard. Before Martin left to mingle with the guests, all three scanned the room. It was easy to spot the donors who hadn't attended the Mass. They sipped their drinks and flashed their cocktail party smiles as they greeted acquaintances. In a matter of minutes, however, the hum of conversation softened as the guests coming from the Basilica told the others of the startling petitions offered by the woman who did the Prayer of the Faithful, adding that she was a secretary who worked at the Catholic Center.

Florence Merriman, now with her husband Marcus at her side, was surrounded by almost a dozen of the guests. "Margaret was very quiet in the sacristy before the Mass," she said. "We hardly spoke after we said hello. I thought she was a little nervous…but so was I."

Her listeners inched closer, expecting Merriman would go on.

"I thought Archbishop Gunnison might faint. I don't know how he made it through the rest of the Mass."

"Florence," Archbishop Cullen said moving into the group

surrounding the Merrimans. "Florence," he repeated, "thank you for slipping out of the sacristy so quickly and quietly after the Mass. The archbishop was mortified."

"How is he?" Merriman asked.

"He's upstairs in a suite the hotel provided," Cullen said, thinking it best not to answer her question. "He'll come down when the meal is served." Then, making careful eye contact with each benefactor in turn, added, "Thank you for coming this evening. And thank you for all you do for Catholic Charities." Cullen forced a smile, gave Florence Merriman a brief hug, shook hands with Marcus Merriman, and started to move on.

"I've known Archbishop Gunnison for twenty years, Archbishop," Merriman said holding on to Cullen's hand. "I don't believe for a minute he abused anyone. Not for a minute."

Florence took her husband's elbow and led him and the archbishop a few steps away from the others. "Is there anything to this, Charles?" she asked in a whisper.

"This isn't the place," Cullen answered, coloring, "We'll talk soon," he promised.

Monsignor Aidan Kempe, shaken by the disastrous turn of events and furious with the unthinkable, unforgivable behavior of his own secretary, was surrounded by his base—conservative, wealthy Catholics convinced their church was under attack by a liberal secular media exploiting isolated cases of sex abuse to attack and diminish the moral influence of the Roman Catholic Church. Standing to the side of one of the three open bars serving the banquet guests, Aidan Kempe, master of damage control, spoke in measured tones to a growing circle of benefactors.

"Margaret Comiskey has worked for the archdiocese for more than thirty years. It's the reason she was invited to do the Prayer of the Faithful. But I noticed a change come over her in the last week or so. For a while I thought she wasn't feeling well, but she denied there was anything wrong."

The expressions on the faces around him, sober and thoughtful, stoked his confidence. "I suspect there are personal and family issues behind her inexplicable behavior at the Mass." Kempe noticed a few nods that seemed to say: *Yes, that must be it.*

"We need to keep her in our prayers," the monsignor added, striking an appropriate pastoral note. Standing on either side of the reception room, Moore and Havel noticed the same phenomenon—individuals breaking away from the milling guests to make cell phone calls or standing alone with heads bowed, texting. What they had witnessed or just now heard from guests who attended the Mass was too good not to be shared with family and friends.

Bryn Martin finally worked his way through the subdued guests to Ella, Nora, and Ian. Nora gave him a brief hug. "I'm so sorry, Bryn. I know Margaret is a friend."

Bryn turned to Ella who said quietly, "It was as bad as I feared. And I can't reach her. She's not answering her cell or her home line."

"If you hear from her, let me know," Bryn said. "She's going to need friends around her."

"How are the guests dealing with this?" Ian asked.

"I've probably talked to a few dozen so far. They've all been unfailingly polite. A few asked rather carefully how Archbishop Gunnison was doing. He's resting in the presidential suite. One or two wondered what Margaret did at the Catholic Center. No one has asked the one question everyone wanted to ask. Was there any substance to Comiskey's final petition? But it's got to be on the minds of a lot of people in this room."

Bryn exchanged a quick glance with Ella.

"How in God's name," Ian asked without expecting a response, "will Gunnison handle the closing remarks?"

"I have no idea, Ian. Aidan Kempe will likely have a talking point or two for him. Listen, I'll stop by your table as soon as the dinner is over." Then as an afterthought. "We were so focused on a man with a laser."

Giorgio Grotti removed his scarf, revealing a black clerical shirt and white plastic tab collar. He folded the scarf and placed it in the left-hand pocket of his overcoat before walking confidently to the Sheraton's registration desk.

"Good evening, Father. May I help you?" asked a smiling clerk wearing a Sheraton Hotel name badge that read "Ashley."

"Good evening. I'm Father Peters. I think Monsignor Kempe left an envelope for me."

"Oh yeah," she answered brightly. "He dropped it off just a few minutes ago."

At seven forty-five, thirty minutes after Grotti picked up the key-card to Archbishop Gunnison's suite, the banquet manager emerged from the kitchen and approached Bishop Martin.

"We're ready to serve the salads, Bishop. If you like, we can flick the lights to start the guests moving into the ballroom?"

"Yes, go ahead," Martin responded dreading the next two hours. He turned to look for Moore and Havel and found them standing nearby.

"It's time to get the archbishop," Martin said, holding out a key-card to the presidential suite. "I'll call his room and let him know you're on the way up."

As Moore and Havel walked to the elevators, Martin tapped in the telephone number of the presidential suite. Archbishop

Cullen, his face wet with perspiration, approached him.

"This is strange," said Martin. "I'm calling Wilfred's room to let him know that Moore and Havel are on their way up. No answer."

Cullen frowned. "I wish he would have listened to us, Bryn. He's making a big mistake in coming to the dinner. If Margaret knows Gunnison has abused minors, then it's really over for him. He'll be lucky to relocate in Florida and avoid a media exposé."

"He can't stay in Baltimore, that's for sure," Bryn said, looking over Cullen's shoulder at the guests meandering into the banquet hall.

Cullen put his hand on Martin's forearm, holding him in place. "You know, Bryn, we're going to have to let her go."

"That won't be necessary. Margaret knows she can't work at the Catholic Center. She tendered her resignation with that prayer."

On the way to the dais, Martin stopped at the circular, candlelit table where Ella, Ian, and Nora were taking their seats. The very sight of his sister calmed him, despite the adrenaline that had fueled the last few hours. Bryn nodded at Ian, who understood as well as anyone might that this high-church drama was unfolding like a medieval morality play. Ella's face was drained of color with worry for Margaret, but her eyes, intelligent and deep, were difficult to read. What he thought he saw, mixed with her concern for Margaret, was a penitent's remorse. "I'll come to your table as soon as the after-dinner remarks are over," he said, recovering his focus. "They'll be short."

Before Bryn reached his place next to Archbishop Tardisconi, his cell phone vibrated. "Bishop, its George Havel. You need to get up here to the archbishop's suite immediately. Bring Archbishop Cullen with you. It's not good, Bishop, it's not good."

Archbishop Cullen was already on the dais, but hadn't taken his seat. Martin walked to his side, leaned in, and whispered in his ear. Both men moved as quickly as Cullen's legs would permit to the steps at the side of the dais and toward the closest door. As the elevator rose to the twenty-fifth floor Bryn's stomach dropped. What more could go wrong?

"I don't feel good about this, Charles."

Cullen didn't respond. He leaned against the back of the elevator, staring at the floor. Stepping out of the elevator they faced an elegant sign in Edwardian script that read "Presidential Suite," an arrow underneath pointing to the left hallway. Moore and Havel were standing outside Gunnison's room, the door slightly ajar.

"Archbishop Cullen, Bishop Martin...you need to prepare yourselves for what you are about to see," George Havel said softly.

Duane Moore pushed the door open, "We're so very, very sorry," he added. He closed the door as Cullen and Martin, nerves now on edge, glanced around the two-story suite overlooking the Inner Harbor. A striking spiral staircase leading up to the second tier stood between them and the floor-to-ceiling windows.

"He's on the other side of the staircase," Havel said as he and Duane led the two bishops in silent procession.

Wilfred Gunnison's face was a purplish blue, his eyes open and bulging, though eerily unfocused. His head was bowed, listing slightly to the right. A thick hotel bathrobe belt suspended the archbishop by his neck. It was tied to the banister pole halfway up the staircase. One of the chairs from the dining room set lay on its side just inches from Gunnison's dangling feet. Cullen and Martin could not help noticing he had stained himself.

"Dear Jesus, dear Jesus," Cullen mumbled, tears running down his pink cheeks. Then "Holy Mother of God," he wailed. Bryn, speechless, took him by the elbow and directed him to the closest chair.

"Bishop," Havel said to Martin, "We need to make some calls."

Martin nodded as Moore called the Baltimore Police and the county's medical examiner's office while Havel used his cell phone to contact the hotel's security officer. Martin realized he had his own call to make and touched in Kempe's speed dial number on his cell.

"Aidan, this is Bryn. If I'm not mistaken, Wilfred's physician is one of the guests. You know him. Ned Gannon. Get him and get him up to Wilfred's suite as soon as you can. I can't say anything more right now." Then turning to the two laymen, Martin asked, "Did you find a note or any kind of message?"

Both Moore and Havel shook their heads. "We should have advised you not to leave the archbishop alone," Havel said speaking for Moore and himself.

"He insisted on it," Cullen reminded the two men.

Martin nodded in agreement, trying to shake off his own feelings of guilt for leaving Wilfred by himself.

Then Archbishop Charles Cullen did what he should have done immediately on finding his predecessor hanging from the banister pole—he prayed the prayer of absolution and commended the soul of Archbishop Wilfred Gunnison to a loving and merciful God. Martin, Moore, and Havel, heads bowed, prayed in silence.

Then Cullen added, "Eternal rest grant unto him, O Lord."

"And let perpetual light shine upon him," the three shaken men said in unison.

The four stood in silence—Cullen and Martin looking in disbelief at the grotesque scene before their eyes as the implications of the tragedy sank in.

"Let's move to the dining area," Martin said softly to Cullen. "We have to say something to the guests. They've been seated over thirty minutes, maybe more." Before Cullen could respond,

225

they heard two sharp knocks on the door. Kempe and Ned Gannon entered with two uniformed police officers and the hotel's security chief. Moore and Havel led them around the spiral staircase. Aidan Kempe's knees almost buckled at the sight of Wilfred Gunnison hanging from the railing. He turned away as soon as he saw Gunnison's distorted face, reaching for a handkerchief which he immediately pressed to his mouth.

"Aidan," Cullen said softly as he and Martin led him to the sofa. "This is unspeakably hard for all of us, but I know you were close to Wilfred."

"Oh God, Oh God," Kempe moaned as he sank into the sofa.

Cullen and Martin understood the disbelieving shock in Aidan Kempe's eyes—what they didn't understand was the shear, raw terror welling up in Kempe's breast.

Forty-five minutes after the guests had been seated, Archbishop Charles Cullen, Bishop Bryn Martin, and Monsignor Aidan Kempe climbed the two steps to the dais. The guests had finished their salads and were now keenly aware of Archbishop Gunnison's absence. Cullen moved to Archbishop Tardisconi's side and informed the already-stunned diplomat of what he was about to announce to the restless guests. It was a courtesy Tardisconi's rank demanded. He took the news without any visible sign of emotion. More than anything else, the Holy See's ambassador to the United States hoped he would soon awaken from a very bad dream.

Archbishop Cullen moved to the microphone at the table-top lectern at the center of the speaker's table. Bishop Martin stood to one side, the ashen chancellor of the archdiocese to his other. For almost half a minute, Cullen stood at the lectern in silence, striving for some semblance of composure.

Twenty-seven floors above, a team from the medical examiner's office hefted the lifeless body of Wilfred Gunnison onto a gurney.

"Dear friends. There is something quite terrible and tragic I need to tell you. What I am about to say, I say with profound sadness and a broken heart. Bishop Martin, Monsignor Kempe, and I have just come from Archbishop Gunnison's suite." Cullen paused and reached for a water glass and sipped. Then he sipped again. "It appears," his voice hinted at cracking, "that Archbishop Gunnison has taken his own life."

Cullen heard gasps across the room. The ballroom fell silent. Even the servers didn't stir.

"I can't say anything more at this time," Cullen continued. "I ask you to join me in prayer for our brother and friend." The assembled benefactors of the archdiocese, the prelates at the head table, and the hotel's serving staff all bowed their heads.

"O God, we have gathered this evening to give thanks to you for the life and ministry of Archbishop Wilfred Gunnison and to honor him for his fifty years of priestly service. Now, in disbelief and profound sorrow, we pray for his soul. We ask you to embrace him with your love and mercy. And we ask you to bless us, we who don't understand, we who sit in stunned confusion and unspeakable sadness, with the consoling presence of your Holy Spirit. Grant Wilfred, our brother and bishop, peace and a holy rest. We ask this, O God, in the name of Our Lord and Savior, Jesus Christ. Amen."

A weak "Amen" could be heard at some of the tables. The guests sat stunned, many blinking back tears, a few crying openly.

Cullen turned to Martin, who stepped to the microphone.

"Archbishop Cullen and the others at this head table know of your respect and affection for Archbishop Gunnison and for Catholic Charities of Baltimore. We came to honor him this evening. Let's still do that. We beg for your understanding as we call this evening's gathering to a conclusion. Your entrees are now being boxed in the hotel's kitchen and we have arranged for students from Loyola College to distribute them to the homeless of our city. At this time a van load of students is on its way to the hotel."

Martin looked up to see a hand waving to him from the kitchen door. "It appears the students are already here. Believe me, these young men and women know how to find the poor and homeless of our city. They will do their best to make sure the dinners prepared for you will not go to waste." Most of the guests looked relieved to bring the tragic evening to an end. "Archbishop Cullen asks that you return to your homes now. Thank you for your understanding and your prayers for Archbishop Gunnison. God bless you."

The guests rose from their tables and moved, hardly speaking, to claim their coats and find their way to the garage.

Bryn Martin worked his way through the stunned benefactors to find Nora, Ella, and Ian. "I have to meet up with the students in the kitchen and then with Archbishop Cullen. I'll call you as soon as I'm free. Can we meet at your place, Nora?"

"Of course. We'll be up for some time. Come over when you can."

Nora hugged her brother and whispered, "I'm so sorry, Bryn."

Shaking her head, Ella said to no one in particular, "Can it get any worse?" as she tried to calculate the impact of Gunnison's death on her friend Margaret.

Martin, with his eyes tearing and mind racing, turned and headed toward the hotel's kitchen. He pushed through the swinging doors and felt a wave of emotion rising in his throat. A dozen or more Loyola students stood shoulder to shoulder with kitchen staff and servers boxing dinners of sea bass and tenderloin fillets. In their midst, as if the major domo of the hotel's kitchen, Archbishop Cullen moved from student to student and to the hotel's employees, offering a personal word of thanks to each of them. Bryn heard one student respond, "No problem, Archie."

Loyola senior Mary Ellen Brennan hugged the archbishop. "We're so sorry about Archbishop Gunnison. We can't believe it."

Cullen wanted to say thank you, but the words wouldn't come.

"Charles," Bryn whispered into Cullen's ear, "we need to get back to the suite."

34

Giorgio Grotti, aka Monsignor Giancarlo Foscari, hoped the calming play of lights on the Inner Harbor might calm his racing heart. He walked close enough to small groups of bar crawlers to hear their chatter and laughter. Their pseudo-innocence appalled him—naive, superficial Americans out for a good time on a Saturday night. They were blind to the evil that was rotting their souls. But Giorgio Grotti wasn't blind to evil. By the grace of God, he was now a holy warrior fighting evil. In his own humble way, he too was a protector of the Brotherhood of the Sacred Purple. He broke away from the pedestrians and found a secluded doorway among the buildings facing the harbor. He glanced to his left and right, pulled his scarf up around his neck, and then punched in M's number on his mobile.

"I have completed the assignment."

"For the good of the church," M said with the fatherly concern of a spiritual counselor. Then abruptly, "Call tomorrow afternoon, Rome time. Good night, my son."

Archbishop Cullen caught up with the papal nuncio at the door of the ballroom as he scanned the hallway for his driver.

"Archbishop," Cullen said breathing hard from the unbearable strain, "we will do our best to make you as invisible as possible to the media."

Lorenzo Tardisconi nodded weakly. No one knew better

than the nuncio that it was not good for a Vatican diplomat to be present at the breaking of a clerical scandal, especially the suicide of an archbishop of the Roman Catholic Church.

"I would appreciate that very much, Archbishop Cullen." Cullen understood that by using his title rather than his first name, the nuncio was expressing his profound displeasure at the unthinkable ecclesiastical debacle that had just fallen upon him. "And," he added sharply, "make sure my office is informed of the funeral arrangements."

"Of course," Cullen said, ignoring Tardisconi's tone.

Looking over Cullen's shoulder for his driver, the nuncio said coldly, "I'm not sure if my schedule will permit me to attend the archbishop's funeral. Right now I must contact the Secretary of State, who will inform his Holiness of Archbishop Gunnison's sudden death. But you, Archbishop Cullen, must stay in regular contact with the English-speaking desk at the Secretariat of State and the Congregation of Bishops." Tardisconi paused, realizing he was lecturing the archbishop of Baltimore. No matter. The evening's bizarre events demanded directness. Then, trying to find a more conciliatory tone, he offered, "It would be a courtesy to the Holy Father and to the Holy See to avoid the indignity of an autopsy."

Cullen looked into the nuncio's eyes. What he was proposing was nothing less than an order. "I will expect your call the first thing in the morning."

Without another word, Archbishop Lorenzo Tardisconi turned from Cullen. Catching the eye of his driver, he stormed out of the hotel.

Doctor Ned Gannon spoke softly to the physician on duty at the medical examiner's office. "Please inform the medical examiner that Archbishop Gunnison held a Vatican passport as well as a

U.S. passport. That made him a citizen of the Vatican City State. In the name of Archbishop Cullen, I'm asking that you honor the Vatican's request that he be spared an autopsy."

Across the room, Charles Cullen took the chair at the head of the presidential suite's dining room table. Bryn Martin and Aidan Kempe, seated to his right and left, were each drafting a statement to the media and a personal statement for Archbishop Cullen to issue to the Catholics of the archdiocese. Someone, thoughtfully, had ordered coffee from room service. Cullen poured himself a cup. The three of them needed to be armed with some kind of statement before they left the Sheraton.

"Tomorrow," Cullen said looking like he might collapse, "right after our Masses, we meet in my office. We can't start planning for Wilfred's wake and funeral until I talk to the nuncio."

Martin and Kempe nodded.

"I'm not sure," Cullen said looking at his two aides, "what to do about Comiskey's accusatory petition. If it's going to come out, we would be better off to get it out ourselves before the media does."

Again Martin and Kempe nodded.

"Charles," Bryn said evenly, "we need to be ready to respond to Margaret's accusations."

Looking at his two aides, Cullen said emphatically, "Should either of you get questions about the allegations against Wilfred, make it clear I am committed to proceed immediately with a thorough internal investigation and that the archdiocese will cooperate fully and completely with the civil authorities." Cullen looked from Martin to Kempe. "We heard the rumors..." his voice trailed off. "But they were only rumors. I never heard of any formal complaints or allegations."

Martin lowered his eyes and thought what he wasn't free enough to say: *And you never really wanted anyone on your staff to look into those rumors.*

"Aidan," Cullen said firmly, "I want you to review your files and I want to know if there are any allegations against Wilfred that somehow may not have been brought to my attention." He held Kempe's eyes. Kempe looked away first. "And see if there is any way we can reach out to the individuals Margaret named. See if you can get their full names."

Kempe tried to look composed and in control, but he wanted to scream. He closed his eyes and rubbed his temples. *What had Giorgio done? Wilfred didn't have the stomach to take his own life. But I'm not a psychologist. Maybe Wilfred did commit suicide.* Kempe told himself to stay focused, and in that split second of clarity he understood his desperate wish was but a futile attempt to escape the horrible truth that cramped his stomach and lungs.

Monsignor Aidan Kempe, self-proclaimed master of deftly-worded media statements, master of the art of ecclesial spins, could neither write nor say anything. He stared at the lined, yellow paper in front of him. *What if Cullen and Martin find out the truth? What if the police find out? And how did Comiskey ever get hold of those names?* Without looking up from the blank legal pad under his clenched hands, Aidan felt Charles' and Bryn's eyes on him.

"I need to use the bathroom."

Kempe closed the door behind him and sat on the side of the tub. He rose almost immediately, raised the toilet lid, and vomited the evil, terrifying mass in his stomach. But the fear remained. Kempe stood up slowly and flushed the toilet, went to one of the sinks, splashed water on his face and wiped the spittle and droplets of vomit from his lips with one of the hotel's hand towels. He stood leaning on the sink counter and slowly raised his eyes. A scared, perspiring middle-aged man stared at him in the mirror. He needed a drink. He needed to talk to M. But what would he say? For the first time, Aidan Kempe's confidence in the Brotherhood of the Sacred Purple was badly shaken.

It was after midnight when Bryn joined Nora, Ian, and Ella. An open bottle of single malt scotch on the coffee table had barely numbed the pain of the evening. Ella Landers, veteran diplomat and one-time CIA operative, looked defeated.

"I'm afraid for Margaret," she said, looking straight ahead. "I could never have imagined the change that has come over her the last few weeks. I would never have believed her capable of doing what she did."

Bryn looked to his sister, the professor of psychology. "What do you make of this?"

"It appears Margaret has suffered some trauma, some shock to her inner world or belief system."

"Nora," Ella said slowly, glancing quickly at Bryn, "Margaret suffered a terrible shock recently. Do you remember the victim's name she read first? It was Mark. Mark Anderlee is her nephew and godson. They are very close. She thinks the world of him."

Bryn knew very well what was coming. Nora and Ian were drawing their own conclusions.

"About two weeks ago, Margaret's nephew told her that Archbishop Gunnison had abused him when he was in high school, or maybe it was the summer before his first year of high school."

"Dear God," Ian said, taking Nora's hand.

"Margaret didn't handle the news well, and I'm afraid I didn't help the situation. Actually, I believe I made it much worse."

"What do you mean, Mother?" Ian said speaking for the other two as well.

"I can't go into it right now. Perhaps at another time." It wasn't Ella Landers' embarrassment at her poor judgment that kept her silent about the after-hours invasion of Monsignor Kempe's office. It was her concern that she not implicate any of them, especially Bishop Martin, in the sad affair.

The doorbell rang, surprising everyone but Nora. "You've got to be hungry. I've ordered some Chinese."

They moved to the dining room. Nora carried in plates from the kitchen while Ian and Bryn opened the cartons.

"I've been calling Margaret every fifteen minutes," Ella said. "She doesn't answer."

"There was a black SUV waiting for her at the curb outside the Basilica," Bryn said. "So she's not alone. It may have been her nephew that picked her up. You'll hear from her, Ella. You'll hear from her."

They ate in silence for a while.

"You know," Ian said hesitantly, "if this were the late Middle Ages, Margaret might be in some danger." He stopped abruptly, cursing his thoughtlessness.

"What are you saying?" Ella said with growing disquiet.

Ian had opened the door, now he had to walk through it. "I'm going back to our conversation at your dinner party, Mother, when I mentioned the Brotherhood of the Sacred Purple." He glanced at Nora. "Thanks to Nora, I discovered the archives of the Carmelite Monastery in Towson. According to one of their earliest chaplains, a Jesuit by the name of Combier, the Brotherhood was willing to do whatever was deemed necessary to protect itself. To protect its stated mission to save the church from reformers who wanted to decentralize papal authority, the church's 'supreme center,' as they referred to it. The priests and bishops of the Brotherhood really believed there was a hidden conspiracy to weaken the papacy, a conspiracy of insiders who wanted to undermine the imperial governance of the church."

"Violence in the name of God," Nora said. "It's nothing new. I remember reading of a cardinal who said he only lied in the best interests of the church. If you can justify lying for the good of the church, it's not that big of a jump to justifying physical violence."

Ella wasn't sorry she had asked Ian to go on, but hearing again of the Brotherhood only added to her worry.

Bryn was sure that Ella knew of Kempe's association with a group of Baltimore priests—and one dead archbishop—who called themselves the Brotherhood of the Sacred Purple.

Ella touched the resend button on her cell and silently begged Margaret to answer. The others waited to see if Margaret would pick up.

Ella shook her head.

"You did it, Aunt Margaret. You did it," Mark said as he drove a circuitous route to his Inner Harbor condo. He didn't think they were being followed, but he would continue driving north for a few more miles before heading back into the city. He touched the Sig Sauer P226 in his coat pocket. No one was going to hurt his Aunt Margaret.

"Yes, I guess I did," is all a drained Margaret Comiskey could say.

Two hours after Margaret stumbled out of the side entrance to the Basilica, she stepped into Mark's Inner Harbor condo. The harbor lights were striking—and strangely comforting.

"Would you like some tea?" Mark asked.

"Something stronger. I need something stronger."

Anderlee went into his kitchen and came back with two ice-filled glasses and a bottle of Jack Daniels. They sat for a while without speaking. Mark watched as his aunt placed her glass on the coffee table and squeezed the fingers of her right hand with her left.

"You're cold," he said as he got up and went to the hallway closet for a blanket.

"When you told me what you were going to do, Aunt Margaret, you kept me out of a heap of trouble. I was thinking of doing something pretty stupid. But your plan was better than mine—far better."

Margaret pulled the blanket around her and sipped her drink. Mark had never seen his aunt look so frail, so very tired.

"Are you okay?"

"I don't know. I know I ruined Gunnison's jubilee. And if what I said about him gets into the papers, I've ruined his reputation. But the man's a pervert. A hypocrite. And it's not just what he did to you, Mark. There were others. I found out there were many others."

"Aunt Margaret, why don't you stay here with me tonight? I don't want you staying alone in your house. It's just better for you not to be alone."

Margaret shook her head. "I'll be all right."

"I'll stay with you."

Margaret hesitated. "If you don't mind, I think I would feel better with you in the house."

"Just let me grab a few things."

Before turning out the lights to his condo, Mark slipped his Sig Sauer into his duffle bag and helped his aunt into her winter coat. The attached hood came down over her forehead, hiding her eyes. Mark thought she looked a like a monk or nun.

"Thank you, my dear, dear Mark," Margaret said softly as they walked to the elevator. "I really don't want to be alone tonight."

Mark pressed the button for the garage level. When the doors opened, an older couple, two of Mark's neighbors, stood waiting to enter. The woman was in tears.

"What's wrong?" Mark asked.

The man, whose name he had never caught, said, "We were at Archbishop Gunnison's jubilee dinner." Putting his arm around his wife's shoulders, the man stammered, "He's dead. The archbishop apparently took his own life."

237

Margaret's knees buckled and Mark dropped his bag in an effort to keep her from falling. "How awful," Mark responded automatically, holding on to his trembling aunt. If the two neighbors had been at the Mass, neither one seemed to recognize the woman before them as Gunnison's accuser. It may have been the hood, or perhaps they skipped the Mass and went straight to the dinner. It didn't matter. What mattered was his aunt. He was afraid she would collapse. "Good night," Mark said abruptly, leading Margaret carefully to his Explorer.

Before he could put the key into the ignition, Aunt Margaret, tears running down her cheeks, sobbed, "Oh God, Oh God! What have I done?"

35

Aidan Kempe noticed the slight tremor in his hands that grasped the outer edges of the Sunday edition of the *Baltimore Sun*. He had spent a sleepless night dealing with the shock of Gunnison's tragic death—he couldn't bring himself to say "murder"—and wrestling with terrible, baffling questions he kept repeating. How did Comiskey come to know what she obviously knew about Wilfred's mistakes as a young priest? How did she know the boys' names? How would Wilfred's exposure affect the Brotherhood? He had to call M, and soon. And without even a hint of shame, he pondered how yesterday's events would affect his career.

Kempe's late night call to the paper's city desk editor had paid off. It could have been much worse. In fact, considering the circumstance, it couldn't have been much better. Below the fold, in the left lower corner of the front page, the headline read: "Retired Archbishop Dies Suddenly at Inner Harbor Hotel." The article was brief.

"Retired Archbishop Wilfred Gunnison," it said, "celebrating his fiftieth ordination anniversary at a fundraising dinner for Catholic Charities at the Sheraton Inner Harbor Hotel, was found dead yesterday in his presidential suite shortly before the start of the dinner. The cause of death remains undetermined.

"A spokesperson said the archdiocese would issue a statement later today.

"Archbishop Gunnison was praised at a Mass in the Basilica

of the Assumption preceding the dinner as a strong supporter of Catholic Charities and Catholic education."

Kempe folded the paper and rose from the table. No mention of Comiskey's outrageous prayer. That was a break. Yes, it was a break, but he had influenced it, more or less. More, he thought, than less. Wilfred's death would certainly be featured on the 6:00 p.m. local news. He glanced at his watch. He had time to get to his office before meeting with Cullen and Martin. Aidan Kempe had to know before the meeting if his private files had been opened.

The chancellor unlocked the door to his outer office, Margaret Comiskey's office. The desk was bare, as were the walls. All her belongings had been removed. He opened the top drawer to her desk. Empty. Then the side drawers. Empty too. He stood still for a moment shaking his head. *How could you do this? You betrayed me, Margaret. You betrayed the church. You betrayed the holy liturgy with your treasonous attack on Wilfred. God forgive you.*

Kempe, terrified of what he might discover, unlocked the door to his inner office and stepped cautiously inside. He saw it immediately. An envelope lay squarely in the middle of his desk. It was addressed to him in Comiskey's handwriting. But at this moment the letter was of secondary concern. He was moving now in slow motion and eased himself into his desk chair. His private file drawer looked intact. *Let it be locked.* It was. *Thank God,* he said under his breath. He unlocked it as if it might have been booby-trapped. Again he whispered, *Thank God.* Everything was there—his journal, the cash and check book, his private notes, account records. *How could she have known?* There were no signs of forced entry. *How could she have known?* he asked himself again. He had the only key...the only key.

Only then did Kempe pick up the letter and reach for his letter opener. It was short. Only three sentences.

Monsignor Kempe,

    I hereby resign from my employment at the Catholic Center of the Archdiocese of Baltimore.
    By the time you read this letter, my reasons for terminating my association with the archdiocese will be clear to you.

Kempe bolted upright in his chair as he read the third and final sentence.

    Instead of Daniel 5:7, you might read Luke 14:11.

                     Margaret Comiskey

The bitch. He knew the reference to Luke 14 without having to reach for his Bible. "For all who exalt themselves will be humbled, and those who humble themselves will be exalted."

But it was Comiskey's citation from the book of Daniel that chilled him: "You shall be clothed in purple." *Daniel_5:7* was the password to his personal computer. How in the name of God almighty could she know that?

Charles Cullen arranged for sandwiches and coffee to be brought to his office. The three men seated at the archbishop's conference table, each bone-tired from a restless night, knew they would be there for as long as it took. A statement had been promised, and the media would hold them to it. Controlling how the circumstances of Wilfred's death were made public would help defuse the scandal that was certain to erupt in a matter of hours. It could make the difference between two or three days of bad publicity or two or three weeks, or more, of painful stories and media probing.

Both Martin and Kempe brought working drafts to the meeting.

"Before we take a look at your drafts," Cullen said, "we need to consider some points I find tricky. First, do we say that the cause of Wilfred's death has yet to be determined by the medical examiner or do we acknowledge that it appears he took his own life? I don't think we can wait for the report from the medical examiner. And maybe that's to our advantage. Second, do we say anything about Margaret's prayer? If we do mention it, how explicit should we be? And three, should we emphasize that Wilfred, over the past few weeks, has been anxious and depressed? I think we agree he had been anxious, and we might rightfully assume depressed, since the laser beam incidents."

Both Martin and Kempe took notes.

"Finally," Cullen continued, "can we honestly state that we are unaware of any formal allegations made to the archdiocese or to civil authorities against Wilfred?" Cullen looked at Kempe. "Is that accurate, Aidan?"

Kempe nodded that it was.

Cullen's instincts said don't push this. Not now, anyway, but soon.

"Let's take a look at your drafts," Cullen said, somewhat irritated. Kempe seemed eager to get his draft on the table first. Cullen caught Martin's eye as Aidan slid copies to each of them.

For Immediate Release

The Catholic Center, Archdiocese of Baltimore
Sunday, February 25, 2007

With deep regret and profound sadness, we announce that Archbishop Wilfred Gunnison, the retired eighteenth archbishop of Baltimore, died suddenly, on Saturday, February 24th, prior to a Catholic Charities fundraising dinner in honor of the archbishop's fiftieth ordination anniversary.

While the cause of death remains to be confirmed by

the county's medical examiner, it appears that Archbishop
Gunnison may have taken his own life. In recent weeks
those close to the archbishop saw indications of anxiety and
depression in our beloved shepherd, community leader, and
friend.

Funeral arrangements have not been finalized.

Archbishop Charles Cullen has issued the following
statement:

"The sudden and tragic death of Archbishop Wilfred
Gunnison has deeply saddened the Catholic Church of
Baltimore. I ask the faithful of our archdiocese and all the
people of our community to keep Archbishop Gunnison
in their prayers. We commend our brother Wilfred to our
merciful and loving God."

Cullen and Martin read the statement again. It had its
strengths.

"Let's see your draft, Bryn," Cullen said.

Martin slid copies across the table to Cullen and Kempe.

<u>For Immediate Release</u>

The Catholic Center, Archdiocese of Baltimore
Sunday, February 25, 2007

From the Office of the Archbishop

It is with deep regret and a heavy heart that I
announce the sudden death of my predecessor and friend,
Archbishop Wilfred Gunnison, the eighteenth archbishop
of Baltimore.

On Saturday, February 24th, Archbishop Gunnison
was celebrating his fiftieth anniversary as a priest.
The celebration included a Mass at the Basilica of the
Assumption of the Blessed Virgin Mary and a fundraising
dinner for Catholic Charities. In the short time between

*the Mass and the dinner, Archbishop Gunnison was found
dead in his reserved suite at the Inner Harbor Sheraton
Hotel.*

*The cause of his death remains to be determined by
the county medical examiner. However, we have reason to
believe the archbishop took his own life.*

*I can report one consoling note. Archbishop Gunnison
made a brief spiritual retreat at St. Mary's Seminary in
Emmitsburg just days before his death.*

*I ask the good people of Baltimore, especially their
civic, religious, educational, and business leaders, and
in particular the faithful of the archdiocese, to keep
Archbishop Gunnison in your thoughts and to remember
him in your prayers.*

*May God strengthen and comfort us all in this time of
sadness and loss.*

Cullen looked up at his two advisors. "These are both good,
but I need to put my own mark on the statement—more or less."
Cullen offered a slight smile. "I'll be drawing on your drafts,
though. I tend to agree with you—at this time it's best not to al-
lude to Margaret's accusatory petition. Let's hope the media does
not pick up on it. But we need to be ready if it does."

"If you two don't mind," Cullen went on, "I'd appreciate it if
you would stay close by for the next hour or so. I'll call you when
I'm ready to send the release to our Communications Department. The two men got up to leave when Cullen added, "You
both look tired. Try to get some rest."

Kempe let his guard down only after returning to the sanctuary of his Catholic Center office. He locked the door behind him, walked to his desk and lowered himself into his high-backed chair. So Cullen and Martin believed Wilfred committed suicide. Of course they would. So would everybody—everybody except M, Giorgio Grotti, and the chancellor of the Archdiocese of Baltimore. But could M and Giorgio really get away with it? God help the Brotherhood if they couldn't. He suspected Cullen would draw more on Martin's draft than his own. Cullen had never really trusted him, at least not the way he trusted Martin. But there were bigger concerns weighing on his mind than the press release about Wilfred's death. *Am I really an accomplice to murder? Might I go to jail?* And the two other thoughts that were vastly perturbing—what else did Comiskey know, and how did she come to know it?

The maddening questions brought his anxiety back full force. Kempe had to call M, though he dreaded it. M, more than ever, held his career in his hands. And more than that—Aidan Kempe was now afraid of the man. There was no doubt now that M would sacrifice him in a minute for the good of the Brotherhood of the Sacred Purple. His fingers trembled as he tapped the numbers of M's mobile phone. There was no answer to the first rings. He checked the desk clock. Almost two p.m.—six hours later in Rome. M was probably at dinner. Just as he was about to hang up, there was a connection.

"Yes?" M said in English, recognizing the U.S. country code.

"It's me. I take it you have heard?" Kempe asked, assuming Giorgio had reached him before his call.

"Yes. What a shame, what a shame. Who would have thought the archbishop was so profoundly depressed?"

"Yes," Kempe said hesitantly, almost choking on his words.

"Who would have thought his Excellency was so depressed?" Their faux surprise, cloyed with starched formality, bordered on the obscene. But it meshed seamlessly with the unreality of their clerical world. They played their game with little awareness that a game was being played.

So, Kempe realized, they would proceed under the illusion that Wilfred's death was a suicide. Of course, there could be no other way. Kempe waited for some allusion to Giorgio, but none came. He understood now, with frightening clarity, that M held in his hands not only his career, but his life.

"I need to inquire about this woman," M continued, "the woman who offered the Prayer of the Faithful at the Mass." *He knows about Comiskey!* "She is your secretary, is that not right? How is it that she believed our friend misbehaved?"

"I don't know," Kempe answered lamely. "My files contained only a few references to the allegations against the archbishop, a few notes. I am most scrupulous about their security. I am sure neither she nor anyone else ever had access to them. I have been very careful."

Not careful enough, Kempe imagined M thinking.

"Is it possible that this woman knows about the Brotherhood?"

"No. No, I don't think so. She knows only that I meet monthly for dinner with a small number of priests. Friends. She thinks it's for fraternal support—an evening that's social in nature."

M remained silent looking out at the lights of Rome, trembling in deep twilight. He was not convinced. *Oh Aidan, you disappoint me. How do you know what she thinks?* "I assume she is no longer your secretary."

"No. I mean yes," Kempe stammered, "she's no longer my secretary. She left a letter of resignation on my desk when she left work on Friday." Kempe said nothing about Comiskey's citation of Daniel 5:7, did not admit she may have accessed his personal computer. "She has terminated her relationship with the archdiocese," he added definitively.

"We shall see," M said vaguely. "Do everything you can to distance our deceased friend from the Brotherhood. Do you understand my meaning?"

"Yes, Bishop," Kempe said emphatically. "Yes, of course."

"Good evening, then, Monsignor." M broke the connection.

Kempe, with M's voice still in his ears, called Tom Fenton.

"Tom, it's me."

"Christ Almighty, Aidan, what the hell is going on? Herm and the others and me—we're in shock. We can't believe what Wilfred did."

Kempe ignored him.

"I just got off the phone with M, with Murex himself. It's necessary that we keep the monthly meetings suspended indefinitely. More than ever, we need to distance ourselves from Wilfred."

"Well, that's what you said at our last meeting. So, we don't meet until you give us a signal. I'll call Herm, Eric, and Paul."

"Good. Do that. I'm up to my neck in dealing with the media and the funeral plans."

"Aidan," Fenton asked directly, too directly for Kempe, "how did Comiskey find out about allegations against Wilfred? I thought you had his past mistakes under wrap, under control?"

"I don't know. But I'm going to find out." Kempe went silent for a few seconds, then added, "Tom, we have to assume she might know about the Brotherhood. Call Herm, Eric, and Paul right away."

"I spoke briefly with Eric and Paul in the sacristy after the Mass. They were really shaken. I didn't get a chance to talk to them at the hotel. I'm afraid they may be coming a little unglued. But I'll manage them."

Kempe knew he could confide his secret with absolutely no one. Not even Tom Fenton or Herm Volker. Nor could he say anything about Comiskey having the password to his computer. "Wilfred's suicide has us all shaken." He paused, trying to think. "It would be a good idea to call Paul and Eric regularly, even every day. We don't want them breaking down and talking to their classmates—or to anyone else."

Giorgio closed his mobile phone and started planning how to execute his new assignment.

As soon as M had concluded talking to Kempe, he had placed a call to Giorgio.

"Yes," he had said in response to M's question. "I know who she is. I know where she lives."

"Unfortunately, this woman has become a threat," is all that M had to say.

Giorgio had his instructions. This, too, would be a delicate and challenging operation, though definitely less dangerous than the last. This time he was free to choose the time and place. But M's tone had made it clear. He was to act soon...for the good of Holy Mother Church.

36

The Monday morning following Gunnison's death, Mark Anderlee and Margaret Comiskey sipped coffee at her kitchen table. "I think I'm feeling a little better," she sighed. Mark didn't believe her. She certainly didn't look any better.

"It was good of you to spend the last two nights here, but I'm going to be all right."

"Promise you'll call me if the media hassles you," Mark said. "Just say you have nothing to say. And let me know if anyone from the Catholic Center calls. I can afford to get you a good lawyer if they threaten you with legal action. Don't be afraid of them."

Margaret tried to smile a thank you. But Gunnison's suicide had hit her hard. From the moment she heard the news in her nephew's parking garage, her will for revenge had melted into a swirling pool of regret. But her will for the truth to get to Archbishop Cullen and Bryn Martin hadn't. They needed to know why she did what she had done.

"Aunt Margaret, it's not your fault Gunnison took his life. The stuff he did would have come out sooner or later." Margaret really doubted that Gunnison's abuse would ever have been discovered. But Mark was only trying to comfort her. She nodded, as if in agreement.

Mark got up to leave, bent down and kissed his aunt on the cheek. "I'll be calling every few hours," he said, moving for his coat and the duffle bag resting on the living room chair next to her front door.

"Mark," Margaret said gently, "that gun of yours. It makes me nervous."

Mark nodded. "It will be out of your house in a minute. It's in my bag."

"And I have a favor to ask. Would you drop the package on the dining room table at FedEx? It's addressed to Bishop Bryn Martin at the Catholic Center. I'll feel a little better if Bishop Martin and Archbishop Cullen understand why I did what I did."

Mark would have done anything to help lift his aunt's guilt.

"Make sure it's same day delivery." She consulted her watch and nodded. "And get a tracking number."

"Done," he said. "And don't think of reaching for your purse. Let me pay for this."

"Thank you."

"Love you, Aunt Margaret. Bye."

Giorgio placed his coffee cup in the beverage holder of his rented Honda Civic, parked four houses from Comiskey's, and watched Anderlee walk to his SUV. He scribbled the time and Anderlee's description onto a note pad. He had to be the driver of the vehicle that whisked her away during the Mass. Maybe he was her son? M hadn't mentioned any family. But how would he know, living in Rome, if Comiskey had family in Baltimore? Giorgio thought of calling Kempe but decided against it. The less contact with him the better.

Returning his attention to the assignment at hand, Giorgio calculated the best opportunity would be early evening, with still some daylight—she would be more likely to let him in—and less of a chance for the media to show up. Giorgio turned the ignition key. Too risky to wait this close to the house. In a few hours he would return to pay this woman an official visit from a Vatican emissary.

Margaret walked back into her kitchen and put her mug of tea into the microwave. She was glad Mark had stayed with her the past two nights but now, to her surprise, she wanted only to be alone. Bryn and Archbishop Cullen would soon be wading through the contents of Kempe's private files. If they couldn't forgive her, maybe they might understand a little. The two other copies from Kempe's files were wrapped and tucked away on a shelf in her basement. She had planned—before Gunnison's death—to send one set to the *Baltimore Sun* and maybe the other to the prosecutor's office right after the jubilee celebration. But now that didn't seem right. *He's dead already*, she told herself. For the first time since Mark had told her of Gunnison's abuse, Margaret Comiskey felt a need to pray.

A half hour later, Margaret knew it was time to call Ella Landers.

"Ella, it's Margaret."

"For God's sake, Margaret, I've been worried sick! I must have called you a dozen times since the Mass. Where are you? How are you?"

"I'm at home. I go from being kind of okay to being a mess. Mark stayed with me the last two nights. He told me to turn off my cell and unplug my land line. I'm sorry. I should have called you. But I didn't want to involve you in this any more than I have already."

"I'm driving up to see you," Landers said emphatically. "I'll be there in an hour."

Margaret was waiting at the door as Ella came up the steps to her porch. Once inside, they embraced without speaking. As they finally stepped back, both women had tears in their eyes.

"I'm so sorry I got you into this, Ella. It wasn't fair of me to ask you to do what I asked you to do."

"One of the things I learned as a Foreign Service officer," Ella responded softly, "—and, between you and me, as a CIA operative—is that working to get the truth out is always a noble endeavor. We got the truth out, even if it never is acknowledged by the church."

Margaret squeezed the tissue in her hand and raised a hint of a smile at the most comforting words she had ever heard—a kind of absolution.

"Over the years," Ella went on, "I've come to think it's more difficult for the church to get the truth out than it is for our government. Both institutions stand ready to sacrifice the truth for the corporate good. We don't always have to broadcast the truth, but if we deny it, we're in terrible trouble."

They sat in Margaret's living room, small but uncluttered—like a convent parlor. A picture of Mark, taken at the time of his graduation from Loyola Blakefield, rested on the side table next to the sofa. Another, in his army uniform, rested at an angle at the end of the mantel of her fireplace.

"Something happened, Ella, when Mark told me he was abused by Gunnison. It's like I grew up." She smiled at Landers. "And for God's sake, we're in our sixties. *I'm* in my *sixties!*"

"Age really doesn't matter, Margaret. I've seen senior field operators who were literally shattered when they discovered the shadow side of the Agency. Some came unglued. Some resigned. Some just disappeared…and one lives in Silver Spring."

Margaret sat stunned. "Oh Ella. You haven't judged me." She

wanted to cry. "And I have no idea what you have endured, what you've been through. I've always idealized your life overseas…so very different from my maddeningly routine life at the Catholic Center."

"Not so different, really," Ella said thoughtfully. "I worked for the most powerful government in the world. You worked for the most powerful church in the world. We both worked for empires. And empires don't work anymore—secular or religious. If I am sure of nothing else, I'm sure of that."

"Still," Margaret said, "what I did at the Mass was wrong. And now the archbishop is dead. I should have just sent the papers from Kempe's drawer to Archbishop Cullen. I should have let Cullen deal with Gunnison."

Ella shrugged as if to say, "Maybe."

"When I found out Gunnison abused other boys as well as Mark, I discovered my own shadow side, as you put it. I discovered I could hate. I wanted revenge, like I've never wanted anything more in my life." Her eyes filled and she reached for a tissue. "I couldn't think of anything else. Revenge, only revenge."

Ella sat still. But her silence held its own message. It seemed to fill the living room with a quiet wave of compassion. Margaret let her friend's warmth wash over her like a second baptism.

"You know what I want to do right now, Ella? I want to go to confession."

37

I an Landers took his place at the seminar table and opened the manila folder with his notes on the Council of Trent. He felt a chill in the room, a tension unusual for this point in the seminar. Then he noticed him. Joe Constanza sat rigid and red-faced with what Ian took as a simmering anger.

"Dr. Landers, I saw you at the Jubilee Mass for Archbishop Gunnison last Saturday. I was one of the seminarians serving."

"Yes, I saw you." Landers looked around the table, unsure how many of the students were aware of the retired archbishop's fiftieth anniversary Mass and his tragic death. "Some of you know that soon after the Mass that Joe served for the archbishop, Archbishop Gunnison took his own life."

Most of the students nodded.

"Why," Constanza blurted, "would someone do what that lady did?" His speech was clipped, like the ra-tat-tat of machine gun fire. "That was calumny! She tried to destroy the archbishop's reputation during his ordination anniversary Mass!"

The high drama had the students on the edge of their chairs looking from Constanza to their professor and back. Ian had to acknowledge the tension and passion in the room beat anything he could say about the Council of Trent.

"The archbishop was so mortified that he couldn't face the people at the dinner." Constanza realized some didn't know about the dinner, so he added, "There was supposed to be a fundraising dinner for Catholic Charities after the Mass."

The clarification gave Landers an opportunity to intervene, but he let Constanza finish his rant.

"I don't believe Archbishop Gunnison did anything wrong," Constanza barreled on. "Even if he had done something wrong, you don't use the Mass to accuse him!"

Nolan Connors nodded in emphatic agreement. The other graduate students sat motionless, ratcheting up the tension in the room.

"What happened Saturday evening," Landers said evenly, "was a tragedy on many levels. As Joe knows, I'm sure, the Catholic Church teaches that all persons are entitled to their good name, to their reputation. So publicly decrying or challenging someone's character is always a serious matter. Maybe in the days or weeks ahead we will know a little more that might help us understand—I don't say excuse—what took place at the Mass."

Constanza bristled but did not respond.

Ellen Stark sat in momentary silence. She wanted to ask, *Well, did the archbishop abuse boys or not?* but thought better of it. Landers knew the answer, but it was an answer he held in confidence. She took another tack. "If, and I say if...*if* the archbishop sexually abused minors, he wouldn't be the first bishop to do so. Remember that Pope Julius III picked up a fifteen-year-old boy on the streets of Parma and made him a cardinal."

"It's been almost forty years since the clergy abuse scandals surfaced in the U.S. and in many other parts of the world," Landers said. "But as historians, you know there is evidence of clergy abuse of boys and girls, of young men and women, dating back to the early second century. Pope Julius doesn't stand alone. Can you think of any other examples?"

"Wasn't it St. Basil," John Pointer asked, "who had child-molesting monks flogged and held for six months in their cells, like in solitary confinement? And that was in the fourth century."

Another student leaned forward, signaling he wanted to offer a follow-up. "In fact, there is a second century commentary on the gospels that says, 'Thou shalt not seduce young boys.'"

"All right," Landers said in approval. "We know the sexual abuse of children and minors is, sadly, nothing new—in the church and in society in general. And from the historical evidence we have, it seems that in every age the abuse was hushed-up and at the same time met with considerable denial." Landers paused here.

"Professor Landers, what do you think caused the cover-up and denial?" Pointer asked.

"For a very long time," Lander said deliberately, "we just didn't want to believe that adults, especially the clergy, would do such a thing—abuse innocent children and young people in their teens. And there are still people today who think the clergy abuse horrors are exaggerated by anti-Catholic bias. But even in the secular sphere, there is mounting evidence that we simply don't want to admit the extent of physical and sexual abuse in our homes and schools and churches."

Joseph Constanza twitched in his chair, his anger mounting. Landers was turning what happened to the archbishop into a history lesson. Bristling, without glancing back at Landers, he got up and left the room.

38

Trying not to stare, Bryn Martin took the measure of the archbishop. In spite of his full, round face and fleshy neck, Charles Cullen's jaw was set and his blue-gray eyes, though watery, were focused—like a general's features, Martin thought, engaging in battle. The photocopied contents of Aidan Kempe's private file drawer were spread out on the conference table.

Cullen looked up to find Martin studying him. Cullen scanned the papers on the table, his pink cheeks now bright red. Abruptly, he walked away from the table, then turned to Martin and said in the tone of a commanding officer, "Read Margaret's note again."

Martin opened a manila folder and took out a handwritten note on a white piece of stock copy paper.

Dear Bishop Martin,

Enclosed you will find photocopies of materials contained in Monsignor Aidan Kempe's private file drawer.

I ask you to share this information with Archbishop Cullen in the hope that you might both come to understand why I did what I did at Archbishop Gunnison's Jubilee Mass.

I regret deeply the archbishop's tragic death. I now realize it may have been better to have sent this package to you and left the matter in your hands.

At the time, I did what I felt I had to do. I can only ask for your prayers.

> Sincerely yours,
> Margaret Comiskey

Both men sat still, trying to comprehend how things could have come to this.

Finally, Cullen said, "Honestly, Bryn, the last thing I wanted to do with Wilfred's funeral arrangements still not settled was to read through these papers from Aidan's file. But you were right. I had to see this stuff first hand. This isn't just scandalous. It's criminal!" Cullen continued in a tired but steely voice. "Kempe's funneled thousands of dollars of the archdiocese's funds into off-the-books accounts that he alone controlled."

"Maybe *hundreds* of thousands of dollars." Martin added.

"What's worse," Cullen went on, "is his handling on his own and in his own way reports of clergy abuse." There was no rhythm to his speech, Martin noted. He had hammered out each word in a staccato stream heavy with his own rising heat. "He's taken it on himself to personally shield Wilfred and half a dozen others. We'd be naïve to think none of them has abused again."

Cullen paced from his conference table to his desk and back again.

"God Almighty, Bryn, what if the media gets hold of this?"

Martin was grateful that Cullen had thought first of the young people his priests had abused before raising the specter of a media frenzy and the storm that would follow.

Cullen sat back down at the conference table and stared towards the window. He sat suddenly erect. "God damn it, Bryn, they knew! They knew! Both Wilfred and Aidan knew what was behind those laser hits. Both of them were aware of Mark Anderlee. They were playing us all along."

"Yes," Martin said, "and hoping a hundred thousand dollars

would make him go away. And keep him quiet."

"And this Brotherhood of the Sacred Purple. What's that all about? Self-appointed guardians of orthodoxy and bishop brokers! Not only that, they have a Vatican godfather, this mysterious M. And *Wilfred* was a member, for God's sake! We have yet to bury the man, and now this on top of everything else."

Martin knew this was not the time to brief Cullen on the Combier papers. That would have to wait.

Cullen got up from the conference table and walked back to his desk but remained standing. He was quiet for a minute, then turned to Martin, still seated at the table, and said, "He's no longer chancellor, Bryn. Kempe's finished."

On the Wednesday morning after Archbishop Gunnison's death, Bryn Martin was back in Cullen's office. Aidan Kempe, he knew, had been informed by Cullen himself to be ready to come to the archbishop's office when called.

"Do you want me to stay?" Bryn asked.

"Yes. I want a third party present."

"You might also want one of our attorneys to sit in on the meeting."

"I've thought of that," Cullen said, "but it's better if it's just you and me."

A mistake, Martin thought. But he didn't say so.

"Before I call Aidan in, tell me," Cullen said, "how did Margaret get copies of the contents of his private file?"

"I can't figure it out either. Margaret, or someone else here at the Catholic Center, must have had an opportunity to duplicate or photograph all this stuff. But Aidan is scrupulous about his privacy. All I know, all we know, is that Margaret somehow got her hands on Aidan's private papers."

Cullen tried to let the mystery go for the moment. But it

rankled both bishops. Charles and Bryn sat thinking…and feeling rather dumb.

Cullen came back to the task at hand. He had important pastoral matters to see to. "Right after the funeral, we begin reaching out to the victims listed in Aidan's journal. We're going to their homes, if they'll have us." Cullen's mind raced on, "Make sure we report the accusations to the county authorities. And have every priest Aidan was protecting in my office the day after we bury Wilfred."

Martin nodded.

"Wilfred's funeral," Cullen said wearily, "is the least of my worries." He glanced at his watch—it was just past eight—and reached for his phone. "Let's get this over with."

Both Cullen and Martin were mildly startled by the sharp double knock on the archbishop's office door. Kempe was reporting as directed—but apparently not at all intimidated by his curt summons to the archbishop's office.

Cullen, standing behind his desk, pointed to one of the two upholstered chairs facing him. "Sit down, Aidan."

Kempe ignored Martin and stole a quick glance at Cullen's conference table. It was covered with piles of paper. Cullen's conference table was never cluttered with papers or anything else.

Martin pulled the matching chair to the left of the archbishop's desk and sat down. Kempe continued to ignore him.

After what seemed an eternity to Martin, Cullen sank slowly into his chair and studied the legal pad in front of him. Kempe stared blankly, as if expecting the blow to come. Cullen spoke evenly and with precision. "I've discovered, Monsignor, that you have been aware of allegations of sexual abuse by a number of our priests—including Archbishop Gunnison."

Kempe stirred in his chair without any sign of concern.

"Allegations," Cullen went on, "that were never brought to my attention or to the attention of the police."

"I have no idea what you are talking about, Archbishop," Kempe said formally.

"A short time ago a package was delivered to the Catholic Center. Its contents appalled me."

Kempe held Cullen's gaze. Without turning his head, he sensed Martin's eyes on him. He felt nothing but contempt for this liberal lackey named bishop in his stead. He still felt stung by that insult. Passed over by Bryn Martin, for God's sake. It was the Brotherhood's most personal, most painful defeat.

Then with only a hint of a crack in his composure, Kempe turned and looked at the conference table. *Comiskey!*

"You have taken it upon yourself," Cullen said glancing at the pad in front of him, "to personally handle a number of clergy abuse allegations without bringing them to my attention or to the attention of the vicar for priests. The accused clergy, and here I include Wilfred Gunnison, continued in ministry."

Kempe made no response.

Cullen picked up the pad and tilted his head to see through the reading lens of his glasses. "You have appropriated archdiocesan funds to buy promises from victims and their parents not to prosecute or sue."

"That's correct," Kempe said smugly. "In these cases I determined they could be handled best by resolving them personally. I offered the alleged victims and their families counseling, some modest financial help, and the assurance that the priest in question would receive treatment and not be a danger to others."

Cullen's neck and face flushed red.

"I hope you realize," Kempe said in a condescending tone, "that the money paid out comes nowhere close to the exorbitant amounts alleged victims are receiving today. And," he threw Martin a glance, "I provided you and your auxiliary bishop with deniability if any of the victims should have sued or gone to the authorities." His tone suggested Cullen should be grateful.

"May I...?" Martin asked, looking at Cullen.

The archbishop nodded.

"Did you ever apologize to any of these victims for the abuse they suffered?" Bryn asked.

"I didn't think it was my place to apologize for claims of alleged abuse by a handful of our priests without real proof of the legitimacy of the accusations. The last thing we wanted was the police investigating priests—and the media circus that would follow."

Cullen listened incredulously.

"No," Kempe continued, more forcefully, "I determined that minimal financial settlements, even against unproven accusations, seemed the best way to proceed. I believe I spared the church scandal and that I protected the dignity and authority of priests and bishops. I believed then, and I still believe, that I acted prudently—in the best interests of the church."

"And I suppose it was in the best interests of the church," Cullen pressed, "that both as financial secretary and as chancellor, you appropriated archdiocesan funds to be used as you saw fit."

Kempe leaned forward in his chair. "Both as financial secretary and as chancellor, I made numerous financial decisions that saved the archdiocese hundreds of thousands of dollars. And I did so with discretion and prudence."

Kempe's scornful expression matched the tone of his voice. Cullen gripped the arms of his chair.

"After Wilfred's funeral," Cullen said evenly, "I'm authorizing a thorough audit of your office and the financial department. And I mean thorough. If there is evidence of fraud, I won't hesitate to report the findings to the prosecutor's office."

Kempe's face tightened in contempt. Cullen wasn't through.

"I have evidence that you received thousands of dollars a month from four of our pastors. It looks to me like this was parish money. What was that all about? And what's this purple purse and the Brotherhood of the Sacred Purple?"

Kempe felt his face coloring. "I consider the matters you just raised personal and private. The pastors' contributions you mentioned—they were not payments—were discretionary funds used to shore up the orthodox teachings of the Roman Catholic Church."

Cullen wondered, but did not ask, *And just how did you do that?*

Kempe, stirred now by his own indignation, was unrelenting. "There are numerous priest support groups, priest fraternities, if you like, in the archdiocese. You yourself have encouraged your priests to join such groups. The Brotherhood of the Sacred Purple is a priest support group. You can hardly object to that. If we keep a very low profile, that is our right."

Charles Cullen pushed the legal pad to one side and leaned back in his chair. He stared at Kempe briefly before going on. "I've discovered you have a list of priests who are being considered for the episcopacy. And another list of bishops your Brotherhood was promoting for advancement to more important—"

"That too," Kempe said quickly, "is personal and private. This may sound rather immodest, but from time to time I'm consulted by members of the Congregation for Bishops on the suitability of priests for the office of bishop."

Before Kempe arrived in his office, Cullen had decided not to ask him about M. That piece of information needed to be pursued most carefully and through discreet channels. The archbishop looked from Kempe to Martin. Bryn, like the master of ceremonies he once was, sat alert and ready to intervene if necessary in the church drama unfolding in front of him.

Kempe broke the brief silence, "This audit you mentioned.

It cannot, of course, include my private files. They're not subject to any scrutiny—not even by you, Archbishop. I'm sure you understand that your 'evidence,' as you call it, had to be obtained illegally."

Martin thought this was Kempe's best shot so far. He should have anticipated it and warned Cullen to be ready for it.

"So," Kempe bored ahead, "I'm asking you, and I have a right to an answer, how were these papers obtained?"

"I don't know," the archbishop said and then turned to Martin, "nor does Bryn. Tell me, is anything missing from your file? Papers or money? Any sign of forcible entry?"

"No," Kempe replied, "nothing seems to be missing or disturbed."

"Well," Cullen said, "you can hardly report this to the police."

"Of course I wouldn't report it to the police," Kempe said testily. "But I want to know how copies of my private files, files that are my personal business, were invaded. And I plan to find out."

"Perhaps some of the papers, your journal entries, and the nature of your Brotherhood, as you've insisted, are none of my business. The money that went into your purple purse, however, money that came from our parishioners, might well be my business. And it's certainly my business that you failed to bring to my immediate attention the names of young people abused by our priests. And you failed to inform me of the priests who were accused. That's *my* business, Monsignor, that's *my* business!

"And," Cullen paused for emphasis, "I neither need nor want any 'deniability'...from you or from anyone else! Is that clear?"

Kempe didn't respond. As before, he held Cullen's gaze. The three churchmen sat, staring without speaking. Kempe finally lowered his eyes.

Archbishop Charles Cullen rose from his chair. Kempe and Martin also stood.

"Monsignor Kempe," Cullen said formally, "You have done

serious harm to the archdiocese. I'm relieving you of your responsibilities as chancellor—as of this moment. You may keep your residence at the cathedral rectory for the time being. Officially, you're awaiting assignment."

The archbishop tried to read Kempe's eyes. The cold look he saw said, *Don't mess with me, Cullen. Don't mess with me.*

"As you say, Archbishop. As you say." Monsignor Aidan Kempe turned and walked deliberately to the door. He closed it quietly behind him.

"Aidan is probably right, Bryn," Cullen said, turning towards the documents scattered on the table. This stuff can't be used in any formal proceedings, civil or even canonical. But wherever this goes, we're put in a very precarious position."

They were quiet for a bit, assessing the ramifications of Kempe's duplicity.

"By the way, Bryn, make sure our former chancellor has a prominent role in Wilfred's funeral. He should be one of the major concelebrants."

Bryn nodded.

"I'm still wondering," Cullen went on, "how in the world Margaret got her hands on these documents."

"I will do my best to find out."

Martin didn't tell his archbishop that he had a hunch.

39

Monsignor Aidan Kempe, feeling the full weight of gross misunderstanding and false accusations, walked back to his office trying to control a mounting rage. *So this is how they persecute their prophets, their faithful stewards.* Cullen was mistaken if he thought this was the end of his career. Although he had to be wary of M, he had friends in high places, he had money, and he had priests who owed him big time for saving their skins. Aidan Kempe knew how to play the game as well as any of them.

"Awaiting assignment," Cullen had said. So, what's the worst he can he do? Assign me to a parish? No doubt as far away from the Catholic Center as possible. Monsignor Aidan Kempe, former chancellor of the Archdiocese of Baltimore, leader of the Brotherhood of the Sacred Purple, arch-defender of the church's orthodoxy, reached for his handkerchief. His eyes were burning. He was unaccustomed to the feeling.

Safe now in the sanctuary of his office, Kempe moved to his favorite window. It was yet another bleak, gray, late February day. Cullen had treated him like some common employee—and in front of Martin. His archrival had witnessed his humiliation. The two would pay for what they had just done to him. But now he must think clearly. There was a time for everything under heaven. And their time would come.

Pushing aside his anger at Cullen and Martin, Kempe understood his real enemy was Comiskey. He hated her for her sacrile-

266

gious betrayal. How did she obtain the names of Wilfred's accusers? And how did she obtain copies of almost everything in his private file? And what if there were other copies? Where might they be? Maybe Martin was behind all this. Kempe thought it was rather unlikely. Martin was too much of a Boy Scout. Only a professional thief would have been able to open that drawer without signs of forced entry. But then why leave the cash? No, whoever opened his file was not looking for money. This enemy was not a thief. And this made him—or her—all the more dangerous.

Comiskey was the key to it all. Kempe knew she had been shocked and upset by the scandals. Most Catholics were. And most Catholics would have been shocked to find out their retired archbishop had been accused of abuse himself. But there had to be something more, something else going on for her to do what she had done. He thought he had had a reasonably good working relationship with her, and Comiskey appeared to have been on friendly terms with Wilfred. Then, out of nowhere, Kempe remembered the name of the first victim she mentioned at the Mass—Mark. *Mark Anderlee? Dear God! She knew Mark Anderlee.* There was that sudden change in her mood right around the time Anderlee had confronted Wilfred. Had she discovered that Wilfred had abused Mark Anderlee?

Kempe got up from his desk and moved to his outer office, now emptied of Comiskey's personal belongings. Its stark bareness a silent cry of accusation. He tried to picture her credenza. There had been pictures of her nephew and godson—as a high school graduate and as an army sergeant. Comiskey had mentioned him by name numerous times, but he had never really paid attention. Kempe sat down at her desk and let the realization sink in: Mark Anderlee was Margaret Comiskey's nephew and godson.

Kempe stood up abruptly and went back into his office, closed and locked the door. He now had Comiskey's motive. She wanted to destroy Wilfred. But how had she gotten her hands on his files? He would find out. And he would destroy her. Right now he had to call M. Then he needed to transfer the contents of his private drawer to a safe-deposit box. He touched in M's number, hoping to catch him before his midday siesta. M picked up on the third ring.

"Excellency, it's Aidan. I'm calling to tell you that we've been compromised."

"Tell me precisely what you mean, Monsignor," M demanded.

"I'm afraid it's no longer the case of one woman knowing some names and knowing about the Brotherhood. Someone, somehow, invaded my private file and made copies of its contents. Archbishop Cullen, himself, has copies of what was in this file."

M stated coldly, "And we have to presume, do we not, that others do too? Do we not have to presume, Monsignor Kempe, that others have information about the Brotherhood, information that was your responsibility to safeguard?"

Kempe's breathing became shallow as his T-shirt stuck to his damp armpits.

M's voice remained even but icy. "Might copies of your private file reach civil authorities?"

'That's not likely," Kempe responded quickly. "However the contents of my private file were obtained, they were obtained illegally. Our laws prohibit illegally obtained evidence from being used in criminal proceedings."

M remained silent, unnerving Kempe all the more.

"Excellency, believe me," he rushed on, "there's really nothing to prosecute. I broke none of our laws. The media would only be interested in the priests accused of sexual abuse."

"And would they not be most interested in allegations against Archbishop Gunnison?" M asked rhetorically. "So, let me see if I understand, Monsignor. It's not only this one woman, your secretary, who has copies of your private file with information on the Brotherhood. Is that not the situation?"

Kempe squeezed his eyes shut. He had no answer.

M paced in impatience in the ensuing silence. Eliminating Aidan's secretary would do little good for the Brotherhood of the Sacred Purple now.

"Monsignor," M said speaking slowly but with force, "as far as you and your priest companions know, there is no such thing as a Brotherhood of the Sacred Purple. You have never heard of such a society. Do you understand?"

"Absolutely, Excellency." He could live with denial with the best of them.

"*Bene*," M responded.

Kempe hesitated, then added, "You should know that Archbishop Cullen has relieved me of my responsibilities as chancellor. I am awaiting assignment—probably to a country parish as far away from the chancery as possible."

"This is your cross, Monsignor. This is your cross."

M walked to the window of his apartment and found the lighted dome of St. Peter's Basilica soothing. It was magnificent, ageless, indestructible. So, he believed, was the Brotherhood of the Sacred Purple. Suddenly, his eyes opened wide—the secretary! He had a call to make. Giorgio.

40

Margaret Comiskey stood at her sink washing the cups and saucers from her tea with Ella. So, she mused, I was an atheist for a few weeks. Maybe that's some kind of record? For the first time in almost a month, a smile softened her lips.

Years ago, she had placed a framed copy of the prayer of St. Francis above her sink. She read the first line: "Lord, make me an instrument of your peace." Peace, she now understood, couldn't keep company with hatred. The exploding hatred and relentless desire for revenge that so surprised her were sinking behind a distant horizon, like a fiery red sunset. In the ensuing twilight, Margaret was finding her religious footing. But she would never again be naïve about the church.

Drying the dishes she thought of Mark. She had told no one but Mark of her plan to expose Archbishop Wilfred Gunnison at his Jubilee Mass. He had reacted strangely, she remembered. He had looked away once he understood what she intended to do. When he turned back, his expression had softened. He looked as if he was calculating something. "Aunt Margaret," she remembered him saying, "Your plan is so much better than mine."

Her doorbell's chime startled her. Margaret finished drying her hands, and moved through the dining room to the front door. Through the side pane of glass that framed the door, she saw a man in a black overcoat. His coat was open, revealing a black clerical shirt with a Roman collar. She knew many of the archdiocesan priests, but this one was unfamiliar to her.

"Miss Comiskey?" he asked as Margaret opened the door.

Margaret nodded, "Yes, may I help you?"

"Good afternoon. Or good evening. The sun is almost down." He spoke formally, with a distinct European accent. "I apologize for stopping without calling first. But you will understand in a moment why my visit is urgent. I am Monsignor Giancarlo Foscari."

He handed her a small, cordovan leather wallet framing a laminated Vatican identification card with his picture and the Holy See's seal. Beneath the seal were two unintelligible signatures with small crosses before each name. Margaret knew the signatories were bishops.

"I won't take much of your time. I'm here investigating for the Holy See the recent allegations brought against Archbishop Wilfred Gunnison." Foscari paused, a sign of respect for the deceased prelate. "May I come in?"

Margaret stepped back and let the Vatican official into her living room, then pointed to the chair Ella had occupied less than an hour earlier. This, she thought, seemed to be incredibly swift action on the part of the Vatican.

Giorgio smiled. This would be relatively easy. The tricky part had been getting into the house without alarming her. Now that he was inside, he would spend only enough time to get her to relax and to accept the story that he was a Vatican emissary. If the house had a basement, all the better. Her snapped neck would be the tragic outcome of an accidental fall down a flight of steps leading to a concrete floor. After a few questions about Gunnison's reported misconduct with young boys, he would ask for a glass of water. He would be careful not to touch anything, and when Margaret went into the kitchen, he would follow unobtrusively. While her back was to him, he would approach her from behind. She would die quickly.

"Tell me, Miss Comiskey," Foscari asked, "did you ever see the archbishop display inappropriate behavior at the Catholic Center, or anywhere else, for that matter?"

"No, I didn't."

She had expected the Vatican investigator to ask how long she had worked at the Catholic Center, how closely she may have worked with the archbishop, what she thought of him. But no, only this direct but vague question about "inappropriate behavior." He wasn't taking notes. He didn't have a tape-recorder. Suddenly she felt uncomfortable. In all her years working for the church, she had never heard of Vatican investigators operating in the U.S.

"I don't mean to impose," Foscari said smoothly, but may I trouble you for a glass of water?" Margaret thought of the wall phone in the kitchen. If she got him a glass of water, she could place a quiet call to Mark.

Margaret forced a smile. "Of course, Monsignor." She rose from her chair and started for the kitchen. Without turning she heard the priest stand. "Please wait here," she said over her shoulder. "It's no trouble." But he was following her into the kitchen. Margaret shivered. Why in God's name had she let him into her home? A sudden shock of fear ran through her.

The priest was no longer smiling as he stood in the doorway of the kitchen. Then, to her surprise, he slowly, devoutly, blessed himself—making the sign of the cross, whispering in Italian. What he was about to do he was doing under holy obedience!

He was wearing rubber gloves.

Giorgio regretted that he wasn't able to approach her from behind. Still, the terror in her eyes had no effect on him.

Margaret stepped back against the sink counter. She was trapped. As he moved toward her, both were startled by the ring of his cell phone. Giorgio hesitated, trying to decide whether or not to answer. He took a step back and reached into his pocket.

"Yes?" He listened without taking his eyes off Comiskey. Margaret stood frozen, her lower back pressed hard against the sink's counter edge. After listening for only seconds, Giorgio closed the phone and put it back into his coat pocket.

He took another step—but this time backwards. He held her in his gaze as he took still another step backwards. Then, walking swiftly toward her front door, he said coolly,

"Ah, *scuzi.*" He caught himself, "I am so sorry, but I must conclude our interview at once. Something quite urgent has come up."

Running to the door, Margaret locked it behind him, then leaned against it, shaking uncontrollably. Impulsively, she moved the curtain to see if this intruder was really off her porch. She saw him moving quickly but without running to a car parked several houses down the street.

Margaret, her mouth parched and her lungs heaving, ran to her phone. Her first call was to Mark. He would be right over. She reached Ella's answering machine and asked her to call as soon as she could. Ella would hear the trembling in her voice. Her third call was to Bryn Martin. He, too, would be there as soon as possible. In the meantime, he told her to call a neighbor to come and keep her company—and to turn on all her lights.

Margaret sat at her kitchen table wearing two sweaters and sipping a glass of chardonnay. Her hands had finally stopping trembling, but her eyes bore the strain of the last three hours. Mark and Bryn Martin were seated on either side of her. Her nephew had been polite but reserved when she had introduced him to Bishop Martin. He was cutting him some slack, Margaret was sure, because he was his aunt's friend. But he would wait and see.

"I'm sorry about what happened today to your Aunt Margaret," Bryn said to Mark. "And I'm sincerely sorry about what

Archbishop Gunnison did to you when you were a boy." The apology caught Mark by surprise. He had been waiting to hear that apology for twenty-five years. He turned his head away from Bryn, afraid of the swelling behind his eyes.

"Archbishop Cullen will be calling you soon," Bryn added gently. "I hope you will let him come to see you."

Mark seemed to signal yes without saying a word.

Margaret, Bryn, and Mark sat at the kitchen table trying to make some sense out of the intrusion by the self-identified Vatican investigator. Two Baltimore police officers had left a half hour earlier, saying that a detective would be calling sometime the next day. In the meantime, they would run a criminal records check on Giancarlo Foscari and place a call to the State Department.

"His identification looked official," Margaret said. "But as soon as I let him in I felt I made a mistake. He caught me off guard, I guess."

"I'm interested in the description you gave the police," Bryn said speaking to Margaret. "On the tall side for an Italian, you thought. Muscular upper body, perhaps in his middle thirties."

"Yes, and his English was good. Just a slight accent."

"I think I may have seen him at the Mass," Bryn interrupted, "There was a man sitting in the back of the Basilica wearing a black coat with a scarf wrapped around his neck. I couldn't tell if he was in a collar or not. One of our security people saw him leave the Basilica through the main entrance right after you went out the side door. A minute later he came back in."

Mark looked up. "He might've gotten the license plate number of my Explorer."

Ella Landers arrived and, after a long, silent embrace with Margaret, joined the circle at the kitchen table, feeling like she was sinking into a well of guilt. By agreeing to the Catholic Center operation she had put into motion a process that placed her life-long friend in mortal danger. Now briefed on the details of the intrusion and still fighting through the web of self-incrimination, Ella asked, "Who was this Monsignor Foscari working for? And why did he want to harm you? And who called him as he stood here in your kitchen?"

Both Ella and Bryn were thinking of the Brotherhood of the Sacred Purple and Ian's find in the Combier papers. Exposing Gunnison as an abuser had put the Brotherhood in jeopardy. But the file's other contents, now in the hands of Archbishop Cullen, might be the Brotherhood's death knell, at least in the U.S.

"If your former boss, this Kempe guy, had anything to do with this, Aunt Margaret, he'll be sorry," Mark said evenly.

"I'm going to spend the night here, too," Ella said firmly.

Margaret nodded. "Thank you. I would feel better with you and Mark in the house."

Martin was the first to get up from the table. He approached his shaken friend and hugged her. "Thank God you are safe, Margaret. I'll call you tomorrow."

Ella walked Bryn to the door. "We need to talk."

"Yes, I know," he responded. "And soon. I'll call you in the morning."

41

"This gets more bizarre by the hour." Charles Cullen said to Bryn. "You're telling me a man conducting a Vatican investigation, with Vatican credentials, was in Margaret's home—you believe with intent to kill—but fled after receiving a phone call?"

"Margaret thought she was about to be murdered when his cell phone rang. He put on gloves. He blessed himself."

Cullen frowned, then asked, "She's not alone, is she?"

"Ella Landers and her nephew are with her. She's still badly shaken."

"Of course," the archbishop said.

"You should know, Charles, that the description of the intruder she gave the police matches up pretty close to the man we spotted in the back of the Basilica at the start of Wilfred's Mass."

"I need time to piece this together," Cullen said almost in a whisper. He sat thinking for a minute, then with force in his voice said, "I want to talk to Margaret. Right now. Would you call her for me?"

Martin reached for the phone on Cullen's desk and called Comiskey's number.

"Margaret, its Bryn. How are you?"

"Better," she answered. "Rested."

"Good. I'm glad you got some sleep. I'm calling from Archbishop Cullen's office. He would like to speak with you."

"Just a minute. Just hold for a minute, please," Margaret said.

Putting her hand over the phone's speaker, she looked across the kitchen table at Ella and Mark. "It's Archbishop Cullen. He wants to speak to me."

Mark shook his head. "No way. Just hang up."

"I think you should, Margaret. Really," Ella said.

Comiskey took a deep breath, mustering her courage. "Bryn? All right. Put him on."

"Margaret? This is Charles Cullen. Bryn just told me what happened last night. I am so very sorry."

"Thank you, Archbishop. I'm still shaking. It was foolish of me to let him in."

"Bryn mentioned you're not alone. And you shouldn't be, of course, until we find out just what is going on. Who's behind this. Please let Bryn know if there is anything I can do to help you get through this ordeal," Cullen said gently.

Margaret reached for the box of tissues on the table. She had to wait a moment before she could reply, "I want you to know how sorry I am for what I did at Archbishop Gunnison's Mass. Something very dark came over me when I discovered that my nephew had been abused by him. I don't expect you to understand, but I do hope you'll accept my apology."

"Perhaps I do understand, Margaret. I'm trying to understand."

"Thank you, Archbishop, that's all I ask."

Cullen hesitated for a moment, then said, "Bryn told me that Ella Landers and your nephew stayed with you last night. If Mark is still there, may I speak with him?"

Margaret again put her hand over the speaker. "Mark, the archbishop wants to speak with you."

Mark shook his head emphatically.

"Please, Mark. Please speak with him."

Margaret held the phone in his direction. Mark realized he was nervous. Conscious that his hand was shaking, he reached

277

across the table to take the phone from his aunt. "Hello," he said cautiously.

"Mark, this is Archbishop Cullen. I wish I could say this to you in person and not over the phone, but I am very sorry. You were terribly wronged by Archbishop Gunnison. If you will let me, I'd like to come to visit you and tell you again in person how very sorry I am."

Mark's eyes blinked rapidly then closed as if he were in pain. Margaret sat, silently praying he wouldn't explode.

"I…I've been waiting for twenty-five years—for a freaking quarter of a century—to hear what you just said. I shouldn't have had to wait that long. I hope you understand that."

"I know," the archbishop said, "I know. I apologize that you had to wait all this time for an apology."

Mark abruptly dropped the phone, rose from the table, and went into the living room. Margaret and Ella heard this veteran of Iraq, this hardened army sniper trained to kill, sobbing.

Ella picked up the phone as Margaret went to sit with her nephew, and to weep with him.

"Archbishop?" Ella asked. "This is Ella Landers. Margaret and I were both present when you spoke with Mark. Thank you for whatever it was you just said. He couldn't continue the conversation. I think you understand."

"Yes, I think I do," Cullen said. "Please tell Margaret and Mark I'm praying for them both and, when the time is right, I want to visit them."

"Of course," Ella answered. "And when the time is right, perhaps a week or two after the funeral, I'd like to have you and Bishop Martin and Margaret down for dinner again."

"I would like that very much. I really would like that. Good-bye, now."

When Bryn Martin got back to his office, he found a phone message from Duane Moore.

"Duane? It's Bryn Martin. Just got your message."

"Bishop, George Havel and I have been asking a few questions of the staff at the Sheraton. We've come up with a few things you should know. Like soon."

"Can you come in this afternoon?" Martin proposed. "Around two?"

"We'll be there."

"Bishop," Moore began, "George and I feel that we kind of let you down. So, we decided to ask a few questions of the staff at the Sheraton. Once I mentioned 'FBI,' we got all kinds of cooperation. One of the registration clerks, a Patricia Crawford, was on duty the night of Archbishop Gunnison's dinner. She remembers a priest dropping off an envelope at the registration desk for a Father Peters. The priest said Father Peters would be picking it up soon. Sure enough, less than five minutes later, a man approached Crawford identifying himself as Father Peters. She gave him the envelope."

"Crawford's description of this Father Peters," Havel said, "matches our profile of the man sitting in the back of the Basilica for Archbishop Gunnison's Mass. Duane and I think it's the same man."

"So do I," Martin said. "There's been a development." Moore and Havel exchanged a glance, then looked to Martin, waiting for him to go on.

"Yesterday around five, a 'Monsignor Giancarlo Foscari,' a self-identified Vatican investigator—a man who matches our friend in the last pew of the Basilica—came to Margaret Comiskey's home. His credentials looked authentic. She let him in.

"Margaret is certain," Martin continued, "that he was about

to kill her when his cell phone rang. After listening to the caller, the guy turned and ran out."

"She's a lucky woman," Moore said.

"Very lucky," Martin added. "I checked with the Holy See's Secretariat of State. There is no record of anyone connected with the Vatican by the name of Giancarlo Foscari. Nor did the nuncio's office in D.C. have any information on him." Havel and Moore sat processing what they had just heard. "That's all we have right now."

"We have a little more from Crawford, the hotel clerk," Havel said returning to their interview with the hotel staff. She told us that 'Father Peters' went almost immediately to the bank of elevators. What if Kempe," Havel paused. "What if Kempe left a key card to Archbishop Gunnison's suite for this Father Peters? Gunnison was alone in the presidential suite for at least twenty minutes, maybe thirty. What if this guy went up to the archbishop's suite, flashed his Vatican ID, and the archbishop let him in?"

"I'm afraid you might have an assassin on your hands, Bishop," Moore said, looking to Havel for support.

"Any idea who he's working for?" Havel asked.

"Maybe," Martin said, regretting immediately his evasive answer and what it revealed.

An awkward silence followed. Duane Moore and George Havel, life-long faithful Catholics, stood at the very edge of the curtain separating the church's clergy from the laity. Both men felt their friend, Bishop Bryn Martin, had just put them in their place.

That very morning, Giorgio Grotti, using an Italian passport bearing his given name, boarded a Continental Airlines flight at the Baltimore Washington International Airport for Houston, where a connecting flight would take him to Bogotá, Colombia.

Since arrangements had been made for Archbishop Gunnison's indefinite retreat, M thought it prudent to have his driver and personal aide spend three or four quiet weeks in the seclusion of a convent nestled in the foothills overlooking Colombia's capital. The clear air and the prayerful quiet of the sisters' convent life would surely cleanse his soul and help him to see that he had acted in the best interests of the church.

42

Three weeks later

For Archbishop Charles Cullen, Silver Spring, Maryland, seemed like another country. He eased his overweight frame into the chair to the right of Ella Landers. His auxiliary bishop sat to Ella's left, and to his left sat Bryn's sister, Nora. Ian sat across from Nora. Margaret Comiskey, uneasy in the presence of the archbishop, sat at the opposite end of the table from Ella. Mark Anderlee, had sent his regrets. It was just like his mother, Ian thought, to host a dinner party including the archbishop of Baltimore and Margaret Comiskey, nudging along their silent reconciliation at a table of communion.

"Would you lead us in grace, Archbishop?" Ella asked.

Cullen closed his eyes. "Loving and merciful God, we are still stunned by recent events. We sit in confusion and grief, yet in hope." He paused. "We pray for all the victims of abuse, by priests and others, including Margaret's nephew, Mark. We also lift up to you our brother Wilfred. Bless him with your unfailing mercy and goodness. Bless the church of Baltimore, in need of your healing spirit. And bless this meal. Bless Ella, our host and friend, who has invited us to her table."

Cullen paused again. "We thank you, Lord, for delivering Margaret from harm's way. Keep her safe in your love."

Ella felt a lump rise in her throat at the archbishop's gracious and generous words for her friend.

"And may we see in the food and drink before us a sign of your abiding presence and love. We ask this blessing in the name of Jesus, the Christ. Amen."

There was a momentary pause as Ella's guests caught one another's eyes, now bonded by the shocking death of Archbishop Gunnison and Margaret's encounter with the mysterious Vatican "investigator."

"Archbishop," Margaret said after mustering her courage. "I want to anticipate a question you and others might have."

The archbishop looked at her with intent but kindly eyes.

"You may be wondering how I came into possession of Monsignor Kempe's private files." Margaret looked for a brief instant at each of the dinner guests—all except Ella. "I'm afraid I simply can't say."

Ian took a sip of water. *Mother,* he said silently.

"It would be wrong of me to explain how I obtained the copies. I'm sorry, but I just can't answer that question. I hope you understand."

All but the archbishop glanced furtively at Ella Landers. Ian turned his gaze to Nora, who returned his look with a conspiratorial wink. Ella Landers, retired diplomat and former CIA operative, smiled at Margaret. Their eyes were soft now with the watery glaze of mature friendship. Ian saw the archbishop tilt his large head a degree to the right, in what looked like a silent salute to Margaret's resolve to keep her secret.

The pregnant pause was somehow peaceful, binding the six table companions in a conspiracy of silence. Ian shook his head. *Never,* he had learned long ago, *underestimate your mother.* He saw Charles Cullen, last to join the loop, look to the poised and confident woman seated to his left, his mother, with undisguised regard and admiration. *So,* Cullen seemed to be thinking, *what I heard was true. Ella Landers, Foreign Service veteran, was also a CIA operative.*

During the drive back to Baltimore, Cullen turned and looked at Bryn, his profile changing from shadow to light as the headlights of the cars heading south on the Washington Parkway washed across his face.

"I'd like to know," Cullen said, "if what I suspect is true."

Bryn smiled. "Me too." He didn't have to ask what the archbishop's suspicion was. "Maybe it's better we don't know for sure."

"You're probably right," Cullen agreed, looking now straight into the darkness. They were quiet for a while.

Bryn broke the silence. "The first time I had dinner at Ella's, Ian told us about the Combier papers he and Nora had discovered in the archives of the Carmelite monastery—and about the medieval Brotherhood of the Sacred Purple. Now, we know, by way of Aidan Kempe's papers, of a Brotherhood right here in our archdiocese. What do you think we should do about it?"

Cullen thought for a few moments. "I'm not really sure, Bryn. But I think we should consider informing the nuncio of the Brotherhood in a confidential memo."

"After that," Bryn said, "I'd just let it go. You can't prove there is a Brotherhood of the Sacred Purple active here. Aidan would simply say it's a monthly gathering of priests for prayer and fraternal support. As for the monthly contributions the pastors made...well, we still have the remnants of a feudal system. I mean our pastors still have considerable discretion when it comes to matters of money. I don't know if I would go there."

They drove in silence for a few minutes.

"This M, their Vatican superior or protector," Martin said, "has probably shut the Baltimore Brotherhood down."

"If he hasn't shut it down," Cullen added, "they're going to be so deeply underground that we'd never hear about them."

"As to their promoting reactionary candidates for the episcopacy...well, I don't think you should go there, either," Martin said, remembering Cullen's efforts to have him catch the eye of the nuncio at Wilfred's jubilee dinner.

Martin took Cullen's silence as agreement.

They passed the exit to Andover. Martin knew he would have the archbishop at his door in less than half an hour. Maybe it was the wine at dinner, but he could see now that Charles had a right to know the theory Havel and Moore had raised. If he was going to tell him tonight he would have to tell him now. Bryn took a deep breath.

"There is something I need to tell you, Charles."

Cullen waited for Bryn to go on.

"It's possible that Wilfred's death was not a suicide."

Cullen turned to his left, searching Bryn's face, the seat belt pressing uncomfortably across his chest and stomach. "What are you saying?"

"There was a man dressed in black sitting in the back of the Basilica during the Jubilee Mass. He had a scarf around his neck so we couldn't see if he was wearing a collar. But at first glance I took him for a priest. Both Duane Moore and George Havel kept an eye on him, even though Moore was sure he wasn't the man with the laser."

"I never noticed him," Cullen said.

"Right after Margaret named Wilfred as an abuser and made her exit from the side door, this guy got up and ran out the front door of the Basilica. Moore followed him out. Whoever he is, Moore saw him watching intently as Margaret got into Mark's SUV. He didn't take his eyes off her until she was out of sight."

"I take it Moore and Havel think he was the Vatican investigator that went to Margaret's house."

"I do, too," Bryn said. "But I don't want to get ahead of myself." He sensed Charles' breathing change as the archbishop took this information in.

"Mother of God." Cullen whispered.

"A day or two after the dinner," Martin continued, "Moore and Havel went to the Sheraton and asked a few questions of the staff. One of the clerks on duty in the lobby the night of the dinner remembers a priest—we're sure it was Kempe—leaving an envelope to be picked up by a 'Father Peters.' Her description of Father Peters fits our dark stranger in the back of the Basilica."

"Let me get this straight," Cullen broke in. "Are you saying that it was Aidan who left the envelope at the registration desk for this Father Peters? And this Father Peters fits the description of your dark stranger? Martin didn't have to answer. He simply nodded as they approached the Baltimore Beltway.

"I was uneasy when Wilfred insisted on being alone before the dinner," Cullen confessed, reproaching himself for not insisting someone stay with the shaken jubilarian.

"It's possible, Charles, that this Father Peters had a keycard to Wilfred's suite. Wilfred was alone for almost half an hour..."

"God Almighty, Bryn, are you suggesting Wilfred was murdered?" Cullen sat stunned. "Why," he whispered, "would anyone want to murder Wilfred? Harm him? Embarrass him? Expose him? Okay. But murder him?"

Cullen ignored the seat belt pressing uncomfortably across his ample hips and tried to calculate the possibility of this bizarre scenario. His mind racing, he tried to slow his breathing, feeling a line of moisture build on his upper lip.

Breaking the silence, he turned to Martin. "Who is aware of this possibility?"

Martin stole a glimpse at his reeling archbishop. "Just Moore and Havel, you and me. And, of course, if there is anything to this, Aidan Kempe." Martin didn't tell Cullen of his decision to let Margaret know that Wilfred Gunnison may not have committed suicide.

Cullen just shook his head. *Lord have mercy on us.*

Bryn Martin turned left into the driveway of the archbishop's residence and pulled up to the side entrance. The dashboard clock read 11:55. Cullen opened the right side door of the car and slowly, awkwardly, climbed out.

Bryn couldn't smother the memory of another archbishop being delivered to the same side entrance at about the same time of night.

"Thanks for driving, Bryn. Call me when you get in to the Catholic Center tomorrow. I need to sort this out. It would help to have you listen to my thinking about it all."

Martin said simply, "Sure. Good night, Charles."

"Good night." Cullen was too disturbed to smile. "I'm afraid I'm in for a restless night."

Before backing out of the driveway, Bryn watched the archbishop enter the side door of his residence. He took a few deep breaths and rested his head against the head guard of his seat. Years ago, as another archbishop's master of ceremonies, his life had taken a turn in this driveway.

The lights blinked on inside the archbishop's house.

Peter Bryn Martin, auxiliary bishop of Baltimore, put the car in reverse and backed out of the driveway, telling himself, at least for the second time in his life, that he wasn't sad at all.